SOME BONES MAY REMAIN

A crime thriller

S. WHITTINGTON

Some Bones May Remain

Copyright © 2023 by Shawn Christopher Whittington

First Edition printed July 2024

Cover Illustration © 2024 by Shawn Christopher Whittington

ISBN: 979-8-9865545-8-7 (hardcover)
ISBN: 979-8-9865545-7-0 (paperback)
ISBN: 979-8-9865545-9-4 (eBook)

LCCN: 2024914029

Printed in Denver, Colorado (USA)

Published by Inward Crossing Publishing
www.swhittington.com

For my father,

my brother,

and in loving memory of my mother

1956 – 2018

Works by S. Whittington

Novels

Ravage and Requiem

Falter
Rupture
Wither
Shatter
Quarrel

Other Works

Some Bones May Remain

Table of Contents

I: The Raptor

A gangly shadow garbed in an ash-colored coat and a black fedora atop his bald head strutted in the misty midnight. The waxing moon shone upon him just over the Sangre De Cristo Mountains like a silent, ghostly eye opening amidst the clouds, a mystic stranger in the heavens witnessing the gaunt interloper below. The man peered up at the moon with his cheeky smirk and regarded the sphere and its halo ringing the sky, gleaming on his curious blue eyes.

Accomplices in the dark.

He promenaded through a parking lot with the gait of a gentleman towards an all-night diner outside of Westcliffe, striding with a casual posture he had perfected over the years. His back was straight with his hands in his pockets, like folded wings ready to take flight at any moment. But not yet. Why rush things? He was in Colorado, after all, the Rocky Mountains. Every day was a holiday for him, for life was far too short, and *somebody* had to live it before it was all said and done.

No one would live it for him.

And who was he to live life for someone else?

Life was sacred, precious, each breath a gift from above, for none were promised tomorrow. But with such great boons came great responsibility; it was not something to be squandered or abused. At all. That was the code, the philosophy, the very bones of civilization. And there were too many of those who violated this code. Far too many. Constantly. And when one violated life…there were consequences.

Not everyone was worthy of life.

But he needn't look far to find them; he need only bother looking.

And the parasites of society would present themselves…waiting to be exterminated.

The hunt was on.

As he trod through the fractured asphalt to the diner's glass door, he took another look at the moon nestled in the clouds, seeing a few flakes of snow twirling down to the restaurant's petite patio area. His smirk widened as a frigid wind blew, unable to penetrate the fleece lining his jacket, gray as death.

"Another storm comes," he rasped in his smooth, gravelly voice, then he breathed in through his nostrils. "Such sweet, sweet mountain air."

He entered the vacant, rectangular diner, the opening door dinging and alerting the curvy, plus-sized blonde waitress behind the counter. She looked at his worn, clean-shaven face and smiled.

"Hello," she chirped.

"Good evening," the man greeted, removing his fedora. He approached one of the barstools at the counter, his piercing blue eyes fixed unblinking on her round face. "I love your hair, by the way."

9

"Aww, thank you." She grinned, stroking the curly locks, bouncing just above her shoulders. "Just had it done today."

"If only more men would appreciate women and the travails you go through, especially in this day and age." The man brushed his gloved hand over his shimmering bald scalp. "Alas, chivalry is a dying art."

The waitress groaned. "You can say that again. Wish my ex-husband shared that sentiment."

"Such a shame," the man remarked, feigning pity. "He knows not what he lost; he struck gold, and he threw it all away."

"What?" she asked, scrunching her face, then giggled. "Oh, right, the, uh…the hair." She let out another sigh. "What can I getcha tonight, hun?"

"Could I trouble you for a cup of coffee?" the man requested, then squinted at her nametag. "Miranda? Such a pretty name."

She fluttered the lashes of her dark-brown eyes. "Well, I like it too. Sugar or cream?"

"Black, please."

"We also have freshly-baked pumpkin pie, one of our specials tonight."

"Mmm," the man hummed. "Sounds delectable. I'll think about it."

He winked at her. She grinned at him again as her stocky, buxom shape sauntered to the coffee pot. With her pudgy fingers, she poured the steaming caffeine into a pallid mug. "You're not from around here, are you? What's *your* name, hun, if I may ask."

"Friends call me Sam," the man claimed. "Just passing through. Your little town of Westcliffe is rather quaint. I like it. Lovely scenery. Very peaceful."

"Sam," Miranda said as she finished pouring. "I have a cousin named Sam. He lives out in California working with real estate."

"How enterprising," Sam commended.

"Yep," Miranda muttered, then handed him his coffee. "So is *this* gig."

"I'm sure," Sam agreed.

He took a seat on the ragged barstool, placing his fedora on the counter and took a slurp of the piping-hot drink, then he examined the rustic diner, gently swiveling to his left on the leather cushion.

The compact restaurant exuded the languid splendor of a log cabin home, corresponding to the region's alpine atmosphere and its abundant history of pioneers and the Old West. Adjacent to the bar were a row of small booths, their edges chipped with wear and tear. Portraits of Hollywood gunslingers, including autographed photos of Clint Eastwood and John Wayne hung overhead. Other accents of cowboy life and even a few Native American trinkets were also present on the walls, ranging from rusty horseshoes, bull skulls, wagon wheels, axes, and other knick-knacks of the sort. Halloween décor scantily populated the place here and there, comprised of merely two ceramic jack-o'-lanterns, a wiry black cat wearing a witch's hat, and a few stickers of cute cartoonish ghosts stuck on some of the windows with the age-old phrase: "Trick or Treat!" scrawled below one of them, while another simply said: "Boo!"

Sam smirked at the quirky seasonal decorations, then back at Miranda. "You like Halloween?"

"Love it!" Miranda boasted. "Only other day I like more is Christmas."

"Your black cat is amusing."

"Yeah," she said, approaching the artificial feline, observing its arched back and plastic tinsel fur. "Looks the way I feel right now." She puckered her lips to one corner of her mouth as she cleaned off a space on the counter from a recent patron. "I tend to like dogs more, though."

"So do I," Sam concurred. "Dogs are more…appreciative than cats."

"Yeah—I mean, cats are okay, I guess," Miranda rambled, grabbing a wet rag from the sink. "I mean, I…I don't…I don't really have a *huge* problem with them. Like, my kids like 'em, so it's fine, I guess. Cats just get snobby and…I don't know."

"Dogs are more trainable than a cat," Sam told her. "One can condition it to obey. They are more cooperative, more…submissive. The cat, on the other hand…is shrewd, always toying with its prey, a lot of times just for mere sport. It wants *us* to submit to *it*." He shook his head. "And we're told that it's 'instinct.' Makes one wonder…." He raised his coffee cup. "But the dog…the dog is well-mannered, playful…useful…always obedient to its master, adherent to its training all throughout life, performing tricks in exchange for treats, never asking questions."

"Right?" Miranda chuckled, rubbing the white countertop with the damp cloth. "I saw a cute little sign in the store the other day. It said something like: "Dogs have owners. Cats have staff."

"Very true," Sam said, then he took another sip of his coffee. "Very, very true." He rested the mug on the counter, then cleared his throat. "Now, do you…ever get trick-or-treaters in here?"

"Not really," Miranda said, wiping the rest of the counter. "I mean, we put out a little bowl of candy for customers and for kids that might come, just in case, but…" she scrubbed harder, "we usually get some…unsavory characters in here."

"Is that a fact?"

"Yeah." She sighed. "I'm a tough ol' gal, though. I can hold my own." She scrubbed a small stubborn coffee stain on the counter. "Too many people these days got thin skin. They shatter like glass at the first insult, always on their phones and what not. Bunch of crybabies. Gotta be tough. Stand up to little shits, know what I mean?"

"I hope you don't think that of me."

"No, not you!" Miranda chuckled sheepishly. "You're okay."

"That warms my heart on this glacial night," Sam said.

He noted the fridge behind the counter, stocked with cans of soda and bottles of cheap beer behind its glass door. Miranda smiled again at him, cocking her head with her plump arms akimbo.

"You talk funny," her voice twanged. "Are you a poet or something?"

"In a manner of speaking," Sam flirted.

11

The door opened and closed behind him with another ding, followed by the squeaking of old tennis shoes and mischievous snickering. Sam turned as Miranda's sanguine expression evaporated, eyeing three scrawny young men in jackets and torn, baggy blue jeans sitting three barstools away from them. Each punk wore shit-eating grins. The one in the middle wore a silver coat, appearing to be dominant over the others. The one on his left was clad in a padded jacket of yellow with gray patches, while the other one sported an orange hoodie.

White trash. Pretending to be black.

"This is the *third time* these damned little brats have been in here this week," Miranda griped under her breath. "Why can't they just get the hell outta here already?"

"Who are they?" Sam murmured.

"Some Yuppie crackheads from outta state," Miranda huffed. "I called the cops on 'em last time. 'Course, they didn't do anything; they're just a waste of tax dollars. Justice system's a damned joke everywhere ya go. Then, *I* got chewed out and wrote up by my boss by trying to ban them from the diner."

"Is that right?" Sam mused.

"Man, we got Betsy *and* Mr. Clean tonight!" the man in silver taunted.

All three of the grungy misogynists erupted with disparaging laughter. Miranda gritted her teeth, clenching her fists. Sam's smirk only widened at the three; they were just asking for it.

"Boy, how lucky are we?" the one in orange sneered.

"Well, that *is* the question, isn't it, gentlemen?" Sam mocked coolly, then he shot a surreptitious glance at Miranda, then back at the miscreants, showing them his wallet chockfull of hundreds. "Depends on how well you all play your cards tonight."

The three's expressions instantly hardened, eyeing the cash as Sam put his wallet away.

"Why the sour faces?" Sam asked, then nodded at a nearby booth. "Let's talk business."

"You a cop?" the leader in silver snapped.

Sam shook his head. "No."

"How're we supposed to know that?"

"How am I supposed to know *you're* not cops?" Sam teased. "I'm just a man looking for a good time, that is…if you have the cargo I'm looking for." He peered through the window at the moonlight. "The night *is* young, after all."

The leader whispered something in his two friends' ears, then he nodded at the booth. "A'ight, old man. Let's have a seat."

Sam turned to Miranda, then handed her a hundred-dollar bill, pointing at the beer. "A round for the mates and I, darling. And…keep the change…as a tip."

He winked at her. Miranda's eyes widened, taking the money, then she examined the bill in the light with leery eyes and verified its authenticity, muttering obscenities. She opened the drawer and slipped the cash under the money tray, then factored in the tip on the machine's keyboard and finished ringing him up. As she fetched the booze and opened each bottle, Sam took his fedora, then he and the three drug dealers migrated to the nearby booth. They all eased into their seats, squinting at each other.

"A token of my good will," Sam claimed as Miranda brought the beer.

"'Preciate it," the leader thanked soberly.

Miranda said nothing, already plagued with goosebumps forming along her round arms.

Sam placed his hat on the table, then raised his beverage. "A toast…to a momentous night."

"What's so momentous about it?" the leader scrutinized.

"As I said," Sam replied. "Depends on how well you play your cards."

Cautiously, the three men picked up their drinks, indulging him and clinked the bottles together, then each took a swig of the alcohol, its pilsner froth washing down their throats.

The leader cleared his throat. "Tastes like shit."

"Not the best in the world, I must admit," Sam said, examining the beer label, "but it will have to do…for now." His smirk widened again. "You'll be able to buy something better later."

"Thanks for the shit beer," the leader criticized. "Who are you?"

"Call me Sam. And you are…?"

"Savage," the leader said, then pointed a thumb at the man in yellow on his left. "This is Bungie." He glanced at his lackey in orange on the right. "This over here is Blaze."

"What up?" Blaze said.

Bungie nodded upward at Sam.

"Cute," Sam mused, taking another gulp of beer. "A little bird told me you have some schwag up for grabs."

"Says who?" Savage raised an eyebrow.

Sam leaned in. "A…little…bird."

"Right," Savage rasped as Bungie whispered something in his ear, then Savage shook his head at his accomplice. "Nah, she ain't gonna call 'em pigs again. 'Member what happened the other night?"

Bungie whispered something else.

Sam glanced back and forth at all three of them. Blaze squinted at Sam, then stared at Miranda. The rotund waitress watched them from the corner of her eye.

"Look, it's too late now," Savage told Bungie in his ostentatious gangster lingo. "He be on to us. Might as well make a sale." He eyed Sam. "Ol' Mr. Clean over here's lookin' to peruse our merch. Ain't that a fact, Sammy Boy?"

"I won't tell if you won't," Sam said. "We're in too deep now, anyway. If one of us squeals, we *all* get the slammer. We can't have that, now, can we?"

A crude grin twisted on Savage's face, revealing crooked teeth grimed with countless cigarettes; a few were capped with tarnished gold.

"He's cool?" Blaze asked.

"He's cool. He's good." Savage pensively rolled his lips back over his filthy teeth, then he locked his bony hands together on the table. "But, see…Sammy, we can't do business right here."

"No, you're right," Sam said. "We need somewhere remote. And places around here are limited. Roads are snowed in, and the snowplows stopped after seven. We have to be careful, lest we get stuck somewhere, and if we have to call someone to get us out, we might get searched. Then we all get busted. You feel me?"

"You from around here?" Savage interrogated.

"I'm familiar with the area."

Savage glared. "That ain't what I asked you."

Sam shrugged. "Don't believe me, check your phone."

"What a swell idea," Savage quipped.

He reached into his pocket and unlocked the touchscreen, tapping letters into the search bar.

"Where you from?" Bungie questioned Sam.

"From out of state…but I visit Colorado periodically," Sam furrowed his forehead. "You?"

Bungie nodded. "Same."

"I like that jacket," Sam complimented.

"Thank you."

"Man, this guy…I don't know 'bout this guy, man," Blaze complained, looking at Savage. "Man, he don't know what the hell—"

"Nah, nah, nah, look, look, look, look…check this out," Savage said, looking at the map of blocked roads. "Yeah." He hissed air through his polluted teeth. "It's gonna be rough. See, look." He pointed at one of the highways. "That storm's already snowed in the way we came…and most everywhere else. Traffic's screwed up all over the place, see that shit?"

"Damn," Blaze cursed.

"Wha—lemme see," Bungie asked. "Lemme see that."

"Phantom Canyon Road might be a good place," Sam suggested. "Maybe."

"Where's that at?" Savage said, scrolling through the map.

"I believe it's…west of Pueblo."

"Is it snowed in?"

"Check the map."

"Why, certainly," Savage jested again, typing in the city's name.

As the drug dealers quibbled about what course to take, Sam peeked out at the incoming bank of clouds outside, steadily veiling the moon. Already, he was fantasizing about the remaining night, contemplating, plotting his next move. Always three steps ahead. He couldn't afford to live otherwise. He turned back at Miranda, eyeing the four from behind the counter, then he winked at her again. She furrowed her brow, no longer knowing what to make of her charming newcomer or the origin of his overly-generous tips.

14

And she wanted nothing to do with it.

"I guess we'll be able to take…I-25 to Pueblo," Savage strategized. "Then *maybe* we can follow…Highway 50 going west towards Cañon City. Let's see…I-25—that's going…that's going towards Denver, isn't it?"

"Denver—hey!" Blaze said. "Isn't that…man, isn't that where that Chris Sullivan thing happened recently? That…guy who was like a…wife-beater or rapist…something?"

"Yeah," Sam said with solemn curiosity. "It sure is."

"Speak for yourselves," Miranda grumbled.

"Yeah, man, that shit was all over the news a few years back," Bungie told him. "I think they said it was like…attempted murder or something. They pulled his books and everything! Yeah, I think his wife was on like *Dateline, FBI Files,* and…I forget what other cop shows."

"*Dateline*?" Savage scrunched his face at Bungie.

"You actually watch that shit?" Blaze judged.

Sam's glances alternated back and forth, observing his subjects with the morbid curiosity of a little boy holding a magnifying glass to an ant hill on a hot, cloudless summer day.

Bungie shook his head and shrugged. "Well, you gotta know what the pigs are up to if you're gonna dodge 'em." He scoffed. "Ol' Sullivan's wife probably watched those shows and learned all the tricks in the book. That's why you rarely see any women get busted on there; they know what *not* to do and how to play the victim. They be slippery like that. Probably framed Sullivan's ass for fame and fortune. Got away with it, too."

"You're fuckin' insane!" Miranda snapped at them.

"What makes you think she framed him?" Sam queried.

"Man," Bungie sighed. "I…I really…I—I honestly don't—"

"Pssh! She probably got a book deal or somethin' like that too outta the whole she-bang!" Savage sneered. "I don't know what women complain about so much. All they gotta do is squeal 'Rape!' and the world waits on 'em hand and foot, gettin' all pampered an' all that by the media, then they say they get paid less than men do! Yeah, right! Friggin' joke, man!"

"Oh, shit." Miranda snorted, struggling to stifle a cackle. "Cry more. Please."

"Look at all the women who are doctors and lawyers—they ain't doin' without!" Savage ranted. "What about the poor bastards who work in construction, gettin' paid a fraction of what those spoiled bimbos do? Those bitches ain't doin' without!" He snorted and shook his head. "Meanwhile, we fellas up in here havin' to hustle and risk our lives and all that shit, all because the stupid system wants to screw us over at every corner and turn, 'cause we get arrested for shit we didn't even do, then we can't find work 'cause of our record. Then they call *us* the 'crooks' because we have no choice *but* to resort to selling this shit 'cause they pigeonholed us into this, and we got nothin' else! Gotta survive somehow or 'nother! The thug life chose me, not the other way around! See what I'm saying?"

15

"Oh, my God!" Miranda chuckled bitterly. "Change your frickin' diapers already."

Savage glared at Miranda.

"It certainly *seems* like that, doesn't it?" Sam gently countered Savage's biased presumptions, turning his head and regarding Miranda's increasingly flustered disposition behind him.

"Man, it *is* like that—the hell you talkin' 'bout?" Savage protested, slamming his hand on the table and baring his teeth.

"Maybe if spoiled Yuppie skinheads like you weren't so damned spineless and stopped pretendin' to be Eminem, maybe you'd stand a better chance," Miranda griped.

"You say somethin'?" Savage boomed at Miranda.

"Got a problem with power? Any idiot can treat women like shit, you crazy bastard." Miranda shrugged and shook her head. "Have you ever tried being a man…instead of havin' your parents pay for everything?"

"That's pussy's really cookin' over there, ain't it?" Savage harassed.

"My pussy's a lot tougher than yours is," Miranda chuckled. "Shit, you look like a pit bull hate-fucked itself with a used Q-Tip—and nobody knows who the father is!"

Bungie and Blaze guffawed, almost falling out of the booth. Savage rolled his eyes and shook his head.

"Real-life Jerry Springer shit is all you are." Miranda put her hands on her hips. "Must have been the runt of the litter."

Savage grew unusually calm and looked out the window. "Bitch, you *would* know."

"Oh, go back to hell already!" Miranda fulminated at Savage.

"You need to make it squeaky-clean, Betsy," Savage jeered Miranda, then blew a kiss at her. "I wanna be able to see my face in that."

"I'm gonna be wearin' your nasty-ass honky face like a damned shoe in a minute," Miranda grumbled, scrubbing harder.

Savage blew another kiss at her. "So sweet."

Miranda glared at the shotgun and the box of shells behind the counter, then back up at the four shitheads. Violent emotions without names coursed through her veins like a molten hurricane. How the hell were these gutless worms not dead yet? It would be so damned easy to obliterate this quartet of pompous fuckers. Yet, her eyes were drawn back to the faded pictures of her kids taped to the wall. Then back at the gun. She sighed and continued cleaning. Parenthood spared them her wrath.

And spared her from doing life without parole.

Yet if they didn't leave in the next two minutes, nothing would stop her from skull-fucking all four of them with a good dose of buckshot.

"All politics aside," Sam said, then took another swig from his beer. "What do you gents say? And thank you for reminding me about…Chris Sullivan."

"Why?" Blaze inquired.

Sam shrugged. "Just a thought."

16

Blaze scoffed. "Weirdo."

Sam grinned. "A weirdo that wants to get smashed on your stash tonight."

"Yeah, boy!" Savage agreed aloud, then slapped his hands and rubbed his palms together.

"And…as a bonus, after we…conduct business," Sam proposed, "I know of a place in Denver where we can celebrate. I'll give you a hint: the dollar decides how far you can go with her."

"Oh, shit!" Savage whooped.

"Ooh-*whoo*!" Blaze howled.

"Crazy old man." Bungie smiled. "Hope you packed some Viagra."

"*I'm* not worried," Sam retorted smoothly, then he stood up and donned his fedora once again. "Shall we…before the storm worsens?" He strode to the counter, then whipped out another hundred for Miranda. "For you and the children. Are you going to be all right?"

"Like I told ya earlier, hun," Miranda huffed, feigning a smile, "I'm a tough ol' gal. I hold my own. One day at a time."

"I admire that." Sam nodded. "Thank you so much for your kindness. Stay strong."

"Thank you," Miranda said bemused, taking and checking the bill as Sam exited through the glass door.

Savage murmured something to Blaze, then all three of them got up and walked out of the diner, following Sam out into the parking lot. With a small remote on his keychain, Sam unlocked his black pickup truck and opened the door.

"Nice wheels, boss," Blaze admired with his hands in his hoodie's pockets. "V8?"

"V6," Sam replied, rubbing the dashboard. "But she gets me where I need to go. Four-wheel drive…with a hemi."

Blaze whistled in adoration as he briefly peeked at the clean interior and examined the upholstery. He smelled the cab, reeking of the scent of a new car. He squinted. It was spotless! Not a single speck of dirt, food stains, or anything; even the polished exterior seemed to have been just waxed, devoid of any abrasions or scrapes.

Clean.

Way too clean.

"Excuse me," Blaze said.

He walked back to his two accomplices standing around their pale, muddy SUV.

"Well?" Savage asked.

Blaze shook his head and looked back at Sam. "No ham radio, no strobe lights, nothing. I guess he's legit. I don't know, though." He glanced at the others. "I think he stole that truck just today."

"Well…we might have to take a chance on 'im, boys," Savage said, glancing at the incoming snowstorm. "All these wussy stoners out here haven't been exactly…all too eager to check out our supply…and business has been slow. Hadn't had much luck, especially with all the gas we've burned makin' our way out here. Been a long trip. Might as well make it worth our while."

"What if he pulls somethin' on us?" Bungie questioned.

"We got this." Savage glanced at the revolvers below the SUV's console. "If he tries somethin' on us, we'll smoke 'im first." He smiled. "Might smoke 'im anyway. Take that fat wallet of his."

"You know, I don't think he had a…credit card or…phone or anything," Blaze observed.

"So?"

Blaze shrugged. "Just noticed is all. Kinda weird—look, let's go, already. I'm freezin' my balls off out here!"

"A'ight." Savage said.

Sam shut the door to his vehicle, then approached them. "So, want to follow me?"

"Say, look, uh…Sam," Savage said. "How's about…*you* follow *us*?"

Bungie and Blaze looked at him, eyes wide.

Savage raised his phone. "I mean…I got directions."

Sam paused, then he smiled, tipping his hat at them. "Sure. As you wish."

"I'll drive nice and casual for ya." Savage grinned. "See you there, boss man."

"Likewise," Sam replied.

With that, he stepped back to his truck as the three degenerates entered and started up their white SUV. Sam opened the door and slumped into the driver's seat of his vehicle and cranked the engine with a vehement thrum.

"Chris Sullivan, huh?" Sam said, adjusting his rear-view mirror. "Looks like I'll be making *more* than one stop this go-round." He backed out of the parking space, watching Savage's dingy SUV leave the lot, then he pursued them onto the road. "For all they that take the sword…will perish by the sword."

They departed into the night as the storm fully shrouded the moon, blinding the sphere and blanketing the mountains with even more darkness. The clouds sprawled like a shadowy wingspan taking flight, soaring down the Sangre De Cristo peaks, engulfing the summits like the ethereal maw of the netherworld. Sam grinned as he closed in on the three; he felt as if taking wing with the invading tempest overhead as the brisk, icy gusts waylaid into the sides of his truck, like updrafts beneath an eagle's deft glide.

He was one with the mayhem.

He eyed his prey. Amateurs. Against a professional, a living calamity. The scum knew not what they were dealing with. Not yet. Yes, the night was still young, and the parasites he sought had presented themselves.

Along with so much more.

He gleefully wrung his gloved hands around the steering wheel, his heart racing.

The hunt was on. Again.

II: The Wake

The next morning, two federal agents, Vince Redman and Theo Nash, exited their black SUV, both clad in bulletproof vests, as they advanced on the grisly murder scene deep within Phantom Canyon's gnarled bowels, just west of Pueblo. The overcast sky shone like silvery stained glass with the platinum sunlight gleaming halfway through the opaque shroud above, its brilliant beams and the canyon's serene landscape a parody to the gory atrocity before them.

Redman was a bald, rotund African-American and a senior officer at the bureau precinct in Denver, having entered his mid-forties. He wasn't going to let age faze him, though, and the way he saw it, he could retire when he was dead. Retirement was for old people. Already, he had beheld his fair share of the worst scumbags and their heinous acts…and there were plenty more where that came from. This was nothing new to him, not that he ever took any pleasure in it. Who in their right mind would? It was all part of the job—and somebody had to do it, damn it. And as painfully cliché as it all sounded, in all his years of policework trying to work his way up the ladder, he never once had been licked on a case.

Not yet, at least.

Nash, on the other hand, was a toned Caucasian with a full head of brown hair. He was already into his early thirties, having recently transferred to the FBI and busting his ass all the way from Denver's police department for the past decade. His wife, Laura, did not share his enthusiasm for law enforcement; her guts were always tied into knots, wondering when she was going to be widowed. Nash was no tenderfoot to the force, but as far as Redman was concerned, Nash was still a bright-eyed and bushy-tailed "probey" and an ambitious fresh prick who errantly saw himself as a loose-cannon cowboy.

Nobody had time for his "Dirty Harry" bullshit.

Already, more federal agents and sheriff's deputies were at the sight, including CSI personnel that consisted of Deanna Gordon, a Hispanic female crime scene photographer with her long, wavy hair in a ponytail, and Curtis Tully, an Asian blood spatter expert. Rick Wellborn, one of Nash's buddies he met at the academy years back, was examining the tire tracks with another investigator. A few others of their team were present bustling about, examining footprints in the mud and snow, all garbed in uniform, wearing thick coats, latex gloves.

And permafrowns.

"It was only a matter of time," Redman, the senior agent, muttered to his younger partner.

"It still just seems so random," Nash replied. "Killing drug dealers here in Colorado?"

"Precisely what the Vulture wants us to think, kid," Vince said. "Ol' Bird Man's making a statement is all. He's letting us know he's arrived and on the prowl. It's all a game to this sicko, and having us chase after him makes it seem more sporting. These freaks always have their patterns they follow; they choose, then expand their hunting grounds. We'll get to the bottom of it sooner or later." He sighed, gazing at the bloody display. "And the sooner…the better."

"Geez." Nash furrowed his brows at the three eyeless bodies.

"Morning," one of the deputies greeted as he approached the duo. His mouth was busy chewing gum with his eyes veiled in aviator sunglasses. "Lieutenant Terry Nelson." He pointed at a toned female deputy with a blonde ponytail and a bulky cop with short black hair. "This is Officer Rita Carlson and Harry Brown."

"I'm Agent Vince Redman," Redman introduced, then pointed at his partner. "This is Agent Theo Nash."

Nelson pointed at Nash's wedding band. "You married?"

Nash raised an eyebrow. "What of it?"

"For how long?"

"Five years now."

The lieutenant smacked his gum. "Give it another two years."

Nash rolled his eyes.

Carlson neared him and leaned into his ear. "Don't mind him. He's not too fond of G-men crowding the investigation."

"We're not crowding," Nash muttered. "I'm a cop. You're a cop. We're all cops here."

"I know," she replied.

"We're happy to cooperate with the FBI," Brown claimed.

"I'm touched," Nash smarted.

"So am I," Wellborn added, walking to them and fist-bumping Nash. "Morning, bud. How's the wifey?"

"She's fine," Nash lied, nodding as his friend. "We're fine."

"What do we got?" Redman inquired.

"A damned mess, as you can see," Nelson cursed, still smacking on his gum, as he strutted around the three corpses. "It would appear that the Vulture got more than what he bargained for this time. Shootout took place. One was armed with a .357 magnum, with the other two having 45 calibers. These punks were fighters, but they just didn't know what they were up against."

"Lucky them," Redman quipped as he and Nash each slipped on a pair of latex gloves.

"What sort of contraband were they dealing?" Nash questioned, crouching and examining the cadavers and reddened slush.

"Odds and ends," the lieutenant reported, pacing around as Gordon continued to take photos. "I suspect they were amateurs. Heroin, Xanax, LSD, meth, even a few kilos of coke. Just scrappy gangster wannabes. A bunch of white trash all the way from Florida, with arrest warrants galore and charges ranging from grand theft, armed robbery, sexual assault, possession, DUIs, the works." He pointed at the body in the silver jacket. "Harold Easterling, age 26, alias 'Savage.'" He indicated the dead man in the torn yellow coat. "Gage Madison, age 21, alias 'Bungie.'" He nodded at the carcass in the bloodstained orange hoodie. "And this poor bastard over here was a little renegade from Texas. Darrell Lancaster, age 23, alias 'Blaze.'" He aimed a finger at each forehead, branded with a square eagle insignia. "Looks like the Vulture has roosted here in the Rocky Mountains, for the time being." He shook his head. "Guess he got bored with the West Coast."

"Time of death?" Redman asked.

"Early this morning," Curtis Tully, the blood spatter expert, said as he knelt down. "He's getting more and more creative with his victims."

"Each time he kills, he does something different with the blood," Gordon observed as she snapped another picture at the mutilated bodies.

"As ever, he sees himself as an artist," Tully explained, gesturing at the blood strokes in the melting snow. "This time, he made blood angels out of them, along with some…runes, weird markings, satanic, maybe. He painted 'wings' and 'halos' in the slush, then gouged their eyes out, probably took them as trophies. May indicate some sort of background with the occult or perhaps a mere fascination thereof, along with his sociopathic sadism and vampirism, his blood fetish. Guy thinks he's Dracula." He looked at the agents. "But it's like Deanna said: it's always something different."

"But the insignia is always the same," Redman replied. "The brand on the foreheads."

"Right," Gordon confirmed. "His signature's always consistent. Probably from a metal stamp or…maybe even a ring."

"You sure it's not a copycat?" Nash inquired.

Gordon raised an eyebrow at Nash.

Lieutenant Nelson sighed. "There's always that possibility."

"Unlike the drug dealers," Tully said. "Three other bullet casings were found, positioned up in the snow in a trilobal formation, fired from a 9mm." He pursed his lips. "We also got a call earlier this morning from a local dealership about a brand-new black Dodge Ram missing from their lot. Somehow, he got the key from their office and bypassed the alarm system of the building. No sign of forced entry, no prints, nothing. They even found that their security cameras had been disabled shortly before the robbery."

"We also have some reports of stolen license plates throughout the area," Nelson said, "some around Gold Camp Road in Colorado Springs and even in downtown Denver, particularly around Cheesman Park."

"Why in downtown?" Nash asked. "It's too risky."

Tully shrugged. "Maybe he heard about the urban legends and the alleged paranormal activity that people claim to see there." The analyst shook his head. "He clearly has a perverse fixation on gothic things. Given what we know about him thus far, it wouldn't surprise me if that's what attracted him to that specific area."

"Bastard thinks he's Dracula *and* a warlock." Gordon scoffed.

"Wouldn't be the first," Redman groaned.

"If that's the case, we might want to keep a closer eye on Cheesman Park over in Denver and other areas like that," Nash grumbled. "That place used to be a cemetery. There're still bones lying in that dirt."

"Wouldn't hurt to put additional surveillance in that area and others like it," Gordon agreed. "Especially ones purported to be 'haunted.'"

"I have a hunch it's him," Redman scoffed. "I don't think a copycat would have the guts to be as meticulous and crafty. He's way too slick. It's gotta be him, whoever the hell he is."

"You're not alone in that, Red," Nelson concurred, then looked back and forth at the dirt road and at the crystallized alpine trees above. "My gut tells me he'll probably target residential areas."

"Or it's possible he might switch up his MO altogether just to mess with us," Gordon said.

"Might as well put the whole state on alert," Nash grunted, rising up.

"That may not be a good idea, probey," Redman suggested. "I've noticed that it's when the media gets involved, he goes dormant, waiting for the heat to die down, then he strikes again, catches everybody off-guard. Slippery bastard. Like trying to catch an eel with your bare hands."

"We may not be able to keep a lid on it," Nelson said, peering down the road.

"Why?" Nash questioned.

The lieutenant said nothing, still chewing, then nodded.

They all turned to see a white van with the local news logo on its side.

"Son of a bitch," Redman growled.

"Weasels are always hungry for a scoop," Gordon snorted. "Relentless."

"We'll handle this," Nelson smacked as he, Carlson, and Brown walked towards the van.

Nash's phone rang. He pulled it out and looked at the screen, a number he did not recognize.

Telemarketer, probably.

"Excuse me," he told Redman, then stepped aside to the canyon's jagged wall and reluctantly answered the call. "Agent Nash speaking."

Silence. Only the faint crackle of static teemed on the other end.

"Hello?" Nash demanded. "This is Agent Theo Nash."

"Detective?" a woman's dainty voice chirped.

"May I ask who's calling?"

"Um...this is...this is Lucy...Rosenthal," she claimed. "I don't know if you, like, remember me. You were involved with my sister's...rape case. Mina. Do you remember her?"

"How could I forget?" Nash admitted. "How's she doing?"

"I can't...get a hold of her," Lucy said. "It could be, like, that her phone's just not working or something, but it's been like...four days now. And until I'm sure...I don't want to, you know, jump the gun and file a missing person's report and get the media all creeping back to her house and bugging the crap out of her—that is if I don't have to...because I know she hates that."

22

"Trust me," Nash sighed, eyeing Redman and Nelson cussing the news reporters. "I know."

"So," Lucy continued, "all that said, I'm hesitant to call 911, and I remember you gave me your card...and I was wondering if you, like, had time to *quietly* do a quick welfare check on my sister?"

Nash paused, mulling it in his mind, then he let out a small groan.

Mina was missing?

And the Vulture was loose in Colorado?

He didn't like where this was going. At all.

"Detective?"

"Yeah," Nash blurted. "Yeah, we'll uh...we'll swing by right quick. We're...conducting another investigation right now—but this afternoon, we'll...we'll check on her. Don't worry." He breathed out another sigh through his nostrils. "You doing okay otherwise?"

"Yeah," Lucy said. "I'm just...worried about my sister, that's all."

"I understand."

"Just, if you could, give me a call and let me know she's okay when you go by there."

"I sure will."

"Thank you, Detective."

"Anything else?"

"I think that's all. I have to go."

"Yeah, don't worry. We'll check on her today."

"Okay," she sighed. "Bye."

With that, the nervous woman hung up.

Nash put his phone away and looked at the triad of bodies. "Shit."

"Look, the press has the right to know!" one of the reporters barked.

"Sir, we're not ready to disclose any information at this time," Nelson rebuked. "If you could—sir? Sir! If you could...please be patient, and we'll get back with you and your team as soon as possible. Let's all try to keep cool and relax, and we'll be with you shortly—we'll have a report for you very soon, okay?"

"Red!" Nash called.

Redman turned, then walked back to his partner as Nelson, the deputies, and the reporters continued their bickering. Nash leaned into his ear.

"Mina Rosenthal," Nash whispered. "Sound familiar?"

"Vaguely."

"That was her sister, Lucy, on the phone," Nash said. "She can't get a hold of her. Thinks she's missing. Wants us to make a welfare check."

"She didn't file a missing person's report?"

Nash groaned. "She wants us to check first. Discreetly."

"Shit," Redman cursed, looking around the canyon. "And with this nutjob runnin' loose, that don't spell anything good." He turned back to Nelson. "Lieutenant!"

"Yeah?" he said.

23

"We gotta run," Redman said, shaking his hand. "Give us an update when you can."

"Will do," Nelson chewed, them aimed his hitchhiker's thumb at the news van. "Don't worry 'bout these clowns—I got this."

"Alright," Redman replied as he and Nash entered their SUV. "Better be just a broke phone that girl's got. I can only take so much good news at one time."

"I don't understand why Lucy can't check on her," Nash said as they pulled around the van and onto the road. "I mean…if they're sisters, I mean…."

Redman shook his head. "Maybe she's too afraid of the answer, too terrified of what she's gonna find over there, wanting us to cushion the blow for her. I don't know how well those two get along, with or without the drama that's been goin' on. Mina's afraid of her own shadow—and I get it, you know, after…after all the shit she's been through." He scoffed as he turned on one of the bends. "I just hate it all the more that it was one of our own who did that shit to her."

"He wasn't FBI, though."

"No," Redman sighed again. "But he *was* a cop." He snorted. "Not anymore, though. Now *there's* a pig. Serial rapist on the rampage for what…ten years, give or take? Right underneath everybody's noses, too! And poor Mina got to be the posterchild for it, even though there were…I don't remember how many victims there were. I don't know why the media does that, always singling out that one person in cases like that, just…fixated on that one face."

"Well, it's quite understandable that she wants the media to piss off about it," Nash commented. "Otherwise, she can't move on. I wouldn't want dipshits pestering me about it twenty-four seven. People gotta heal."

"Yeah…" Redman said absentmindedly as he turned on another curve, "whereas Evelyn Whitaker was all about the paparazzi…."

Nash shrugged. "People handle things differently, I don't know."

"Mmm-hmm…" Redman hummed.

Nash raised an eyebrow, seeing the wheels turning in his partner's head, his eyes glazed over in a scrutinizing meditation, shifting back and forth at the road ahead.

"You got that look again."

"What?"

"Those gears are spinnin' about something up in there."

"Boy, I'm watching the road," Redman deflected. "Making sure a damned deer or elk ain't gonna try to launch out in front of us. They're out like crazy prancin' around this time of year."

"You're not…second-guessing any—?"

"Look, let's just make sure that our perp didn't smoke this chick, alright?" Redman cleared his throat. "La Sombra, right?"

"Yeah, I'm getting the address now," Nash replied, slouching forward and tacking on the keyboard on the console, studying the flat computer screen above the ham radio. He scrolled through lines of various files. "Let's see…Mina Rosenthal…La Sombra."

"The shadow."

"Huh?"

Redman glanced at him, then back at the winding road. "That's what it means in Spanish: 'the shadow.' When the Spaniards came over, they came to that valley and noted how the shadow of the mountains stretched over as the sun was setting, looking so bleak and eerie at dusk…even though all valleys kinda do that. I don't know. Guess they had to name it *something*."

"It can be a pretty dismal place," Nash said. "Like a graveyard, even when the sun's shining."

"That's a fact," Redman agreed. "Looks like something outta one of those…Grimm fairytales or something, like Hansel and Gretel is creeping around in the woods…leaving breadcrumbs."

"Or a witch…living in a gingerbread house," Nash jested dryly.

"Is her name Bianca Sterling?"

"Could be," Nash smirked. "Good thing she's on our side."

"Trust me, she's not," Redman said. "She's just doing her job…and so are we." He exhaled again, then lowered his voice. "She ain't the only one, though. I hope I'm wrong."

Afternoon soon came as the two agents entered the suburbs of La Sombra, one of the scrappier neighborhoods. Though the pale sun had at last successfully torn through the obstinate veneer of wavy silver clouds, it did little to remedy the grungy mining town's unusual penumbra. Even its morose inhabitants were infected with the perpetual gloom, all garbed in thick attire, awaiting another brutal winter in the Rockies. Dirty snow caked the evergreens, rooftops, and rent sidewalks, seeming only to amplify the foreboding, unwelcome atmosphere, displaying the unforgiving wear and tear of the brick façades of the two-hundred-year-old shops, bars, cafés, and government buildings all the more prominently, obscure monuments to past strife and hard lives doomed to be forgotten.

A playground for lurking devils.

And Redman and Nash were no strangers to the seedy characters dwelling there or the packs of degenerates from out of state passing through. It wouldn't be the first time they had responded to calls in the area.

So long as it wouldn't be their last.

They pulled up to a small one-story house with pale-green wood paneling stained by weather and mildew, with a worn front porch and stone steps, its white paint peeling. The blinds and curtains were closed, disallowing any light to penetrate the archaic home. Cautiously, Redman and Nash exited their vehicle and approached the residence, the sun still seemingly unable to illumine the neighborhood. All seemed halfway grayscale, as if death itself hung in the autumn air. A harsh gust howled around them. Slowly, they stepped up to the front door. No sign of forced entry. They looked at the windows. No shattered glass, nothing broken. Nash took a breath, then gently released it…and knocked on the door.

"Stay sharp," Redman ordered. "Our boogeyman might be up in here."

Both agents clutched their pieces at their sides, unbuttoning their holsters, ready to draw at any sudden movement. They waited…and waited. And waited. Nothing.

Nash banged on the door. "FBI—open up."

They waited…then they heard the bumping of brisk footsteps on the floorboards. Their hearts raced, bracing themselves for the worst. Then the noise stopped. Redman's nostrils flared as the deadbolt clacked and slid away…and the knob turned.

The door cracked with the brass chain latch still fastened. Both looked…and saw half of a young Asian woman's face peeking out.

"Can I help you?" she chirped groggily.

"Mina?" Nash asked.

"Can I help you?" she repeated, growing annoyed.

"Yeah, uh…" Nash said. "I'm…Agent Theo—"

"I know who you both are," Mina sighed. "Hold on one second."

She shut the door, then undid the latch, then fully opened the door, revealing her tired, petite doll-like form and long unkempt black hair. She had to be somewhere in her mid to late twenties yet could easily pass for a high school teenager. She resembled an irritated ghost, unable to rest, freshly coaxed from her dark grave. Her wiry figure was clothed in an old gray T-shirt, ragged skintight blue jeans, and a dark-blue bathrobe with pink slippers, contrasting with her creamy-tan flesh…with her hand fingering something just behind the door.

"Nash and Redman, right?" Mina asked.

"We were just calling to check on you on behalf of your sister, Lucy," Redman said, managing a pained smile. "She claimed that she's had trouble getting in touch with—"

"Look, tell her I'm fine!" Mina snapped. "Geez, do I have to proclaim my existence to people every single day? I just want to be left alone. I don't want to talk to anybody—I don't want to see anybody."

"I understand," Redman replied.

"No. You don't."

"Okay."

"Any of those shit-headed news reporters with you?" she hissed.

Nash shook his hand. "No, ma'am."

All three of them stood there in an awkward silence as the wind exhaled another harsh breath around them, wailing around the corner of the house like a melancholy poltergeist creaking and popping the decades-old lumber.

"Anything else?" Mina griped.

"No," Redman said.

"Actually, there *is* one other thing," Nash said.

"Theo—"

"No, she needs to know," Nash protested.

"What?" Mina questioned.

"We don't mean to alarm you," Nash told her, "but there's been three people murdered this morning west of Pueblo."

"So?" Mina complained. "People get murdered every day. That's what people do: kill and rape each other…like the pigs they are." She squinted. "Even ones in uniform."

"We think it's the Vulture, the murderer from the West Coast," Nash said, then he pulled out a business card. "So, if you see anything suspicious, give us a call, okay?"

He handed her the cardboard, yet she regarded it with an icy gaze.

"Okay, then, well…." Nash put away the business card. "You know what to do."

"Give your sister, Lucy, a call if you could," Redman recommended. "Have a nice—"

Bam!

Mina slammed the door right in their faces, then hastily locked all the latches back.

"Day," Redman finished, rolling his eyes, then he stepped off the sun-baked porch.

"She can't do that," Nash barked, following his partner. "Hey, you—you're gonna just let her pull that shit on us?"

Redman glanced at the door, then walked to the SUV. "I'll let it slide…*this* time." He groaned. "It's been a helluva day for everybody." He opened the driver's side door. "Evelyn, on the other hand, would've invited us in and made us coffee and everything, just prattle on and on about her fancy book deals and interviews and what not."

"You still on that?" Nash criticized, hopping into the vehicle.

Redman just stared at his partner with glazed eyes.

Nash scoffed and closed his door. "I mean…nobody can be satisfied with something like that, regardless of the outcome, after what he did to her. Chris Sullivan's a prick."

Redman cranked the engine.

"I say those bones have been picked clean," Nash went on. "Done deal. Case closed."

Redman cranked the engine. "Some bones may remain."

"Red, c'mon," Nash sighed. "It's a done deal, man. Case closed."

"Mmm-hmm," Redman hummed, putting the cruiser into gear and easing into the street.

Nash scoffed again. He knew that sound. He'd known Redman long enough to know what *that* meant. His partner had been with the bureau for far too long.

If only he could leave well enough alone.

How Nash loathed the idea of reexamining that festering eyesore of a case, that wretched debacle! He hated Chris Sullivan. He hated anyone who put their hands on a woman like that. The very thought of seeing Sullivan's trashy face again only made him physically sick to his stomach. They had other things to get done. There was a damned serial killer on the loose, for shit's sake!

And one of the most psychotic ones yet.

"Go ahead and pull that case back up," Redman ordered.

"Yeah," Nash groaned, accessing the laptop mounted around the console.

"You don't mind, do ya?" Redman squinted at Nash.

"Nah," Nash lied dryly, tacking away at the keyboard. "I don't mind."

III: Amazons

Bianca Sterling strode on the fractured sidewalk of downtown La Sombra, her chin held high as usual as the biting afternoon winds graced her long, straight, flowing black hair all around her. The Asian-American attorney's eyes curiously scanned the windows of quaint gift shops she passed, debating whether or not to peruse some of them on her day off; it was Saturday, after all. Soon, the Monday-through-Friday grind would slam her once again in Denver's courtroom, as the city mercilessly worked her and Leah Anderson both like dogs with each case.

And they never stopped.

It was like clockwork. As the prosecutor, she was part of the political mechanism, another appendage of the district attorney's office. She was a sleek, voluptuous machine, designed and built to be fierce yet feminine and lovely while programmed by law school and her strict upbringing to shrewdly deal justice whenever and wherever she saw fit. She was cold and calculating, acerbic and embittered by the predominantly-male justice system that merely saw her as just another sweet-smelling piece of meat with tits and legs; if people hadn't known any better, they would have thought her to have an engine in place of a heart and wires and circuitry instead of blood veins and nerves. On the weekdays, she sported her suit, dress shirt, and skirt, with her toned legs clad in dark pantyhose, all positioned on black stiletto heels, always armed with her razor-sharp gaze and spring-loaded sass ready to launch from her rose-pink lips.

Today, however, she clothed herself in her fun apparel: a beige long coat over a pale-blue sweater and bellbottom blue jeans as she clomped down the street in her high-heeled boots—which she adored. Her compact leather purse swayed from its strap, bouncing off her hip to her curt, proud gait, concealing a taser and a can of mace.

She dared anyone to try anything on her.

But all people saw of her was the acidic bitch and not the longing flesh-and-blood woman beneath; she was too arrogant to ask for meaningful affection. Like she had time for a real relationship. No, the occasional one-night stand after an evening at the bar seemed to be the only thing that reminded her that she was still a human being and not a heartless robotic drone of the legal system. She didn't think herself a slut; she didn't need anybody's permission or their approval in order to make love. Sex made her feel alive again, recharging her worn batteries, temporarily sparking her sentience once again. They didn't know her background, what she had to go through...or what she still went through. But their presumptuous criticism wasn't her problem.

The problem was that Saturday was almost over...and it had been a long week.

A very long week.

And she was scouting for a new face, one worthy enough for her woman-hood.

She wasn't exactly keen on doing the wife thing or the mommy thing, though. No, she was what they called "pro-choice" and utterly unapologetic about it; men just did not understand what sort of ball-and-chain children could be, at least according to her. Why brings kids into this miserable fallen world, anyway? If anything, she was probably doing her and the little brats both a favor; Planet Earth just wasn't what it was cracked out to be. Without marriage or parenthood to nag her to pieces, she could operate at top efficiency, never having to worry about all the petty malfunctions that mother-hood could inflict in her systems, that is…until she eventually became obsolete, decommissioned. Replaced.

And permanently deactivated by death's inevitable grasp.

But for now, she was top-of-the-line.

And virtually lifeless.

Somedays, she actually *did* feel like a synthetic amalgamation, mechanical and constantly running on empty. What had made her this way? What had molded her into this mordant catastrophe of a female? Maybe it was the verbal abuse of her right-wing "tiger parents" always pushing her too hard, pressuring her into marriage, trying to make her into a living Stepford wife, a windup doll, a sex toy, a man's plaything, all the while pampering those two slobs she knew as her brothers. Maybe it was being shipped off to Catholic school, being disillusioned by the preachy hypocrites of the faculty, while she fostered a fiery rebellion in her teenage years.

A rebellion she never really grew out of.

The one thing that refused to mature in her.

She wasn't the only one suffering from arrested development, though, however much of it plagued her. She never got to see that *all* teenagers are shitty, whether they get slung into a "religious" prep school by their wealthy, uncaring elitist parents, or attend just a regular public school…all filled with backstabbing, sex-hungry secular assholes, who were just as guilty of hypocrisy and other things. She knew the boys pretending to like feminism just wanted to get into her panties. And with her being a shapely Asian woman, that just made her a more appealing target. Mina Rosenthal knew that just as well as Bianca did, if not far better. Still, there was a twisted part of her that craved the lewd admiration from men, feeling them undressing her with their perverted gawking eyes, no matter how much she despised them.

They had no problem seeing *her* as a means to an end. Why not repay in kind?

Terminate…or be terminated.

That was the *true* nature of society. She was just better at it than everybody else. At least, that's how *she* saw it.

But buried deep underneath her superiority complex, the mildew of a dark shadow had begun to sprout and infest the recesses of her mind, proliferating silently like a creeping mold, threatening to oxidize the components of her wellbeing. What was this emotion? It had only started menacing her recently, ever since…that one case.

But why? She won. She was a victorious warrior.

An Amazon queen.

Yet, like a parasite, it clung to her, breeding inside, gradually worsening with time.

She walked faster, almost jogging, passing the bustling crowds, suddenly feeling as if being watched, then her stomach alerted her to the lack of fuel. Her batteries were running low again. But she had to maintain her figure. Maybe a small cup of pumpkin-spiced coffee with cinnamon, cream, and sugar would subdue her appetite long enough for dinner. She locked on to a stocky chalkboard outside a restaurant's door, advertising the very seasonal beverage she desired, then darted in…and finally stopped.

She took a breath, then released it.

What the hell was wrong with her? What had taken hold of her?

Maybe it was just stress from the workweek. Hopefully.

She swiveled her head…and recognized a familiar face.

She smirked and waved at her. Bianca smiled and waved back, approaching the woman and her family, consisting of her sulking five-year-old daughter…and her suave new boytoy.

"Evelyn, hi," Bianca chimed. "Haven't seen you in forever."

"Been busy," Evelyn sighed playfully, rolling her pale-blue eyes and flicking her long blonde mane over her shoulder, then she looked at the man with her. "Oh, this is my boyfriend, Newton. Newt, this is—"

"Attorney Bianca Sterling," Newton replied, extending his hand. "It's a pleasure."

Bianca feigned a grin, grabbing his palm and shaking. "The pleasure is mine." She looked at Evelyn and pointed at Newton. "Big upgrade from your ex-husband."

"He…sure is," Evelyn replied. "Yeah, Chris is a slob." She glanced at Newton. "But there are a few…exceptions."

"Got him trained yet?" Bianca teased.

"She's getting there," Newton joked.

All three of them laughed, yet Bianca noticed the cold awkwardness polluting the air…and she caught Newton sneaking a few glances, checking the attorney out. Yet it gave her little pleasure this time. Why? What was wrong? He wore a pastel-colored sweater and khaki pants, with a neat haircut, dark-brown hair already graying around the ears. Perfect smile, angular jawline, clean-shaven.

Toned body. Charming.

Blue eyes.

The guy looked like he had all his shit together, a rarity in civilization.

What's not to like?

Evelyn turned to her brunette daughter. "Melanie, you want to say 'Hi' to Ms. Bianca."

Melanie whimpered, turning away from her nemesis, the one who took her daddy away from her. Bianca pursed her lips, trying to maintain her composure.

"Melanie, what did I tell you about pouting?" Evelyn scolded.

The little girl glared up at Bianca with her dark-brown eyes, cutting the attorney deep into the very soul she didn't even know she had.

"My, look how big you're getting," Bianca complimented.

Melanie could no longer stand it. She lurched out of the chair, then stormed to the restroom.

"Could you excuse us," Evelyn said, chasing after her child. "Melanie Whitaker, you listen to me right now, you...."

Their voices faded as both entered the women's room as Bianca heard Melanie squeal to her mother's harsh rebukes. Bianca cringed; it reminded her all too much of how her mother treated her back when she was younger—even slapping her in the face at times.

And no one else ever knew.

"So, how goes the legal business?" Newton asked.

Bianca didn't respond at first, then she jerked to attention. "I'm sorry, what?"

"How's work?"

"Oh—yeah, it, um, it's...it—it goes," Bianca said, shrugging. "It's one of my days off, and I'm just...you know...relaxing...decided to go to...to La Sombra and see some of the shops."

"Well, I believe it's so great that women like you are in the system, contributing," Newton flirted. "Really makes a difference."

"You really know how to butter women up, don'tcha?" Bianca jested, arms akimbo.

"I do my best," Newton laughed.

Bianca giggled back...nervously, then she sobered back up. "So...what do *you* do?"

"Well, I'm in the tech business and..." Newton's voice trailed off as he noticed a gangly bald man enter the rustic bistro.

"Pardon me, ma'am," a smooth, gravelly voice sang.

Bianca turned wide-eyed, beholding the newcomer and his piercing gaze. He was dressed in ashen clothing, with a mischievous smirk across his face.

"Is your name Bianca Sterling?" the man asked.

"Who wants to know?" she questioned.

He pulled out a wallet from out behind him. "I believe you left this in the parking lot."

"Oh, thank you, sir!" Bianca yelped, taking it and checking its contents. "Thank you so much! Restores my faith in humanity."

"My pleasure, Ms. Sterling," the man said. "And might I say you look quite fetching on this frigid yet lovely day in the Rockies."

"That makes two of you now," Bianca chided smugly. "And you are...?"

"Call me Sam," the man replied.

"Newton," Evelyn's husband introduced.

"Pleasure," Sam said, hesitating, then the two men shook hands, locking eyes.

Squinting hard at each other.

"You...local, or from out of state?" Bianca interrogated, admiring Sam's mature physique.

"The latter, I'm afraid," Sam told her, examining the potted foliage in and outside the restaurant and the mountains in the distance. "Came to see the fall colors of Colorado."

"The Rockies don't disappoint," Bianca said, eyeing her new specimen up and down.

"I think Evelyn and I are debating about going to Breckenridge next month," Newton said. "Might do some skiing or something."

"Sounds exhilarating," Sam commented, noticing Bianca's curious eyes.

The door to the bathroom opened as Evelyn and Melanie exited back to their table.

Evelyn looked at Sam. "How ya doing?"

"I am well," Sam said as Melanie took a seat. "Uh-oh."

"What?" Evelyn asked.

Melanie peered up at him, sniffling, her face still moist with tears.

"I think I see something. Hold still," Sam said, reaching for her ear. His hand pulled back and revealed a quarter, then gasped. "Look at that! Got money coming out of your ears."

Melanie smiled as Sam gave her the quarter.

The three other adults chuckled.

"It's magic," Sam replied.

"Yeah, look at that," Evelyn said. "Say, the Tooth Fairy paid us a visit not too long ago."

"I trust the Tooth Fairy was good to you?" Sam asked.

"Uh-huh," Melanie squeaked sweetly, nodding. "She gave me a dollar."

"My goodness!" Sam expressed. "Why, you're rich! I hope Santa Claus treats you well this Christmas."

"Yeah!" Melanie said.

Evelyn laughed. "She's already making her Christmas list."

"I do hope that your holiday is merry and full of cheer," Sam said to Melanie. "And remember: as long as you believe in magic...all your dreams can come true."

Bianca eyed Sam and Melanie. This stranger had produced more of a sanguine attitude in a matter of seconds than her mother or Newton could have. He pressed all the right buttons, in the right sequence, with precise timing. She squinted at Sam. Who was he? Where had he come from?

She had to know.

And who knew? Maybe he was packing something else she was looking for. This wasn't like her, though. She wasn't *this* adventurous. What the hell had gotten into her?

"Well," Sam said, squinting at Newton. "I must be going. It was a pleasure meeting you all."

"Same to you, sir," Newton told him, squinting back.

"I gotta get going, too," Bianca said, then waved. "Take care. Good seeing you."

Sam left the shop, yet Bianca pursued him on the sidewalk.

"Hey, uh...Sam!" Bianca called out.

He turned. "Yes?"

"I...don't usually do this, but..." Bianca bit her lip, stroking her hair with her hands, trying to fabricate a convincing lie. "You...you seem good with children, and I have a friend who—"

"Walk with me," Sam offered.

Both of them strolled down the street.

Bianca looked at Sam. "I have a friend who's...majoring in child psychology, and she has to...do a survey...and I was wondering if I could pick your brain about it." She grinned. "I'll buy you a drink."

Sam's smirk widened, too amused by her wild, contrived claim. He could see right through her. He looked around the valley, the clouds moving in as the sun slouched behind the mountains, then he glanced back at his new acquaintance. His new toy. Chasing after him. It was too easy. But why pass up the opportunity? He had time to kill.

And plenty more.

"Do you know about the Chris Sullivan case?" Sam inquired.

"I was the prosecutor for it," Bianca boasted.

"I tell you what," Sam suggested. "I'll tell you what I know...and you can tell me how you brought down the loathsome Chris Sullivan." He looked around. "But let's do dinner instead."

"Sure," Bianca said bemused.

She took one last look at Evelyn through the window, still griping at Melanie with Newton eyeing her and Sam outside like a hawk. Something was so unsettling about it. She didn't even congratulate Evelyn on her survival story or even order a latte. She turned back to her new companion. What was happening to her? That mildewy dark shadow from before had instantaneously amplified in her mind, the icy claws of insecurity, a bizarre guilt that seemed to originate from nowhere. She was like a computer that had been hacked, infected with a virus, glitching up. And that excruciating conversation with Evelyn and Newton just now had left her short-circuited. This wasn't like her. At all. A woman of her caliber? It was unprofessional. Unheard of! Yet she couldn't stop, captivated by Sam's toned visage, his intellect. And something about that smirk. Those eyes. Something about it all just turned her on, and if she didn't resolve this soon, she was going to blow a fuse.

Sam lifted his elbow. "Shall we?"

Absentmindedly, Bianca took his arm, and both strolled down the street. A man, leading *her* around? Who did he think he was? Yet she failed to let go, like a hijacked automaton with its programming jammed. Her stomach turned within, her confidence having shrunk to nothing in the murk of the uncertainty before her, wrought by her irresponsible morbid curiosity. But she couldn't let Sam know that. She had to be strong, with a pretense of control, as she struggled against this mounting, unexpected system failure.

Her routine…had been sabotaged. And perhaps her weekend with it.

But that was the least of her problems.

As dusk set in, Mina Rosenthal dragged her bare feet to the bathroom, flipping the switch to the fluorescent bulb over the vanity. She eyed her façade. She looked like hell as usual. But those who go through hell end up resembling the part. The nightmares continued to haunt her, spawning more insomnia and paranoia each day. Her brown eyes peered in the mirror at the ghost of her former self, having woke up after sunset like a vampire yet again. She scoffed at the thought of such clichés. The air vent rattled above her as the overworked central heat activated once again, trying to extinguish the ghastly chill in the house. She did her business, took a shower, then brushed her teeth, then exited into her bedroom, looking at her phone. Lucy, her younger sister, had barraged her with yet another salvo of text messages and missed calls, longing to get in touch with her sibling. Her agoraphobia was steadily devouring her, causing her to detest her house more and more with each passing day. Yet she just couldn't go outside; she barely could stand checking her mailbox.

Lest another one of those men come out and attack her.

Disgusting pigs.

And it was a cop, of all things, that robbed her of her peace of mind!

A serial rapist for years, amongst their ranks.

The other cops covered for his ass for at least a decade.

And the gall that Lucy had to sic those two FBI agents on her the other day! Might as well ask to let the cons loose at the nearest prison to have a blood orgy with her, knives out and guns blazing. Lucy never bothered to come over, too busy with her husband and her new baby, yet she whined and complained that Mina didn't return her calls. She claimed to understand what Mina went through, but she didn't. Barely anyone knew the pain or the shame.

Of being a rape victim.

Sure, she had attended "support groups" here and there and had sought out "help" from egotistic therapists and psychologists who saw her as nothing more than a zoo animal to be studied and researched, trying to make a name for themselves. Hell, if they could, they would coin a brand-new disorder, call it "Mina Rosenthal syndrome," where someone drowned in the terror of leaving home or having complete disregard for the opposite sex.

Who, really, could blame her, though?

And how infuriated she was of Evelyn Whitaker!

No, she wasn't on Chris Sullivan's side at all, but Evelyn had no class whatsoever about the damned thing. A regular prima donna. Mina knew

35

fake crying when she saw it; she had grown up hearing Lucy do it on numerous occasions. If only she could hold her head up high like Bianca Sterling, a crusader for women's rights.

But she couldn't. The fear was overwhelming.

There was a time she wanted to have kids. But now, she didn't know. Who would want to bring children into this hateful world? She understood how stressful parenthood could be; she had been a babysitter when she was younger. And if the rapist had impregnated her—and thank heaven he didn't—she wasn't sure if she could truly bring herself to abort her child, even if the father was a monster. They called it a "woman's choice," yet all too often, it seemed like the only "choice" available was to push the "die button" on their unborn. What about adoption? Was that not also a choice? Why not just be an adult and be there for the next generation? Why should a man, or an angry feminist for that matter, decide for her either way?

Mina was a self-aware individual, unbeholden to any sect. She was no robot slave. She was not owned by the political mechanism. She did not rely on the "news" or social media to discern the world around her. She had learned these things the hard way, as her predictable, misogynistic college professors had taken all too much delight in targeting the female students in their classes, whether subtly or blatantly, all the while dubiously masquerading around as "activists" for the marginalized and disadvantaged. No, she was far past that tripe.

For her to be truly independent, she had to make observations and decisions for herself.

Not for a patriarchy. Not for feminism. Or academia. Or government.

Or anybody else.

She was a whole other kind of Amazon.

They didn't understand just how much the line had been blurred. Perhaps this "Vulture" prowling about saw himself as some sort of "abortionist," albeit deranged and bloodthirsty. But wasn't murder technically just another type of abortion? Could murder be construed as legal now, in some crude, roundabout way? How was it any distinguishable from injecting poison into a living embryo or fetus? After all, how did anyone know that human beings were ever alive to begin with? Because their fickle and precarious human preference somehow constituted it? What would people pretend to advocate tomorrow? Pedophiles?

Or even worse things?

What was this wretched, nihilistic future that awaited them?

Human beings lived in a world where racism, sexism, and animal cruelty were all recognized as wrong—and rightly so—yet babies could be butchered without any thought. Because children had no right to live, apparently, regardless of gender or skin complexion. So how could *adults* have any right to exist? How could men? Or women? What was the foundation for such faulty rhetoric?

Because the elitists in society said so?

Society hadn't stopped her rapist from scarring her for life! Society didn't get to decide what she said, thought, and did! They weren't the ones who were defiled by that bastard!

A tear rolled down her pale cheek.

Maybe she needed to start "aborting" men, with the squeeze of a trigger.

Over, and over, and over again.

Until there were all extinct.

At the end of the day, it wasn't like a mother's womb or umbilical cord made much of a difference in terms of what defined a human life. But she also understood the sorrowful reality of life-threatening birth defects or some disease that might kill both mother and child. Perhaps that was the only time abortion may have to be taken into consideration—but it was no less tragic or harmful! And what about the barren women who aspired to be mothers? And not everyone grew up to be like their parents; Mina sure as hell didn't. Bianca certainly didn't, either. It wasn't the child's fault she was raped. And destroying the child would not have put her rapist behind bars, no matter what anyone liked to believe. She shook her head, already weary of the obsessive political stew stirring in her broken mind.

One by one, she turned on a few lights in the house as night fell, then she entered the kitchen and opened the refrigerator, eyeing the Styrofoam box of zesty beef fajitas she had delivered to her home yesterday. Leftovers. Something to nibble on. Better than nothing.

Outside, someone shouted down the street. An argument.

A man and a woman.

She dashed to the window, peeking through the blinds. Yet she saw nothing. It was too distant, too dark, but it just close enough to hear…seeming to emanate from a few houses down.

Where Evelyn Whitaker lived.

She scoffed again. Somebody would call the cops, but it wouldn't be Mina. Let problems solve themselves. She had her fill of the pigs. They clad themselves in their glorified Boy Scout uniforms, thinking themselves as cowboys with their Batman utility belts across their fat waistlines. Just like the ones in Indiana, where she once lived. And the media relentlessly pestered her for a scoop, wanting to prostitute and plumb her for money. They were pigs, too. All of them. So-called "social justice warriors." She knew better. She was one of the few who saw past their smokescreen, their gaslighting. They were xenophobes in disguise. She was intelligent enough to realize they didn't truly care about her; they just wanted to molest her in a different way, a lucrative way, all the while pretending to walk on eggshells, as if she were an alien lifeform from another planet. In their eyes, she was just another means to an end, the poor little Asian girl, the weak damsel in distress through the perspective of the closet racist bigots of the self-styled "open-minded" mainstream.

That's not who she was. But that's what they had reduced her to.

Just another stereotype.

Even those who may have actually had the best of intentions.

How lively and adventurous she used to be! She was part of a volleyball team in college, athletic, a socialite, wanting to travel the world and explore with her family, her sister.

Her best friend.

She eyed a shelf where a few volleyball trophies and medals sat, coated with dust…with a photo of her and Lucy in mountain-climbing gear, grinning in the sunlight. It was the day they scaled Mount Rainier together in the Pacific Northwest. She stared at her reflection again in a nearby mirror, then back at the picture. She was indeed a mere shadow of her former life, her house having become a crude purgatory realm, awaiting the other side.

She huffed and took the Styrofoam takeout, spooning some on a ceramic plate, then covered it with a paper towel and popped it in the microwave, then pressed the button to reheat it. The dish cooked, sputtering and rotating on the turntable, then she walked over to the bookshelf in the living room next to the front door, where her revolver lay: a .357 magnum.

If Vince Redman or Theo Nash had taken another step closer to her….

And if this Vulture killer was loose….

She squinted at the weapon. She had forgotten to take it to her room yet again. And it had been a good while since she had cleaned it…or hit the shooting range, for that matter. She wasn't helpless; she knew how to take care of herself. Her adopted Caucasian father had shown both her and Lucy how to brandish a firearm and how to maintain it, for he knew all too well that both his beautiful daughters would be appealing targets for the depraved in society. But Mina hadn't liked guns before the sexual assault, neither did she fancy the notion of what would happen if she were caught with a concealed weapon. She didn't have a permit. She never bothered to apply for one. Thus, she had refused to carry it in her purse; she errantly thought the can of pepper spray she toted around would suffice.

And it cost her so much.

But now, she was all for the Second Amendment, the last vestiges of her left-wing sentiments having died with that part of her years ago after her rape case. Government would take care of them? Yeah, right. She knew now exactly what those cranky rednecks were talking about—but Donald Trump could still go fuck himself! Not that Obama or Biden were any better, or Bush, the Clintons, or any of those other jackasses. She was self-aware now. She was no machine. She was not subject to society's erroneous programming. She had to be stronger, stronger than Evelyn Whitaker, stronger than Bianca Sterling.

If she had to kick it like Red Sonja, so be it.

She knew what justice *really* was.

She got out a small toolbox and a gun-cleaning kit out of the kitchen drawer, then she took a wad of paper towels and retrieved the revolver from the shelf. She sat down on the couch in the living room, facing the kitchen, then she unloaded the bullets. With the petite screwdrivers, she disassembled the piece on the coffee table and proceeded to scrub the short barrel and chamber with the black brush, thoroughly swabbing it of soot and gun powder.

The microwave beeped before her, yet she had grown too immersed in the maintenance of her armament to pay immediate attention, burnishing the metallic parts with oil. As the minutes ticked by, the spicy aroma of the fajitas permeated the air and eventually caused her empty stomach to yearn for the cuisine, prompting her to put the gun back together. She wiped her hands with more paper towels and aimed the gun at the wall, making sure the sights weren't off. Then she loaded the ammunition back, then slung the cylinder magazine back in with a clicking spin. She stared at the firearm, then at the front door.

She had to overcome her phobias somehow.

If only she knew the way forward.

The future was a fog, the path so murky.

But she was ready enough. Ready for the Vulture.

Ready to stand firm.

She needed her life back. She had to restore her peace of mind.

Even if she had to blow it out of every man's skull to get it.

One at a time.

IV: Bereft

Naomi sighed out steam in the freezing air as she thrust open the door to her house, doing her best not to explode. She stepped over the threshold and into the unkempt living room, then slammed the door shut. She flung her brown fleece jacket on the back of the couch, which had become more of an elongated coatrack with pillows and cushions than actual furniture. With glazed eyes, she briefly surveyed the disorder of her house, a house she rented. Nothing seemed to belong to her anymore, not even herself. She huffed and briskly walked to the kitchen. The sink was still full of dirty dishes and the trash can was on the verge of overflowing. She just didn't have time for shit…and she was utterly sick of trying to get her shit together. Life had a nasty knack for taking a baseball bat and smashing everything she loved to oblivion.

Either survive…or die quicker.

She breathed a soft, dry chuckle and shook her head. Not much of a choice.

She tossed her keys to the counter; they ricocheted against the wall with a loud clack. The veins in her forehead were throbbing again. She let out another heated breath, trying to assuage her mind…and her heart.

The alcohol withdrawals were getting worse.

She eyed the sheet of notebook paper hanging from a magnet on her refrigerator door, titled: DAYS WITHOUT A DRINK. Fifteen tally marks. She took a pencil from the counter and drew a sixteenth on the paper. She emitted another sigh and examined her progress on the sheet. Sixteen days. A hard-won two weeks of anguishing sobriety.

And it was all she had. Other than her new job.

Which she abhorred. Deeply.

But a shitty gig was better than no gig at all, lest she wind back on the streets of Denver. Colfax Avenue was a fate worse than death, especially in downtown. La Sombra was a bit quieter than the concrete shithole of gentrified gray boxes she once dwelt in, a shithole with more dogs than people. Dogs. Everywhere, there were fucking dogs. Dogshit in the grass, on the sidewalk, on the hiking trails tied up in plastic bags and left to pollute the mountains and the wildlife. Dog piss in the elevators, in the hallways. Barking, howling. Shedding. Jumping on everyone, pressing their noses into people's crotches. Ruining everything. The owners were only worse, misanthropic Yuppies, control freaks, letting the dogs do whatever they wanted, letting them run without leashes.

But whose leash were the owners on?

And to think Naomi had once loved dogs.

Gone were the days where animals were just pets. Passing them off as children was flat-out deranged, but alas, that was the stuff of Planet Earth these days, infested with shit-headed hipsters as far as the eye could see and onward. How often they touted their dogs as "rescues," that dogs exuded "unconditional love" when it was nothing more than canned responses, operative conditioning incepted into the mongrel's mind by tantalizing them with food and doggie treats. And the men just used dogs as pussy bait, trying desperately to get into a woman's panties. Dogs walking other dogs. Nevertheless, Naomi refused to consider a so-called "fur baby," "doggo," or "doge" as "emotional support," and it *damned* sure would never be a replacement for her daughter, Aeriel.

Aeriel was her everything.

And everything had been taken from her.

It was another living hell to slog through, along with her new job as a receptionist at the local hospital. Every day, she was forced to don the fake smile and take the routine onslaught of abuse, from toxic phone calls to snobs varying in age to unattended kids—and, of course, dogs too—running and screaming up and down the halls from the waiting rooms. She loved kids, but the lack of decent parenting made these particular ones insufferable.

And all the while, her cantankerous new boss just breathed down her neck. Constantly.

Smile more. Be professional. Conform.

Assimilate.

She placed her hands on the counter and hung her head and scoffed. She might as well be a Stepford wife, a robotic torso bolted to the front desk at the lobby, swiveling left and right, grinning obliviously all throughout the day as a mechanical slave, abiding to programming she didn't want.

Plugged in. Like the rest of the world.

But she needed the money, as bullshit as it was. She scoffed again. Green paper. That's all it was. Dead trees. Deforestation. Either that or electrical signals in a computer system. A number. An amount, one that could be changed at the simple pushing of buttons. And people were starving to death every day, all because they didn't have enough slips of green paper. Not enough electrical signals to live. It was nothing more than another glass wall separating the overprivileged from those like her.

A tear rolled down her face. She felt so trapped.

And the impending Alcoholics Anonymous meeting did not help matters. She gritted her teeth. How she craved a drink right then! A gin and tonic. Whiskey. Something hard. She turned and glanced at the tally sheet on the refrigerator again.

Stay strong.

Just stay strong.

Chill the fuck out, she thought. *Try to. Just try.*

She sighed as she checked her phone, seeing if anyone had answered her nanny applications. No emails. No replies. Nothing…except for another daycare center rejecting her query. She wanted to rip the whole world down. It was like pulling teeth. She knew why she was being rejected. It wasn't even her fault.

And there wasn't a damned thing she could do about it.

Guess she was stuck being an organic answering machine at the hospital for the time being.

She looked at the clock hanging on the wall.

5:32.

"Shit," she cursed, then rubbed her round exposed forehead.

She undid the scrunchy holding her ponytail of curly dark locks in place and allowed her mane to roll past her shoulders. She peered down at her green scrubs, then walked to her bedroom. She sat down on the bed, then unlaced her white sneakers and slid them off, then she stood up and pulled her top off, revealing her petite breasts nestled in her white bra. She took off her pants, then strode to the bathroom. She did her business and flushed the toilet. As she washed her hands, she beheld her tired reflection once again. She wiped her hands on a towel on the rack and observed her lanky body.

She was as thin as a rail, so much so that one of her plus-sized colleagues at work asked her if she were anorexic. Her tattoo-scrawled skin was coppery with her interracial heritage, one she was proud of. Sadly, much of the world still seemed stuck in the Stone Age, and the ghetto she had grown up in was no exception. All the boys teased her growing up, calling her "Milky" all because her mother was white. But that didn't stop their wretched sex fantasies about her mom…or her, for that matter.

Men. A bunch of pigs.

But that didn't stop her from falling for the same damned shit every time.

Just about the waistline of her white panties, she stroked the thin stretch marks, barely noticeable now, then her fingers reached the old C-section scar, an ongoing reminder of a motherhood she would never be able to enjoy again, all because of a small misunderstanding.

If douchebags everywhere did, in fact, have a posterchild—and there were countless contenders all over the place—Rob, Naomi's baby daddy, made for quite the competitor for such a title. Abusive. Manipulative. Snide. Shady. Being the loving empath she was, Naomi made for a soft target for such an asshole. She knew better than to get involved with him…and she did it anyway. Like the mesmerizing event horizon of a black hole tearing a star apart, she too was taken with his superficial charm, culminating to the one-night stand that would change her life forever, forcing her to drop out of college, despite the "pro-choice" junkies at her school desperately trying to convince her to push the "die button" on her unborn little girl.

And she gave birth. By choice.

But it was not to last.

She made the mistake of attempting to make it work with Rob. She had given him an ultimatum: either change his ways and stop dealing on the streets, or fuck off for good. She was successful. So she thought. Another fateful night came when she was pulled over and caught with possession of crack. And lo and behold, the cops cut her no slack for being half-black.

It wasn't her fault. And no one cared.

Men. Fucking men.

Fucking system. Fucking Nazi shit.

Everything fell apart from there, from losing custody of Aeriel to her parents to sinking into alcoholism as a result, eventually leading to a DUI, rehab, and these bullshit AA meetings, drowning in one person's sob story after another.

Were all men like that? Just after ass, titties, and pussy?

Was Chris like that?

Another tear rolled down her face, then she huffed and hastily wiped it away. Chris. *That* Chris. Chris Sullivan. It had to be him. It hadn't dawned on her until just a couple of meetings ago. That shit was all over the news. The ruthless wife-beater. So they said. They crucified him all over national television. But it wouldn't be the first time the media dragged an innocent person's name through the mud.

And look what they did to her.

Besides, she preferred to investigate things for herself. That seemed to be the healthiest route. As far as she was concerned, there was no left-wing, right-wing—and Trump, Biden, and the others in Washington D. C. were all made of the same exact putrid shit. She was loath to allow a bunch of spoiled rich dumb-fucks in the world to tell her how to think and feel. The entire planet seemed to be constructed of sweet lies, glittering with its cheap, tinny glamour, brainwashing every mind to its convenient propaganda, one wave of misrepresentations after another.

Chris would be there tonight. Though there was still a good part of her that was reasonably leery of him, he still did not seem like the misogynistic monster the "news" made him out to be. Though Chris had yet to testify in the meetings—much to the exasperation of Patty, the meeting coordinator—he and Naomi could talk for hours afterward as they confided to each other their personal hells, just the two of them in the parking lot. He was an author. He was shy. He was deep. He was mysterious. How she longed to delve further and further into the fathoms of his soul, to see what really made him tick. But what atrocities might she roil to the surface in the process? Was Chris truly worth knowing, through and through?

Was the truth worth the trouble?

Pain bonded with pain, the morbid romance of life.

Like Naomi, Chris had also lost his little girl, Melanie. He seemed like a nice enough guy.

Then again, so did Rob…and a bunch of other dogs.

And look what happened there. Such was the stuff of sociopaths. Was there anyone she could trust? Why was she the one who had to go off on a limb for people every time? Why the one-sided romances? Why couldn't the ones she loved reciprocate the way she felt about them? Why did she have to fall head-over-heels for them every time? What was this doom in her life?

Why did she have to be alone?

She exited the bathroom and looked at her alarm clock on the nightstand. 5:46.

"Damn it, I'm runnin' behind," Naomi said, then stepped to her closet.

Frantically, she slid on a pair of skinny jeans with holes in the knees, then she slid on a sleeveless black T-shirt and a blue hoodie. Like a crane, she slipped her tennis shoes on and laced them back. She went into the bathroom again and applied a dose of cheap perfume, then briefly fluffed her long curly hair, eyeing herself in the mirror. She was no super model, but she wasn't made of numb plastic either. Already, faint bags were forming under her eyes…along with the beginning of crow's feet. She wasn't what she used to be. College felt just like yesterday, yet it had already been seven years. She knew…because Aeriel was seven by now.

And she wasn't allowed to see her little girl. Ever.

It would do no good to see her now. Aeriel wouldn't even know her, her own mother.

Her own flesh and blood had become foreign to her.

She felt so trapped. There had to be a way out of this hell!

As she entered the kitchen and reached for the fridge door, she stopped and eyed the tally sheet again, then she noticed the rectangular magnet holding the paper. The magnet featured a stern-faced Hispanic lawyer in a suit with black wavy hair down to his shoulders and his arms crossed. The lawyer stood in front of a purple background, with his name displayed in gold lettering: DAVE RODRGIUEZ. Beneath Dave's name, his business phone number and a schmaltzy slogan to his left read in more gilded letters:

YOU HAVE THE RIGHT TO FIGHT BACK!

FREE CONSULTATION

Naomi squinted at the magnet and took a step closer. It had come in the mail the other day, along with the other spam. She had come to the ace of spades of throwing it out with the rest of the shit mail but decided to slap it on the fridge only to hang bills and notes up with. Only now did she stare at it as she read off the services Rodriguez offered. She had been under the impression he only represented those with immigration disputes, which appeared to be his specialty. Car accidents. Wrongful death. Harassment.

Discrimination.

Naomi eyed the phone number again. It was a longshot. But it couldn't hurt to ask. She had a voice too.

And it had been taken from her.

Time to get it back.

She opened the refrigerator door and snatched a can of sparkling water, her only tangible bulwark against the alcohol withdrawals…and it was failing. She had to get through, even though she didn't really see the point. Maybe it was just something chemical. Instinctive.

She hoped there was more to it than that.

But there was only one way to find out.

45

She picked up her keys and walked out of the house, then locked the door, leaving the lights on lest some slobbering gangbangers decided to pay her an unwarranted visitor. With haste, she entered her car and cranked the engine back up. The classic rock played weakly through the speakers again, crackling occasionally from the lack of signal. She sighed again, then clicked her seatbelt on and pulled out of the driveway and back onto the icy streets. As she neared a red light at a four-way intersection, she toggled the knob to the radio seeking another channel.

"...Found dead near—" a male news reporter's voice sputtered as she surfed.

"What?" Naomi snapped as she returned to the news channel.

"Three bodies were found in Phantom Canyon near Pueblo, the result of a drug deal gone wrong and possibly the work of a serial killer, officials say, as the blood of the bodies was painted with strange occult symbols. While officials refuse to comment any further at this time, local police are urging citizens to be on the lookout for foul play and—"

"There's always foul play," Naomi snapped as she clicked the radio off. "All over the the damned—"

Beeeeeep!

A silver truck's horn blared behind her. Naomi looked at the traffic light, now green.

"Fuck you!" Naomi yelled at her rearview mirror, the rolled her window down and flipped off the truck behind her.

The truck's horn blared again.

"Motherfucker!" Naomi blew her horn and sped through the green light, still aiming her middle finger proudly up in the air, letting the frigid mountain air bite her face. She flew down the road, going fifty in a thirty-five speed limit zone.

The truck kept its distance from her.

"Fucking pansy!" Naomi growled at the truck, then she withdrew her arm and rolled her window up.

As she ventured further down the streets, Naomi vented another heated breath. Goosebumps formed on her skin as she pondered the news flash just now. Murders and drug dealers were nothing new to her. Nevertheless, the streets seemed darker in dusk's last light, with the misty black peaks in the distance seeming to loom taller than usual. They suddenly seemed so oppressing, so grim.

So wraithlike.

Everything wanted a piece of her.

She sighed again as she felt more tears welling up in her eyes. Chris was going to be there tonight. She knew he was interested in her. But to what degree, and to what end? Her emotions stood on the edge of a knife. She didn't want to be alone anymore. But she couldn't go another day taking the shit. Her mind was unraveling. Why couldn't this one guy be nice this time? Was he just another dog cruising for another fuck? Why couldn't she just be loved again? Even her own family had betrayed her, so why the hell did *she* have to care so damned much? The system was wrong about Naomi.

Why couldn't the system be wrong about Chris?

She huffed again and shook her head. She had to get her shit together.

Or she would drown in it.

She blinked, coaxing two more tears rolling down her cheeks. So many thoughts now raked across her overloaded mind that she failed to notice another set of headlights behind her: a black Dodge pickup that appeared brand-new.

With a smirking face behind the wheel.

Following her.

V: Two Lanes

A vibrant sunset adorned the skies of Denver's mountainous outskirts as a gray-headed man in a black suit exited his dark-green SUV in the steep driveway of an extravagant log cabin mansion. The multicolored vista of the heavens soaked into the wispy streaks of clouds like vivid paint strokes of gold, orange, pink, red, violet, and blue; its fleeting splendor was juxtaposed from the viridian alpine gloom of the rocky peaks and misty evergreen valley below. All was still dusted with a few traces of the snowstorm days ago. The man plodded up the gravel driveway, gradually leveling out to the rustic front porch. He stopped and admired the craftsmanship of the century-old Pfeiffer estate, belonging to one of Denver's "high-profile" figures.

An old acquaintance.

Above in a towering spruce tree, a lone raven crackled, the only wildlife daring to announce its existence in the encroaching twilight as another brisk autumn wind tore around them, soughing through the surrounding woods. The man regarded the stately bird of yore with his permanent smirk as he proceeded up the steps of the mansion.

"How quoth you tonight on this Plutonian shore?" the man mused, taking one last look at the raven's solitary silhouette, then he reached the doorbell with a gloved hand. "Only this…and nothing more."

He pressed the button.

The doorbell chimed.

And he waited, scratching his faint yet neatly-shaven facial hair: a thin mustache and goatee combo that was somehow a five o'clock shadow just a few days earlier. He squinted, eyes shifting left and right; he had grown unusually indecisive this evening as the question nagged him.

How, exactly, did he want to do this?

A few minutes passed, then another biting gust blew, wailing through the trees and around the corners of the lavish home. The man pressed the doorbell again…then the muffled snarl of an old man sounded on the other side.

"I'm coming, damn it, I'm coming!" the voice barked, then coughed. "That must be him."

The door opened, revealing a stocky man close to his seventies, clad in a denim shirt, dress pants, a thick belt across his plump waistline, and black leather boots polished virtually to a mirror sheen. He sported an ashen toupee atop his head and a well-groomed mustache to match, one that was akin to the anachronistic scruff of a Civil War general. His olive-green eyes peered up at his tall visitor, then a smile curled on his pudgy face.

"Leslie Haney," the short mustached man said in his gruff smoker's voice.

"Your Honor," Leslie replied in a smooth yet gravelly tone. "It's been a long time."

"Damned right it has," the judge replied, shaking his hand. "And it's only 'Your Honor' in the courtroom, Les. Up here, it's just Stan. Stanley."

"Of course," Leslie conceded, then turned to the dwindling sunset. "Lovely view up here."

"It *is* that," Stanley agreed, then shivered from the wind and waved his guest inside. "Well, come in—come in, let's get outta this cold! Got a nice fire goin' in here. Maria went home a little while ago."

"Maria?"

"My maid. She's a sweet little thing."

Leslie crossed the threshold and followed Judge Pfeiffer.

The home was an oversized man cave, eminent with warmth from the fireplace and reeking of cedar, tobacco, burning oak, and gamey scents wafting from the animal pelts and taxidermy proudly arrayed on the walls. A flight of stairs led up and terminated to the second floor, the railings composed of whittled tree roots and undulating boughs. A few chandeliers of elk antlers hung from the lofty ceiling, with landscape portraiture and sepia photographs of the Pfeiffer lineage from the 1800s. Various trophies of moose, bear, deer, and even grouse and pheasants hung on the surrounding paneling of the living room, forever petrified and gazing with their marble eyes. Rugs of grizzly hides lay on the floor amongst the leather couch and recliners, with a shawl of Native American designs draping the sofa's back. A large television rested on an entertainment center of mahogany, the cabinet stocked with DVDs and old VHS tapes, with a few surround-sound speakers peeking throughout the walls and furniture. Above the stonework mantle, two muskets crisscrossed each other over the flaming hearth beneath. Stanley hobbled over with the grace of a goblin, his bad knee evident, then took the poker and rearranged some of the blazing wood. Embers sprayed as the charred chunk fell over.

"There ya go," Stanley said, putting the poker away. "You'll burn now, won'tcha, ya bastard." He looked up at Leslie, standing by the long minibar with a silver tray of glasses and decanters on top. "May I offer you a drink, Les? Brandy? Whiskey?"

"Um, no thank you—uh, say!" Leslie pointed at a nearby photo of a bearded man in a derby hat and suspenders standing in front of an oil well. "Who is that? Great-grandfather?"

Stanley turned. "Uh…more like…great-great uncle." The judge approached the image. "Victor Pfeiffer. People called 'im 'Vick,' though. One of the early oil tycoons out further southwest, Arizona, Nevada, and parts of California—and quite the gunslinger, too. There was a lot of blood. Hadn't been for him, this luxurious home you see before you would not exist…or the beginning of the family's *true* legacy, for that matter. He raised an' ol' deaf boy, then they became business partners for a little while…then sometime later, they had some kind of falling-out for some reason. They basically told each other to go to hell and all that…and that was it."

"That's a shame," Leslie commented.

"Yep, yep." Stanley chuckled. "There's a…there's a funny story…about an ol' preacher who didn't want Vick to buy his land at first, then years later, he got into a financial bind, then came crawlin' right back and beggin' for ol' Vick to buy it."

"Did he?"

Stanley nodded at the photo. "Yep. Even got that poor bastard to renounce his faith, too. Then Vick shot 'im in the head, point-blank—and he was never convicted, either!" He laughed. "Damned Christians with their fake 'holier-than-thou' bullcrap! Jews ain't any better! Yeah, ol' Vick 'drank his milkshake,' alright. Hee hee hee—we're *still* drinkin' it. Dumbass fundamentalists. Bunch of useless, whiny religious trash."

Leslie only maintained his smirk, silently revolted by Stanley's Christophobia and anti-Semitism.

But he expected about as much from the cantankerous, bigoted judge.

"As you well know," Stanley said, turning around and fetching the crystal flask. "I ain't much for fairytales. If I can see it…and if I can touch it, then it's there—it's real." He pulled out a refrigerated drawer of ice from the buffet's built-in minibar, then fished out a few ice cubes. "Sure I can't tempt you with a…Scotch on the rocks? Cigar, maybe?"

"A kind offer, but I must decline," Leslie gently rebuffed. "Knowing me, I might get too smashed to drive back down the mountain."

"I've gotten to be a social drinker myself in later years," Stanley claimed as he poured the whiskey into the rocks glass, then he shambled to his recliner. "Have a seat. Make yourself at home."

Leslie obliged him and eased down on the leather sofa, watching the judge like a cat with his uncanny blue eyes. Stanley took a sip, then cleared his throat as the alcohol scorched down his throat. He eyed his guest, then glanced at his beverage.

"You still doin' litigation over in Boulder?" Stanley inquired.

"Not anymore," Leslie replied. "I retired."

"Been thinkin' about that myself," Stanley said, then took another sip. "Might be the smart move. Never know what the interest rates are gonna do, though. The courts are runnin' me ragged." He scoffed. "They still make witnesses 'swear' on the Bible. Like a book's gonna make those jackasses tell the truth. Like the hand of God is gonna magically appear an' squash 'em like a bug if they lie or something like that. It's all cheap formality."

"You always were a fan of Darwin's work."

"Only damned good thing that ever came outta society was Darwin," Stanley sneered. "Survival of the fittest. The justice system's just there to keep other bastards' little asses in line, so that people like you an' me don't have to be bothered by the scum…scum like Chris Sullivan, and those three little shits they found down in Phantom Canyon Road a few days back." He snorted. "'Oh, wah—I want equality. I ain't gettin' treated fairly. I want more rights than everybody else.' Blah, blah, blah, blah, blah. Boo hoo. Nobody wants to work for jack shit anymore. Zero work ethic. Just want to whine and have everything handed to 'em on a silver platter, all the while tryin' to make us bend over backwards for 'em. Ungrateful shit-eaters." He snorted again.

"I just hope ol' Trump can hold down the fort up there in D. C. We'll see, though."

Leslie grinned. It was just too damned much. The profane judge was just begging for it.

"What's so damned funny over there?"

"Nothing." Leslie shook his head. "It's just been so long. I've missed your...charm."

Stanley squinted at him, then took a slug from his drink. "I ain't about charm. You, of all people, oughta know that. I tell it how it is. I sugarcoat nothing! I call a spade a spade, that's what I do. If people want to get a sore ass about it, then they needed it."

"I guess that's...what I meant, Stan," Leslie swindled. "They just don't make them like you anymore. A dying breed, really."

"Yeah, I don't know where all the men have gone," Stanley slurred, taking another swig. "After the '60s rolled around, those damned sheltered left-wing Yuppies, New Agers and all, just been sproutin' up like mushrooms everywhere. Got women trying to run the show now. And if Bianca Sterling don't mind her shit, it's gonna be her head and that district attorney's who are gonna be next on the choppin' block. Damned heifers!"

Leslie eyed something on the corner of the ceiling. His smirk faded.

A security camera was watching him...and no telling how many more.

Big problem.

Maybe they were all hooked up to a server somewhere, an office, perhaps. But where?

"You...brought up Chris Sullivan?" Leslie questioned.

Stanley eyed him. "Yeah?"

"Whatever...happened to him?"

"Who gives a shit?" Stanley cursed, finishing his booze. "Couldn't have gone far—he's doing AA meetings somewhere local. Down in La Sombra, I think. Damned wife-beater. 'Course...she *did* clean 'im out pretty damned good—I mean...she gave 'im the business. That's why I never bothered with marriage. Connivin' bitches take everything from ya."

"Interesting how you say she was...conniving," Leslie observed.

"Well, you know," Stanley explained. "To be fair...she didn't really have any business goin' behind Sullivan's back and filing for some life insurance policy without his permission. Intuition tells me she...*might* have been up to no good. Statistically, not too long after something like that, a dead body shows up, then the beneficiary, usually the spouse of the deceased, collects the life insurance money, several tens or hundreds of thousands of dollars. But that's not what the case was about! The case was about whether or not he bludgeoned her out of rage and insecurity—and statistics show that men who fit Chris's profile are prone to that sort of violent behavior. The feds study these psychological behaviors, and the evidence simply reinforces these findings, and Bianca successfully proved that in the court of law. Chris and his wife *could* have handled it in a civil manner, and everybody would have been fine and dandy—but that's not what happened!" He scoffed. "Reminds me…of another case years ago. Conroy."

Leslie straightened up in his seat, almost frowning. "Conroy?"

"Yeah," Stanley grunted, rising up from the recliner and pouring another drink. "Blair, I think the wife's name was. Her husband's name was…Henry. They had a little boy." He ambled back to the recliner. "Name was…Sam."

Leslie's eye twitched.

"Those Conroys were a nasty bunch—Blair certainly was. Real bitch. Gambler. Alcoholic. Chain smoker. A regular piece of work. Trailer trash, all of 'em." The judge took another gulp of whiskey. "But she didn't…do anything *illegal*, per se. She accused Henry of…sodomizin' her or somethin' against her will. *He* claimed she assaulted *him* and abused their son. She said it was self-defense and that she did nothin' to Sam—the whole thing was a big damned mess if I ever saw one! Wasn't as famous as the Sullivan case, but it sure did leave a nasty taste in my mouth. Wasn't a whole lot of evidence to go on, a lot of hearsay mainly…but I ended up convictin' the son of a bitch. I sentenced ol' Henry…then he got raped and murdered in prison not too long after that." He glared. "Then that hotheaded little teenager of his cussed me out in the last day of court, said he was gonna slit my throat an' everything for ruinin' his life. Sent his little ass to juvey to cool off for a while! Could've tried 'im as an adult, but I didn't. I was already too sick of that rotten family, anyway." He shook his head. "I don't know what happened to him from there…or Blair."

"I trust juvenile hall did Sam Conroy some good?" Leslie asked.

Stanley shrugged. "Who gives a shit? As long as I don't have to deal with the little fucker." He sampled the Scotch again, then smiled at Leslie. "You still like bowling?"

"I've grown rather…rusty with the years," Leslie told him. "But yes, I still fancy it."

"I got a private alley down in the basement if you wanna go a few rounds. It's a two-laner." Stanley stood back on his feet. "I insist…for old time's sake."

Leslie's smirk returned as he rose up. "Well…if you insist, old friend."

Stanley grinned, revealing a grill of yellowed teeth wrought from his bad habits, then he led the way down a hall, with Leslie surveying the rest of the décor. As they made their way to a staircase, leading downward, he managed to catch a glimpse of a small office nook through one of the doorways, with computer servers and flatscreen monitors showing the feed of the security cameras. His smirk widened.

One less thing to worry about.

Still, how did want to do this?

They proceeded down the dark steps. Stanley flipped a switch, illuminating the quaint game room with a cozy, languid glow, its Victorian woodwork nauseatingly evocative of the 1900s, all complete with a narrow bowling alley of two lanes just as the judge said. In an adjacent gallery, a lavish billiard table sat, with cue sticks lined up on a rack, with more televisions mounted on the corners of the ceiling. A stereo system was inset into an alcove with a vintage turntable positioned on top of a stout end table; its bottom shelves were filled with various vinyl records, ranging from operas, jazz, copious amounts of country, blues, and even some classic rock. Another minibar lay to the right wall of the bowling alley, with a box of Cuban cigars and top-shelf liquors on the counter, including a bottle of genuine imported absinth. Leslie squinted; Judge Pfeiffer had been holding out on him.

Stanley took one final slug of his whiskey, then placed the rocks glass on the minibar, then activated another switch as the pinsetter machine hummed to life. Leslie saw the judge breathing harder, his forehead perspiring.

"You're my guest." Stanley gestured at the heavy balls in the return trough. "You go first. You'll have to take your gloves off."

"As your guest," Leslie said. "I implore you to make the first go."

Stanley squinted, then took one of the bowling balls. "I don't recollect you bein' so…poetic, Les." He took his stance with his thick sausage fingers in the three holes. "It's been longer than I thought, I guess."

Leslie said nothing as the judge sweated more and more, cringing.

"I must've gotten that…fire too hot or something," Stanley panted.

Clumsily, the judge proceeded to the foul line, then cast the ball and yelped, falling over. Leslie watched as the ball barreled into the gutter and into the darkness of the service aisle beyond.

"Ahh!" Stanley shouted, rolling onto his back.

"Tsk, tsk," Leslie said, stepping towards him, his arms folded behind him. "I wonder how many more gutter balls you've rolled in your life, Pfeiffer." He cocked his head. "Did you enjoy your drink?"

"You…bastard," Stanley coughed, eyeing the empty glass. "What did you…do?"

"I won't bore you with the details," Leslie knelt down by the judge. "Let the poison do its work. It's better that way. Fighting it will only make it worse."

"Why, Les?"

"You don't read the obituaries, do you?"

Stanley gawked at him.

"Leslie Haney died several years back from a 'massive heart attack,'" the imposter sneered. "At least that's what the autopsy report read. Rather pro-saic, if you ask me, but let them think what they like. No skin off *my* ass."

"Who are…you?"

"Who, me?" the man mocked, glaring. "I'm just a piece of 'trailer trash' from a 'rotten family' that made you *sooooo* sick." He squinted harder. "Look at what you've made, Your Honor. Your handiwork looms over you at long last."

Stanley scowled at him. "You…you little prick!"

Sam Conroy emitted an unsettling, grating hyena-like chuckle deep in his throat. "I find you Darwinists so amusing. You believe that everything is a random contingency in a chaotic universe of meaningless chemical reactions, that humanity is nothing more than the product of an accident in existence. Then you impose your false rules on society, your pretense of morality, your artificial philosophies of law and order, only for overprivileged, corrupt little shits like you to get your way all at the expense of others, thinking yourselves as glorified gorillas, the descendants of primordial defecation in a steaming toilet bowl billions of years ago. All your lofty politics are merely a means to an end. All you wish to do is to get shit-faced, get fat, fuck each other, then die." He tenderly shook his head. "All I do is accelerate the process. Why should anything matter, according to you? Because you say so? Even before I came, you were already dying…and from what you've told me…your death means nothing, neither good nor bad."

Stanley sputtered, his ears ringing, his sight blurry.

"Oh, what sort of God would allow this, I wonder?" Sam taunted, feigning pity, then he tittered his muffled hyena laugh again. "The heinous things you've committed would make Hitler and Stalin blush." His eyes widened. "Or is that all just another 'fairytale' to you?"

"Don't…do this," Stanley wheezed.

"Oh, but why not? Because you would *prefer* me not to?" Sam tilted his head to his other shoulder. "After all, in *your* paradigm, it's 'survival of the fittest,' is it not? For someone who wants to believe such precarious nonsense, you sure are quite mediocre at it. Look at you now! The last of your wretched family legacy gasping its final breaths! Just another product of the world's collective genetic entropy. All that fossil fuel polluting the earth around us, when it should have been left deep in the ground right where you found it. But greed is bottomless, isn't it? Vick Pfeiffer, that nescient swine you call an ancestor, knew it all too well, I'm sure! Who is to say that he would have dealt with you, his own kin, in the exact same way as his murder victim? How fit are *you* to survive in this society slowly devolving before our very eyes?"

Stanley reached out, trying to grab Sam's shirt collar, yet the Vulture snatched his palm.

"I am a destroying angel," Sam whispered, "and I do not bear the sword in vain."

As the dying judge strained and thrashed, Sam removed a thick ring from his pocket, with a square insignia engraved like an eagle. Stanley watched as the killer took a cigarette lighter, a pocket torch, and ignited it with a click, heating the emblem quizzically.

"Don't die just yet, Stanley," Sam told him, studying the blue flame. "I want you just aware enough for the *pièce de résistance* of my performance to-night." His smirk tightened. "Don't be bitter if I beat you at your own game."

The crooked judge grew more inert, unable to fight back. Sam finished stoking the ring, then he held Stanley down…and pressed it onto his moist forehead. He uttered a gravelly yell as the metal branded him, sizzling his flesh with lazy, stringy smoke. Then Sam pulled it away.

"Now you are mine," Sam said, unsheathing a hunting knife from the interior of his blazer. "There's going to be much more blood this evening…perhaps…too much blood." He caught the gleam of light on the knife's reflective blade. "For what does it profit a man if he gains the whole world…yet loses his soul?"

Stanley twitched, now foaming from the corners of his mouth.

"Quoth the raven, 'Nevermore.' Only this…and nothing more."

Sam Conroy smiled, eyeing the razor-sharp edge of his weapon. Things couldn't have gone any smoother even if he tried. This would be among his finest work. As he carved his whimpering quarry, spilling fresh crimson, he calculated his next moves, glancing at another security camera. That footage had to go.

Not all of it, though. He couldn't have Stanley Pfeiffer dying as a saint; it was unprofessional. No, he had to be exposed for the dirty anti-Semite and thug he was, a nice gift for the feds to find. Perhaps he could procure something else while he rummaged the surveillance office upstairs. He studied the judge's bleeding mouth, gurgling a crude death rattle up at him. Music to his ears! Yet it was missing something; it needed just the right touch. One could not rush perfection. And Sam Conroy was quite the perfectionist, a shameless carnifex. For life was far too short to live in shame. This would be among his greatest works, a prelude to his *magnum opus*. He was a bloody maestro, and violence was his orchestra, each vengeful execution its own carefully-wrought sonnet. All great art must convey the right message.

And he knew just the thing.

As for Chris Sullivan, he remained an enigma, as did his estranged family…especially his little girl. Something was not jiving. And Bianca Sterling was not of much help. Nevertheless, she proved to be quite a delight, watching her squirm the other night.

Pushing her buttons.

The feds would find the lovely attorney as well…soon enough.

And Sam would find Sullivan.

Soon enough.

VI: Wight and Gray

Vince Redman and Theo Nash peered through the windshield of their black SUV cruiser, their faces exuding a worn malaise, watching for any movement on the isolated pavement or amongst the skeletal trees and pastures of dead grass surrounding them. The strangling blanket of night had slithered over the neighborhood hours earlier, accompanied by a bank of fog as yellow leaves silently twiddled down from nearby aspen limbs and cottonwoods. A lone overpass loomed several yards away, partially shrouded in the mist, yawning like the mouth of a tomb in the dim light. Not a single gust of wind was present; even the clouds completely veiled the rising moon, waxing more and more with each passing evening, a silver eye gradually opening, soon to become fully-fledged. Nash tacked away on the console's keyboard, scrolling through names and case files, mainly to occupy his mind; the stake-out was boring him and his partner to pieces.

"Sure he'll strike again tonight?" Nash asked, taking a sip of coffee.

"Nope," Redman replied, his hand halfway over his mouth with his left elbow propped up on the driver's side door, then he lowered it and cleared his throat. "But that's fine with me if he doesn't. Rather it be a *dead* night than it be my *last* night."

"True," Nash said.

"Look, will you get off that thing?" Redman scolded, then pointed at the windshield. "We're supposed to be watching."

"Yeah," Nash said, putting the computer on standby. "Seen anything else?"

"Other than that gray fox earlier? No." Redman sighed. "And they're ain't no damned 'Lady in Gray' either." He shook his head. "Don't even have the Ghostbuster wannabes out tonight hauntin' around, chasin' urban legends."

"Too cold, I guess."

"Yeah, it is." Redman sighed again. "This place is spooky enough, with or without ghosts or goblins. Damned media couldn't help themselves the other day. Had to broadcast that thing about the three drug dealers in Phantom Canyon Road. Probably spooked our perp back into hiding again. It's like chasing lightning; you don't know when or where the scum is gonna strike. All you can do is guess and be where the storm is. It's all a big crapshoot at this point."

Another yellow leaf fell, fluttering down on the windshield, already gleaming with frost from a nearby fluorescent streetlight, the only glow amidst the thick darkness.

"Why is it called Phantom Canyon Road?" Nash questioned.

Redman rolled his eyes. "Because back in the 1800s, there was a guy who was executed at a jail in the area. Not too long after that, people claimed to have seen him walking on the railroad bridge, still in chains and in his striped prison jumpsuit. Some other nuts later on had claimed to…hear…chains rattling with nothing being there. Just some hokey shit is all." He coughed. "Guess our lucky three might get to meet 'im now."

"And the 'Lady in Gray?'"

Redman looked at him. "Do you realize how many places in America alone have legends about a 'Lady in Whatever,' or a 'Crybaby Bridge,' or ghost trains, or the guy who ax-murdered his family, or gravity hills where people *think* that ghost children are pushing their car uphill, when really it's an optical illusion and their really going downhill with their car in neutral? Then you got so-called 'spook lights' when really it's just somebody's head-lights or fireflies or swamp gas." He scoffed. "They see lights on a mountain, and they think it's a damned flying saucer landing." He groaned. "No, I deal with evidence. We're cops; that's what we do. We deal with facts."

"Then why are you wanting to reexplore the Chris Sullivan case?"

"Because," Redman lectured, "I'm smart enough to know that evidence does not speak for itself. It's the *interpretation* of the evidence that gets the say-so at the end of the day. We're trained to study 'psychological profiles' and see patterns in our unsubs, our unknown subjects...and also our *known* subjects." He glared at the rear-view mirror. "But all that does is condition us to be presumptuous and prejudiced. Sometimes, I wonder if I'm any better than the cops who tried to profile *me* growing up...all because I'm black."

"But Chris Sullivan isn't black."

"No," Redman agreed. "He *is* interracial, though, even though he doesn't look like it...and the media had *waaaay* too much fun with that. Made even *my* stomach turn. His dad was white, but his mother was Hispanic. Martina was her name. According to his files, she died of cancer a few years back in Mississippi, where Sullivan grew up. He met his ex-wife, Evelyn, down in Florida, then they moved out here to Colorado. His writing career was fail-ing, and she filed for life insurance without his permission. That's when shit hit the fan...and that's where we came in."

"So, what does that have to do with him beating his wife?"

"Precisely my point!" Redman snapped, his huge index finger raised at Nash's face. "You hit the nail on the head! What *does* it have to do with what he was accused of? We have here a six-foot-tall male who weighs roughly two hundred pounds, he's in his late twenties, has a Hispanic background, has a history of depression, and looks like he's pissed all the time. Even though he's bustin' his ass with his career as an author, he ain't makin' a whole lot of money—mostly likely due to being socially marginalized and politically disadvantaged. You see, in truth, his lawyer's argument...was no less sound...than Bianca Sterling's in court." His eyes widened. "But that's not what we saw, was it?"

"What did we see, then, Red?"

"We saw only what we wanted to see: the poor, little white girl, the blonde-haired, blue-eyed martyr with tears in her eyes and cuts and bruises from a fight she only *claimed* happened...and we were all predisposed to put the pieces together in her favor: Stanley Pfeiffer, the bureau, the media, society—everybody." He snorted. "And I'm just as guilty of it. I've become the thing I hate: just another gun-totin' pig with a badge."

"Vince…c'mon, you're not…."

"I used to run from cops back when I was young. We all did," Redman said, looking at the windshield again. "It was…just a reflex—and we weren't even doing anything wrong." He licked his lips and shook his head. "But in the cops' eyes, we fit their little 'psychological profiles,' all because of some bullshit statistics where they thought black people were more likely to commit crime than white people. They stereotyped us. I thought if I joined the force…maybe I could change some of that." He huffed. "Guess I became just another stereotype."

"Red, you're an individual," Nash told him. "So am I. And the cops who did that to you and your friends and family growing up…*they're* the pigs, not you. They're the ones who have a God complex, thinking they're superior to everybody." He released a slow breath. "Look, um…if you really want to take another look at that case…we will. Leave no stones unturned—because *now*…now you've got me to thinking."

"You're a good kid, Theo," Redman replied. "I think you're gonna be all right."

They bumped fists, then smirked at each other.

"I just want to make sure," Redman said. "I mean…if Sullivan's guilty, he's guilty."

"What was it, really, that made you…start thinking about that?" Nash squinted at him. "It wasn't those three goons we found in the canyon."

Redman shook his head. "Mina."

Nash squinted harder.

"Mina wants nothing to do with the paparazzi. She doesn't want anything to do with us. I imagine that girl is borderline-suicidal. Hard to blame her, though." Redman rubbed the bridge of his nose. "Evelyn, on the other hand…can't get enough of it. Just a little starlet, craving all the attention. Guess I'm being presumptuous again."

Nash shook his head. "It's an observation." He sighed. "I would, however, like to know our next move in this…if we're going to open up this can of worms once a—oh, shit! Shit!"

"What?"

"I forgot about Laura! Our anniversary! It's tomorrow!"

"You mean *today*," Redman said, then pointed at his watch, reading 12:46 a. m. "Right?"

"Damn it!"

"Relax, you caught it just in time." Redman smiled, then chuckled. "Women like surprises."

Nash scowled at him. "Red—"

Redman burst out laughing. "You good. You good." He shook his head. "I don't know, just…make her…pancakes, breakfast in bed or something like that when you get home. They love it when we fellas do shit like that for them. The sun'll be comin' up by then, I think. Nice little sunrise for the two of you lovebirds if the weather's decent." He sobered up. "Glad *I* don't have to worry about that shit anymore. My ex wasn't exactly the nicest gal in the world." He furrowed his brow. "I wasn't all that perfect, either."

"That's not inspiring confidence, Red."

"You got plenty of time, kid—take a breath." Redman perked up, then eyed the ham radio. "Hey, wha…did you…did you turn the radio off?"

Nash looked. "No. Why?"

Redman gawked at it. "It was garbling like crazy hours ago when we first got here."

The radio finally buzzed, whizzing and gurgling in various unstable intervals, as if something was brushing back and forth inside its components. Redman adjusted a knob as Nash heard a sound through the speakers, something like…female whispering, a language he could not make out.

"Bad reception," Nash said, looking around outside.

"Yeah." Redman nodded. "And for the record…those are red reflectors on the mailboxes, not red eyes, so take it easy."

"What about those smudges on the signs?"

"Paintballs," Redman surmised. "Kids come through here and shoot and vandalize the road signs. Even though it's been mostly washed off, you can still see the residue only at night because the way people's headlights shine on them as cars pass. Makes it look like ghost blood or something." His lips curled into a wry smirk. "Local folklore has it that if you see the coyote…it's a good sign."

"And the gray fox?"

Redman scoffed. "They claim it's an evil spirit—look, let's…get back to the—"

His phone rang. Nash looked out to the overpass as his partner answered.

"This is Redman," he said, then he nodded. "Yeah. Yeah. Wait, what? Slow down."

Underneath the bridge, Nash noticed movement in the distant mist. At least…he thought he did. He strained his eyes as goosebumps wracked his skin. Maybe the dim lighting was playing tricks on him. Or just a wisp of fog.

"Damn." Redman sighed. "Alright…we're on our way." He hung up and put the phone away. "That was Wellborn. Our perp struck again. Guess who's on the menu?"

"No telling."

"Judge Stanley Pfeiffer," Redman said, fishing for the car keys.

"Pfeiffer?"

"His maid, Maria, went back to his estate this evening because she forgot her paycheck. She had a spare key. She found him with his throat gouged wide open in his game room with his eyes gouged out," Redman looked at his partner, "with the eyes of the three drug dealers in his open mouth. Blood's everywhere."

"Geez!"

"And he's got the Vulture mark branded on his forehead," Redman went on. "Even drew some kind of satanic runes and something like an Illuminati pyramid around his head with Pfeiffer's own blood, putting one of his severed eyeballs in the middle…like an 'all-seeing eye' or something."

"Let's move, then," Nash said, taking another gulp of the coffee.

Redman cranked the ignition, yet the engine sputtered, turning aimlessly. The headlights flickered, then the motor hushed, the starter merely clicking.

"Son of a bitch—the hell is wrong with this thing?"

The radio buzzed again, the woman's voice seeming closer. Angrier.

"What is that racket?" Nash snapped.

"Somebody in the neighborhood back there pranking us, probably!" Redman snarled, gritting his teeth at the steering wheel. "C'mon, you piece of motherfu—!"

The engine revved. Redman hastily put the vehicle in gear and lunged out into the road, approaching the overpass. Nash looked as they went under, seeing where satanic cultists had painted upside-down Christian crosses on the cement with black paint. Bigots. Desecrating and appropriating a holy symbol. As Nash turned his head, he saw it again…standing in the fog of a pasture…looking right at him.

A fleeting human figure.

Ashen. Eyeless. Garbed in a pale gown.

"Shit!" Nash jerked.

"Boy, settle down over there!" Redman rebuked. "This place is freaky enough without you jumping at shadows."

"I could've sworn I saw something back there!" Nash fired back.

"A tree," Redman growled. "You saw a tree—that's all. Keep your head screwed on."

Nash took a breath. "Yeah…sure." He nodded. "Just a tree."

Redman belted out a guttural breath. "Fuck this place."

The radio garbled with its usual unclear cop jargon once again as Nash looked in the side-view mirror, studying the gnarled cottonwoods, their branches hanging like bony fingers, ready to snatch anyone up; their yellow leaves whirled behind them in the crimson of the taillights, as if hell itself was chasing them down the road. Maybe it *was* just a tree. Maybe he had too much coffee. Maybe his imagination was just getting the better of him. But there was at least *one* boogeyman loose: a slippery grim reaper. An invader. There was something dark at work in Colorado…and perhaps the Vulture was the least of their problems. He swallowed his fear, struggling to ignore the reality.

"Shit!" Redman yelled, slamming on breaks.

Tires shrieked to a halt as they stopped at a second overpass. Redman and Nash got out of the car and drew their pistols, gawking upward at what dangled from beneath the bridge.

Thirteen dead bodies hung from chains and nooses.

All dripping with blood.

And carved with satanic runes.

Upside-down crosses, pentagrams, and incantations in Latin and German were crudely scrawled beneath the bridge, all painted with the red fluid of the victims. Some were civilians, men and women.

Some were dressed in black tactical gear.

Mercenaries. Sacrificed.

"Dear God," Nash rasped.

On the other side of the overpass, another black SUV sat...with a shadowy hooded figure entering the driver's side, muttering something in German.

"Freeze—FBI!" Nash blared, aiming his gun.

Another hooded man appeared from an open window on the passenger's side, brandishing a sub-machine gun.

"Shit—get back!" Redman yelled.

Both agents darted back to their car and hid behind the open doors. The gunman snarled something in German, then blasted a fusillade of rounds at them as the other SUV sped off. Bullets pinged against the doors, then Nash whirled around and fired back, knocking out one of their taillights.

"C'mon!" Redman snapped and hopped back into the SUV.

Nash barreled into the car. The car doors slammed shut as Redman revved the engine. Both of them ducked behind the dashboard as two bullets cracked their windshield. The enemy SUV careened back and forth down the winding road as the two feds pursued the fanatical terrorists into the night. Nash failed to process what was happening. He was stuck in a horror movie, a nightmare come to life.

And it was craving blood.

Everyone's blood.

Bianca Sterling yelped awake on her bed, her sight blurry at first. She rubbed her eyes, feeling like a freight train had its way with her fried brain the previous night. What a hangover. She wasn't operating at her usual optimal performance. Had she blacked out? Or worse? Her murky mind steadily rebooted, straining to recall what happened.

Then she looked down...and panicked!

Her sweater was gone, replaced with a white button-up blouse wide open, exposing her bra, still hooked behind her. On the floor, her jeans, socks, and boots lay on the carpet, revealing her lacy black panties and the creamy-tan flesh of her slender legs.

"Sam," she breathed as she felt around her crotch and thighs.

No residue.

Nothing moist.

An uncorked bottle of champagne sat in a metal pail near the bed, the ice having turned to water. Her champagne glass rested sideways on the floor adjacent to the mattress, the rim still smudged with her pink lipstick.

The other one was gone.

As was Sam.

She got up and examined the sheets. No stains. No evidence of a struggle. And nothing missing from the room, at least as far as she could tell.

Except…for her laptop.

"Shit!" Bianca hissed.

She looked at her desk. That part she remembered. She had left it there before going to La Sombra, before encountering Sam in the bistro.

"That son of a bitch." Bianca's voice quavered. "That fucking—!"

Her phone vibrated.

She answered. "This is Bianca."

"Where the hell are you?" the matronly voice of Leah, the female assistant district attorney, demanded. "It's almost nine o'clock! The case is gonna start any minute!"

"It's Sunday!" Bianca protested.

"No," the other attorney corrected sternly. "It's Monday, dear."

"What?" Bianca gasped, then looked at the calendar app on her phone.

Her eyes bulged. It *was* Monday. Her alarm clock read 8:56 a. m.

Had she been in a coma for over twenty-four hours?

"What's going on with you? You've never been this late before!"

"Leah," Bianca sighed. "I think I might have been…raped."

"What?" she squawked.

"I met this guy Saturday evening, made the mistake of bringing him home after dinner…and…I must've blacked out and—"

"Oh, shit," Leah said. "He must have spiked your drink, because you don't…."

"I know," Bianca said. "I'm gonna get him. I'll get that bastard!"

"Go to the emergency room, get 'em to do a swab, a rape kit—make sure!" Leah recommended. "Girl, I am so sorry, look—what was…what was his name?"

"He claimed his name was…Sam. White guy. Blue eyes. Completely bald. Clean-shaven. Maybe…mid-forties, I don't know." She sighed. "Has a smooth, raspy voice, very suave and…rhetorical in personality."

"I'll let the FBI know right away," Leah said. "Okay, well…I'll cover for you. Don't worry about coming in, then. I've got your back."

"If Pfeiffer gives you any shit, you let me—"

"Pfeiffer?" Leah chirped. "No. Didn't…didn't you hear?"

"Hear what?"

"Bianca," Leah said, "the Vulture got him last night. They found footage of Pfeiffer making anti-Semitic comments to some…guy, that his ancestor murdered a preacher, and they even found…swastikas in his office drawer— they're thinking he was a closet Neo-Nazi, part of a cult or something." Her breath shuddered. "And his visitor *also* had a…smooth, raspy voice, too, but the camera never saw his face. He destroyed the other footage and the servers, sparing only that little bit. The Vulture wanted them to find it."

Bianca froze, trembling. She had never screwed up this bad before.

"Bianca…are you there?"

"Yeah, yeah," she replied.

"You don't think that...your guy is...."

"I need to go to the hospital!" Bianca squeaked. "I need to see that footage, too. Maybe I-I can—I can identify it, his voice!"

"Bianca, please be careful. That guy knows where you—"

"I know! I know!" Bianca almost sobbed.

"Look, sweetie, just calm down. Just take a breath," Leah comforted. "If he wanted you dead, we wouldn't be having this conversation right now—and it may not even be him. Could be just some random dirtbag or something trying to get his sick kicks with you. He's not gonna get away with this, trust me." She sighed again. "Did he mention anything when you two were at dinner the other night? Do you remember?"

"He asked me about...the Chris Sullivan case. Like...everything. All the details."

"He and his family need to be warned."

"Evelyn, sure," Bianca said, slipping her blue jeans back on. "Chris can go fuck himself!"

"C'mon, now. That's not how we roll. You're a big girl. You're better than that!"

"*Everyone* is better than Chris Sullivan, Leah."

"That's not—ugh!" Leah groaned. "Look, just go to the hospital and call me back. The trial will probably be in session by then, so I may not answer right away. Just...send me a text or something. I gotta go—they're starting."

"Alright, will do." Bianca said. "Good luck."

"Same to you, dear," Leah sighed. "Try to stay alive."

With that, the assistant district attorney hung up. Bianca's lips quivered. She actually let that...thing in her house? Who was he? What was he? Was he even human? And what was this morbid fascination he had with Chris Sullivan? Why now? Those bones had been picked clean.

Right?

Her mind was still scrambled. Should she go ahead and call 911? Or was Leah already sending the feds to her house to investigate? Better not touch the crime scene. She shook her head, slipping on a pair of leather moccasins, too dizzy to put on shoes. Golden rays of the morning sun shone through the blinds and against her translucent white curtains. The majesty of the mountain sunrise over Denver only mocked her, making her sicker, like fiery fingers accusing her, shaming her, condemning her for her naïve foolishness. For what Sam had done to her. She tried to fight back the tears welling up in her eyes.

Tears of mounting terror.

She exited the bedroom, then flew out of her house and to her silver sedan, then started the engine, almost peeling out of her driveway and down the street. She sniffled. Sam would be back for her. Her pride was shattered. She could almost feel him savoring the horror that choked her, feeding off it from afar like some sort of otherworldly entity. She glared and bit down on her jaw, constricting her grip around the steering wheel, trying to focus her brain into gear, her heart thrashing in her chest. It was all a game to these freaks…and now she was in the crosshairs.

But not if she got him first.

She opened the glove compartment. Her silver Beretta was still there, along with an extra clip of ammo. Her breath seethed in and out through the grill of her clenched teeth as she eyed the weapon, her flaming sword. Her saving grace.

Redemption.

She slammed the glove compartment shut and gunned the engine faster.

Terminate…or be terminated.

With or without the law.

VII: Cream Sodas

Another cold night fell as Chris Sullivan drove through the streets in his rag-tag truck, a beat-up fossil from the '90s, already an antique…just like him. And he was still in his late twenties! He grumbled, thinking out loud. He had succeeded in being sober for a few days now, and the withdrawals were already taking their ruthless toll on his ruined mind and body. His little girl's drawing was still on the refrigerator door, his only motivation…and a sheet of notebook paper with tally marks hanging just below it. If he was going to be addicted to something, it might as well be that. But if he wanted the method to work, he alone would have to take the initiative.

And it was as hard as hell!

Especially with the frequent nightmares he had been having for several months now, horrific visions of blood, gore. The court case. The sentencing. Dead bodies in California, Seattle. L. A. Florida. Mississippi. Russia. Germany. Everywhere. All cobbled together in phantasmagoric tumult in his mind almost every night. Dreams of flames. Burning wings reaching up to an evening star. A giant ghostly bird crackling with tendrils of lightning over a desert of tombstones, its talons coaxing the dead from their graves, bringing the end of the world, with the sun and moon crumbling. Many of the atrocious dreams were as if he were watching through someone else's eyes, with his bare hands smeared with blood, a traumatic montage of someone else marauding police officers, including the ones who had arrested and tormented him throughout the years. And the nightmares were growing all too constant, plaguing him more and more each day. All too often, he was sleep-deprived. He felt less and less like himself. He couldn't rest.

Neither booze nor sobriety could blot it out.

Maybe it was just a symptom of the alcohol withdrawals…or eating too late.

He couldn't let Naomi know. Or anyone else, for that matter.

His bared his teeth as a flurry of snow blew down on La Sombra, having been a freezing rain earlier, making the rugged asphalt extra slick with ice…and the heater had gone out in his pickup. Lucky him. He had at least another fifteen minutes before he got to yet another useless AA meeting, with the chance of seeing Naomi, the only thing to look forward to tonight. He didn't need another relationship right now, though, if ever again.

Then again, he couldn't help it.

He was a man. And he didn't need anyone's permission or approval to be one—and being masculine did not make him toxic! He didn't hate women. Women hated him. And there wasn't a damned thing he could do about it. So many grown men were still immature and afraid of "cooties," and so many grown women had yet to grow up and graduate from their petulant "girls rule, boys drool" mentality. Even his five-year-old daughter, Melanie, knew better than to behave like that, that is…if Evelyn hadn't already warped her into another ruthless Jezebel spawn. Still, he drowned in their androphobia, their misandry, the wretched gender war ripping everyone to pieces…and he hadn't done one single thing to them.

So he claimed.

He hoped Naomi would see that as well, at least try to see it.

But he wasn't going to hold his breath. She, too, had been through some shit.

She had already proved to be quite different, though. She was so cool, so outgoing…and she was easy on the eyes. They would talk for at least an hour after each AA meeting. She wasn't some neurotic chickenshit man-hater like so many other people…and a lot of douchebags had treated Naomi horribly, from what she'd shared about her life thus far. She was so different from other women, so unique. She was tough, authentic. Compassionate. A rare combination in this day and age. He couldn't get her out of his head. Yet he couldn't help but feel like just another moth to a flame, prone to combusting to its deadly undertow all over again. He didn't stand a chance anyway. It would all blow up in his face like a ticking powder keg, just like every other time. Like so many other things in life, romance was just a crock of shit, fraught with restrictive social formalities. Don't be creepy. Tell her she looks nice. Smile. Have a sense of humor. Get the door for her. Don't overshare. Get the check. Don't come on too strong on the first date. No tongue on the second date. Only get intimate on the third date. Don't be too clingy. Buy her flowers. Buy her chocolates. Buy her diamonds. Buy her a ring.

Buy her shit…and she'll put out.

He glared. It was like trying to program a sex robot to simulate affection. How pathetic.

God help them if that's all there ever was to it. Otherwise, such a woman makes for one overpriced prostitute! Might as well make love to the GPS on his phone and orgasm to the electronic, sultry female voice, autonomously telling him when and where to turn. And sadly, it would probably be just about as sane and productive!

Because that's all society was: a program.

A mechanism.

All were guilty of manipulating others to like them. All were just a means to an end. Individuality and genuine self-awareness were alien concepts to the masses. As far as his shit-headed psychiatrist and her goons were concerned years ago when he was a teenager, he didn't have emotions. They were just chemicals swimming around in his skull. Love was a "manic episode." Anger was labeled as a symptom of his "bipolar disorder." Sadness was just an imbalance of "serotonin" and "norepinephrine" and whatever other meaningless molecules the witchdoctor wanted to allege. There were no actual emotions, only sludge inside of the damp meat of his machine-head. She had even joked that he had been her "personal Guinea pig," only…it wasn't much of a joke. He still wore the literal scars over his body where "fluid" was building up beneath his flesh, where the drugs—that poison—were steadily destroying his body from the inside out, permanently and blatantly disfiguring him, mutilating his torso, stretching the flesh. Only in his last year of college did his psychiatrist finally come clean.

"In all my years of medical practice," she had told him, "you were the hardest one of my patients to diagnose, because I never truly knew what was wrong with you."

And what, exactly, was wrong with him?

He had been nothing more than a hormonal teenager. An early bloomer.

Already six feet tall at age twelve, with people mistaking him for twenty-one.

That's all.

And the cowards of the paranoid world refused to see that, inflicting him at every turn.

All because he was Chris Sullivan.

Eleven years of his life he could never get back. Ever.

And no, he couldn't sue the quack and her clique of over twenty therapists, nurse practitioners, and counselors for malpractice. They were just glorified drug dealers, each supposedly having a Ph.D. Had it been a botched job of trying to mend a broken arm, maybe. But when it came to something of the mind, the corrupt fat cats of the healthcare industry were seen as impervious in the eyes of a crooked justice system. None cared about him.

But he wasn't her "personal Guinea pig" anymore. He wasn't their Frankenstein monster.

He was a prisoner no more. Neither was he their "inmate."

A lab rat no longer.

A bolt of lightning snaked through the sky, its tendrils skirring in the storm…then the thunder snarled down at La Sombra. The snow fell more. Such power. Such force. Austere and immaculate. When he was younger, he used to be terrified of bad weather. But now, he appreciated it, for it mirrored the way he felt deep down, the foreboding tempest raging within.

With his brown eyes, he examined his gaunt visage in the rear-view mirror in fleeting glances.

He looked like shit. He always did.

But so did everybody else, whether they believed it or not.

He was no photogenic mannequin; he was no android. He was the real deal, such as it was. His teeth weren't the best in the world due to his alcoholism and his consumption of soft drink back during his "Guinea pig" days, back when he was a three-hundred-pound fat ass. He had shaved, at least. If he was going to start giving a damn, he might as well look the part. But he was doing it for him, though, no one else. Not even for Naomi. Fuck what other people thought! People were shit. All the wasted time, money, and effort trying to appease people for years, apologizing for things he didn't even do, all the insecure sociopathic people who could care less whether he lived or died, who secretly delighted in his torment—and the trial with him and Evelyn only painfully reinforced it all the more. People would eventually die, or betray him, or simply just lose touch with him for whatever reason, so what was the point of getting too close?

Society was doomed. And the planet wasn't worth saving.

If only he had figured that out way sooner.

He could only hope that Naomi was an exception. But he couldn't let her know that he was *the* Chris Sullivan, the one they had scorned, the one they had falsely accused. The one they had sullied. He hated this feeling. The rotten butterflies in his stomach had come back from the dead.

It was like high school all over again.

He ran his hand through his dark hair, his crown balding, owing it all to Evelyn's spoiled, schizophrenic personality stressing him out, who then blamed *him* for his thinning scalp. The light-tan flesh of his face showed in the grungy streetlights he passed; he almost looked white. At first glance, nobody would ever have guessed that his mother—may she rest in peace—was originally from Puerto Rico, even though he didn't speak much Spanish. But that was the story of his life.

He was either too much of this...or not enough of that.

A weird middle child in society.

Either his suffering wasn't bad enough or exotic enough for people to care about, or he wasn't "high-ranking" enough to enjoy any sort of privilege. He got so sick of telling people about his problems; if anything, they were glad he was dying inside.

Fuck people.

He pulled into the parking lot of a small convention center, the auditorium where they would meet, then he turned the truck off and got out, embracing the wind's unforgiving chill. Another roll of thunder pealed through the clouds, as if heralding his arrival.

If only.

He walked up, took a breath, then burst through, entering the hall of metal folding chairs. Some turned, then looked back up at a middle-aged guy on the stage at a lone microphone, Hank, "testifying" about how he had been sober for two weeks now after running over a bicyclist while driving drunk. To the right of the speaker, a bronze crucifix hung on the wall, with Patty, the corpulent, boisterous female counselor and self-professed "Christian" sitting in a wooden chair beneath it, running this shit show before them.

"Chris!" a woman whispered.

"Hey, boy!" a round black man in baggy jeans rasped, nodding up at him.

"'Sup, Ray?" Chris nodded back. "Naomi."

They waved him over, saving a seat for him in between them. Chris managed a smirk as he fist-bumped Naomi and Ray. She smiled at him, looking him up and down with her dark-green eyes. Like him, she too was interracial, her father being African-American. She was petite and thin as a rail with a coppery skin complexion. Her long, curly black hair curled down to her small breasts, still damp from showering. She donned skintight navy-blue jeans, old tennis shoes, and a snug hooded sweater with azure and gray stripes, contouring to her every curve. She had to be freezing. Was she not able to dress for this kind of weather?

Or was she waiting to see if Chris would offer his coat for her?

He pursed his lips. Women and their churlish, creepy love games, always "testing" men.

Ray was a heavyset man, married with kids, sporting a thick jacket and brown steel-toe boots with a gray beanie on his head. He had been arrested for public intoxication and possession of marijuana. And weed was supposed to be legal in Colorado. About as legal as booze. Only the manufacturing and distribution of pot was legal, and many people did not realize that. He claimed that it was medicinal, but the cops didn't buy the story…because of racial profiling. Chris didn't really have a problem with weed, so long as they didn't exhale the smoke in his face…or mix it with PCP or LSD.

One thing about it, though…it *did* smell like a dead skunk's asshole on fire. Which Ray facetiously denied. He was a cool guy; the pot made him mellow.

Self-medicating.

"Who's up next?" Chris asked.

"*You* are, man," Ray said.

"Nope," Chris rebuffed quietly, waving his hand. "Pass, pass. I pass."

"C'mon, man!" Ray said. "Not this time. Look, it's not good to bottle it up—we all gotta get up there and spill it!"

"We're not gonna judge you," Naomi said in her dainty voice. She put her delicate hand on Chris's back. "We've all screwed up. I know this is all bullshit, but…you don't need to be afraid."

"I'm not afraid," Chris lied.

She rolled her eyes as Hank finished and sat down.

"Thank you, Hank," Patty said, marking something on a clipboard. She looked up. "Oh, good. You made it, Chris."

"Yep," Chris groaned.

"So…I don't think I'm going to give you a choice tonight," Patty said. "I've been lenient with you and everybody, but…you *have* to testify. You have to participate. Otherwise, I'm gonna have to report it to your parole officer."

"Now you're just gettin' nasty," Chris muttered.

"I don't think he's got the balls for it," another man behind him mocked. "He thinks he's better than us…don'tcha Chrissy?"

"Mitch, that's enough," Patty scolded.

Mitch outstretched his arms. "I'm just strong enough to shoot straight, Ms. Patty…unlike a certain self-centered dickhead in this room."

A few people murmured behind him.

Chris glared at the crowd, then at Patty.

So much for the "judgment-free" zone.

"What's it gonna be, Chris?" Patty chirped impatiently.

Naomi and Ray only looked at him, anticipating his reaction. He shook his head. He knew this was coming, like a relentless vise slowly crushing his soul with each passing day. He couldn't even win for losing. Even his secrets were not safe. No one had any privacy anymore. Nothing seemed to be sacred or wholesome. All because people wanted to be people.

"Alright," Chris said, rising up from his seat. "Alright. You want me to 'testify?'" He maneuvered around the crowd, making his way up the stage to the microphone stand. "I'll 'testify' for you. But you ain't gonna like it, though."

"Ooh, somebody actually grew a pair tonight," Mitch taunted.

"Bitch, shut up," Ray snapped at the heckler.

"*You're* the one who needs to grow some balls back there!" Naomi growled.

"That's enough, all of you!" Patty rebuked. "Don't make me call the police again."

They all reluctantly hushed and faced forward. Chris ignored them, unfastening the microphone from its stand, feeling his inner volcano about to erupt once again, this time with an audience: one scrappy motley crew.

They had backed him into a corner.

Nothing left to do but to uncork the shit.

"I...am Chris," he sighed through the microphone, "and I'm...an alcoholic."

"Hi, Chris," the crowd collectively groaned.

"And I gotta say...that this shit's not working out," Chris derided through the amplifiers, "this whole charade we're doing tonight, this...Alcoholics Anonymous thing. It ain't working. At all. Because...this ain't the whole crowd tonight...is it, folks?"

All of them perked up; even Mitch raised an eyebrow.

"We're not all present, Patty," he said to the counselor. "Where are all...the 'social drinkers,' the 'high-profile' people, the celebrities who host all the fancy soirées at their mansions, getting shit-faced, all the politicians who get stoned? Where's Trump? Where's Obama? Bush? Pence? Hillary? Romney? Biden? Sarah Palin? Pelosi? Al Gore? Stanley Pfeiffer? Bianca Sterling? All the other fuckers—I mean, they all gotta be gettin' fucked up on *something* for 'em to be pullin' our strings the way they do, right?"

The crowd grumbled at him. Naomi and Ray silently nodded at him.

"*They* drink. *They* 'self-medicate,' right?" Chris paced back and forth. "But they're not here. *We* are. This ain't all of us tonight. You know why? Do you really want to know why?"

"Well, Chris," Patty interrupted. "First of all—"

"Shut the fuck up over there!" Chris seethed. "You wanted me to give testimony, so I'm givin' it to you—tonight. I'll tell you when I'm finished—you asked for every bit of this, so you listen, and you listen good!"

Patty grew quiet, eyes wide.

"We're all here tonight...because we're not part of the 'high society.'" Chris uttered a crazed chuckle. "We don't have enough money to bypass the system—we're not rich enough to be above the law like those corrupt rich asshole people in Washington D. C. and I don't know who the fuck else. All the corporate bigwigs running the show, corralling us all like livestock, slowly leading us to the slaughter. They're CRAPs: Corrupt Rich Asshole People. It ain't no secret society; stupid, overprivileged rich people ain't no secret. They don't care about us…and *every* election is rigged, I don't care who you think you're 'voting' for—left-wing, right-wing, it's all the same theatrical shit. Democracy is a myth. America is a myth. All America is…is a glorified sociological experiment, a political laboratory…and we're the lab rats, the test subjects. 'Oh, let's fuck this up over here and orchestrate this crisis over there, and let's see how citizens react and respond so our thinktanks can collect data. Then we can manipulate them more effectively.' I mean…that's why they call it 'political science,' right? All at our expense. But it ain't just about money, is it, boys and girls? Oh, no! Because…because they're as shrewd as car salesmen; they could take a pile of shit…and manipulate people to buy it…and they would make millions, so long as the lie is elaborate and convincing enough—in fact, isn't there…isn't there already some 'emoji' that looks like a grinning pile of shit, and people buy it? Don't they do that, already?"

"For real," Naomi whispered.

"But us," Chris went on, growing more heated, roaming the stage, "as far as the CRAPs are concerned, we're just bugs in the system. We do something, we get arrested by the pigs, we get the horns, and we wind up at this clusterfuck called AA. The CRAPs do the exact same thing and worse…and all they do is get a slap on the wrist." He glared up and pointed at the crucifix. "And *He* wants to tell us that 'all things are working for good.' All things? All things. All the rape. All the murder. All the disease. All the medical malpractice. All the war. All the violence. All the disasters. All the false arrests. All the poverty. All the child abuse! All the racist and sexist bullshit! What the fuck's so good about all that, Jesus? You're just gonna continue to allow this shit, or did You just give Satan the reins altogether? What sort of God does all that? You just gonna hang out nailed on that log, sleeping, doing absolutely nothing over there? My little girl is gone because of You! My life is gone because of You! Because of the system! Because of people! Because of society! And You let it all fucking happen! Are You not amused?"

He flung the microphone like a tomahawk at the crucifix, striking the white wall just below it, barely missing it. Patty flinched, narrowly dodging the ricocheting device as the amplifiers pinged and rang with shrill feedback.

"If I was even *half* the monster people make me out to be," Chris rioted at Patty, "your fat head would be rolling down that street right now—'cause I would've taken it clean off, along with Evelyn's! But seeing that I haven't, what's *that* say about your biased ass? I'm a sweetheart, motherfucker!"

Patty gasped and ducked behind a chair.

"Are You enjoying all this, Jesus?" Chris railed. "Is my suffering entertaining You tonight? Are You enjoying the show? Is *our* anguish delighting You on this dark eve? Pray, tell us!"

Thunder blared outside!

Everyone else jumped a mile—even Mitch—looking at the ceiling, alarmed all the more by the lightning's uncanny timing. Then with mouths agape, they all gazed up at Chris, who was still fuming through gritted teeth, scowling up in the direction of the heavens.

"It's almost like I struck a nerve up there," Chris blasphemed.

"Whoo!" Naomi yelped.

"My man!" Ray cheered.

Everyone applauded him, except Patty. As Chris made it back to his seat, nausea burbled inside him. The fiery fallout of his heartfelt fulmination had not granted him the soothing catharsis he had hoped for. The virus of society only sank its fangs deeper into his soul. He stared at the crucifix again, feeling the biting shame wash over him like scalding acid, then he listened again as the storm rumbled again above, like a woken titan, perturbed and vengeful.

But that's all it was anyway, just a storm.

So they all liked to think.

After the meeting, Chris had at last successfully secured a lunch date with Naomi the following afternoon at a local bistro, though she wanted to go "just as friends" and do "separates checks." She had politely declined to wear his jacket when he offered it, even out in the snow. Damned love games. But maybe she just wasn't looking for anything. He would have little choice but to honor that, much to his chagrin, if he could keep it all together and still maintain his newfound sobriety.

And it was as hard as hell.

The two arrived in downtown La Sombra in separate vehicles and sat at a booth next to the window looking out to the street. Both of them ordered sandwiches, with Naomi having a side of fruit and Chris a side of broccoli. There was a stiffness in the air though, an unwarranted tension between them, more from Chris than anything.

"So," Naomi said, dabbing her mouth, careful not to smear her lipstick, "I thought that was pretty cool what you said at the meeting last night. You were like…Spartacus up there."

"I took it way too far screaming at that crucifix," Chris groaned.

Naomi raised an eyebrow. "Why? I mean…I'm not exactly the religious type, but…they're ain't nothin' wrong with callin' a spade a spade. I mean…if God was there, why would there be so much—"

"I blame people and society for that more than anything," Chris interjected. "I just don't know why…God would do this. It doesn't feel right yelling at Him like that, no matter how shitty everything's gotten, I don't know. It's weird." He sighed. "And it wasn't because of the well-timed thunder last night, either. That just made it…weirder."

"You go to church?"

"I haven't been in a long time," Chris confessed. "Not since…."

"The trial?"

Chris jerked back at her.

Naomi smiled warmly at him. "It's okay. Relax. I know. I know you're Chris Sullivan."

"How?"

"Uh, because it was all over the news, and I recognized you from TV?"

"Then why did you agree to come and—?"

"'Cause I'm not a coward, okay?" Naomi gently retorted. "And it wouldn't be the first time the cops screwed something up, especially *this* bad. Probably won't be the last time, either. Friggin' pigs. And Evelyn *did* seem like she was acting in the courtroom, fake crying and all. Not all women were on her side."

Chris furrowed his forehead at her.

"Contrary to popular belief," Naomi went on, "women *don't* stick together. We throw each other under the bus more often than what you think—and *this* chica has seen her fair share of it and been through it herself. There's what the media wants us to think…and then there's getting it straight from the horse's mouth, you know?" She took a sip of her tea. "And I definitely know fake crying when I see it…your ex-wife."

Chris sighed. He didn't like his soft underbelly being exposed.

She averted her eyes. "And you're not the only one who lost their little girl to bullshit."

"You too?"

Naomi exhaled a quavering breath. "Aeriel is her name. I guess she's about…seven now. I got caught with possession of crack years ago—my asshole baby daddy must've slipped it in my car without me knowing. Then I got pulled over one night, all because I'm half-black. They searched the car, and pinned it on me. I tried to tell 'em it wasn't mine, and they wouldn't believe me—they didn't care. Damned pigs. I got arrested for something I didn't do, and I was found guilty anyway…and I watched my life fall apart right before my very eyes. My parents got custody of my daughter…and they still won't let me see her." A tear rolled down her cheek. "She doesn't even know who her momma is; she was a baby when they took her away from me. Now I got a criminal record for that shit…and I cope…by drinking way too damned much, having a blackout here and there. Got a DUI—I'll take responsibility for that…but the possession thing? No. Uh-uh. Like the jury cares; they're just twelve random dipshits selected to decide another human being's fate, their stupid asses fallin' asleep, not listening to the case at all, and all they want to do is go home. Like they know anything! They don't care about us. They only see what they want to see and hear what they want to hear. That wasn't me who did that. That's bullshit. So, no, you ain't the only one who got screwed by the system." She squinted at him. "I just wonder if they did the same thing to you."

"Naomi," Chris said, holding her hand. Her fingers were so cold.

She sniffled and wiped her face. "I'm okay. I'm a big girl."

"You're still human, though."

"Well, so are you."

"Am I?"

Naomi scoffed. "Yes. Why you gotta bottle yours up? It's not healthy."

"Because I'm a man," Chris grumbled. "We're supposed to swallow it all, just eat it. We're not allowed to be weak or pathetic. We're not allowed to cry. We're not allowed to feel pain. We're not allowed to have emotions."

"That's a bunch of bull!"

"Tell that to society," Chris said. "No, I gotta be like the Terminator, over-the-top, be indestructible, unfeeling, show no signs of humanity whatsoever. Because that's what being 'macho' is all about." He huffed. "All people ever do is look at me like I'm some Frankenstein monster, like I'm some creep. I've even had women who would deliberately walk out in front of me and would pretend that I'm following them, just to flatter themselves."

"Ooh, I got a friend who does that shit!" Naomi growled. "I hate that, because then, all these guys...they think I'm like that. No, I try to be fair, give everybody the benefit of a doubt. I try to be level-headed. She's paranoid, thinks everybody in the world's stalking her—and she'll brag about it! It's like a damned fetish to her or something. She fantasizes about that shit, thinks her life is one big soap opera. Watches way too many of those damned cop shows." She glared, shaking her head at the window. "I could slap her teeth right outta her mouth."

"Well," Chris said, "that's all those cop shows are: just soap operas with cops and serial killers. Crime novels, too. A cast of unrelatable characters built like mannequins, with a crappy plot twist here and there for cheap shock value. Weave some gimmicky political commentary, propaganda, and other popular sweet nothings in there, pepper it with steamy romance, murky suspense, a few action scenes, and corny melodrama and *voila*! Instant best-seller. It's all formulaic crap. It's potato-chip fiction. Empty-calorie storylines that all look and taste the same, with maybe a few flavor variations here and there. And none of them are good for you. But they sell like the motherfuckers, though. Might as well be trying to sell Doritos to everybody."

Naomi giggled, then took another sip of her drink. "Well, aren't you an author?"

"I *had*...a zombie apocalypse series going," Chris told her. "Like we need any more of those, either, after talking shit about crime novels and cop shows. Yeah, I...I never finished the last one of the series, but it doesn't matter. I was forced to self-publish because people in the industry wanted to be bigoted and prejudiced towards me, push me around. And I couldn't prove it, and these were people who *claimed* to represent those who are 'marginalized,' when really they're just a bunch of fake shit-headed profiteers trying to exploit people when it suits them."

"Ooh, I feel that. I do."

"They pulled my books after the trial." Chris smirked. "But I *did* try to make my novels a little different, though."

"How?"

Chris sighed. "It doesn't have…a global virus that turns people into zombies. There's an…evil necromancer who resurrects them and kills and converts people into zombie slaves. And I have a cast of characters who each are born with special magic abilities—they're not like superheroes or anything. But they…try to stop this evil necromancer who basically becomes a dictator who's trying to summon the devil with these mass hecatomb sacrifices in this post-apocalyptic world, and he even enslaves living soldiers, threatening to turn them into zombies if they don't comply." He shook his head. "It's like symbolic of what we're going through. The necromancer represents, like, the politicians and rich people of the world trying to manipulate the masses and censor and discredit people who disagree with them, whether they be those Trump fetishists or—"

Naomi busted out laughing.

Chris chuckled. "What?"

"Trump fetishists—I love it! I'm gonna use that now!"

"You should," Chris said. "Either that or it's whiny hipster fanatics who clog up the streets, complaining and shit, firebombing everything."

Naomi's cheer instantly evaporated at that comment. That was the last nerve Chris wanted to strike. Here he went again, his mouth getting him into trouble, if not his writing. Maybe this *wasn't* going to work out.

"It's just…I'm sick of totalitarian government is all," Chris groaned.

"Yeah. Everybody is," Naomi said, then snorted with a smirk. "Trump fetishists. I like that."

"I'm an Independent—I don't vote," Chris admitted.

"Yeah, I'm the same way," Naomi agreed.

"What bugged the crap outta me, though," Chris said, "is that the few people who actually bothered to read my zombie books…is that they'd say it'd make a 'great cartoon,' when I didn't intend anything like that. One chick even said it would make a 'badass anime,' even though I guess she meant well. I'll tell you what would make a great cartoon: real life. It's stranger than fiction. You can't make any of this shit up, what we're goin' through in this day and age." He huffed. "Even my mom kept tellin' people that my books were kids' stuff.'"

Naomi scrunched her forehead. "Zombies are kids' stuff?"

Chris sighed. "Apparently so."

"How is your mom?"

"She passed away a few years back. Cancer got her."

Naomi's face twisted with sorrow. "I am so sorry."

Chris shrugged. "It's just life." He sighed again. "We're just…getting to that age now." He scoffed. "Unemployment's gonna run out soon, and I'm so behind on rent payments, I've already gotten an eviction notice."

"You can't find work?"

"I've been looking for something. Something with a salary, but…Evelyn fucked me over pretty good." Chris scoffed again. "Nobody wants to hire a 'wife-beater.'"

Naomi shook her head. "I don't think you're a wife-beater."

"Why not? Everybody else thinks that."

Naomi leaned in and peered into his eyes. "I'm not everybody else. And neither are you. I don't think your little girl would've reacted so strongly at that trial the way she did on TV, screaming at the cops not to take her daddy away, if you truly were the monster they make you out to be."

Chris just stared at her, silently stupefied by her words.

She was growing sexier by the minute.

Yet, he still didn't really know what her angle was about the relationship.

"And concerning Evelyn," Naomi said, "all they were doing was pampering and elevating one female on a pedestal all at the expense of other people. At the expense of Melanie."

"Well," Chris moped. "Evelyn always gets what she wants. Everything's always handed to her on a silver platter. Always."

"And that bimbo bitch is gonna get hers one day," Naomi replied. "I truly believe that, Chris. Evelyn Whitaker is *not* the queen of women. Neither is Bianca Sterling. They don't represent me. We're individuals, you and I. We shouldn't be stereotyped because of what other individuals do. It's gonna come back on them something fierce. It's gonna be ugly. And they're not gonna recover from it. Ever. The payback's coming, baby, don't you—oh, crap!"

"What?"

Naomi smirked. "I just called you 'baby.'"

"So?"

As Naomi opened her mouth, their tattooed hipster waitress came back up to the table. "Is there anything else I can get you two? Any dessert?"

"Anything on the special?" Naomi said.

"We have chocolate lava cake, apple pie. Even got some crème brûlée." The waitress smiled. "Our root beer floats are pretty good, too—they're my favorite. Homemade vanilla ice cream."

"Mmm," Naomi hummed. "That sounds good."

"Is it Barq's?" Chris asked.

"Always," the waitress chirped, grinning. "Comes in a big glass goblet."

Chris looked at Naomi. "Wanna do that?"

"Uh…yeah," Naomi nodded. "Two root beer floats, please."

"Coming right up," the waitress said, sauntering back to the kitchen.

"You ever had a root beer float?" Chris questioned.

"Oh, yeah," Naomi said. "You?"

"I'm from Mississippi," Chris said. "That's where Barq's was invented, in Biloxi."

"Really?"

"Yeah," Chris told her. "The first bottling of Coca-Cola took place in Vicksburg, actually. See, they boiled sassafras roots to make root beer back in the day, hence the name. I think Hires was the first root beer, though." He glanced out at the window. "I don't think they make it like that anymore."

"No, everything's just…shortcuts and artificial bullcrap."

"First heart transplant was performed in Mississippi," Chris explained. "Elvis Presley grew up there, Brett Favre. John Grisham went to Mississippi State. I think Jim Henson, the guy who came up with the Muppets, grew up in Leland, Mississippi, too. His friend was named Kermit Scott, apparently, which is where the frog puppet came from. There's a historical marker for it and everything."

"You makin' this up," Naomi teased.

"Google it," Chris flashed his teeth. "I dare ya."

"Nah, I'll take your word for it." Naomi rested her chin on her palm, her elbow on the table. "So…why did you leave Mississippi if it's associated with such fame?"

Chris's smile vanished. "You even seen that movie, *Oh, Brother, Where Art Thou*?"

"Mm-hmm."

Chris sighed. "People still think we look and act like that. They look at us like we're a bunch of archaic, inbred savages runnin' around barefooted in overalls—and there *are* still some people who still do that shit, unfortunately." He sighed again. "But they don't see me, the self-aware individual. They're too spoiled and…nescient to see who I am. Back when I was in Orlando, there was a guy, some four-hundred-pound walrus fuckface I was interning for, and the news brought up the Confederate emblem being on the state flag. It was on the TV at a meeting in the restaurant one day. He pointed and said, 'Uh-oh! Look, Chris, your flag's in danger.' I thought to myself, 'That ain't my flag, you bigot.' When I was in college over there in Florida, people would ask me, 'What's Mississippi like? Do you make moonshine over there?' People are so presumptuous! Just a bunch of sheltered, narrow-minded motherfuckers who never bothered to leave the city, being spoon-fed lies daily by the media. If people want to know what Mississippi is like, they need to go see it for themselves—all of it, not just one little place over there. It makes me sick! I ain't no damned Neo-Nazi. I don't lick asshole. I hate country music. I don't do that redneck hillbilly shit. I don't worship Trump—people don't even remember who the hell Trump even is: just another Hollywood shitbag pretending to be a Republican…not that the other dipshits in D. C. are any better." He shook his head. "But that's all they want to see, the damned stereotype. I got shit on by racists for having a Hispanic mother—and people couldn't even get her name right! Her name was—"

"Here ya go." The waitress sang, setting the two root beer floats on the table before them, the pale vanilla ice cream scoops bobbing in the fizzing goblets of the dark soft drink.

"Thank you," Naomi said.

"My pleasure," the waitress replied, then walked away.

Chris and Naomi each took a napkin and wiped some of the thick froth escaping the rim of their goblets.

"Anyway…you were saying?" Naomi asked.

"Yeah," Chris went on. "Her name was Martina. You would not believe how many people screwed that up over the years, calling her Marketta, Margarette, Margarita—like, yeah, sure. My mother's an alcoholic beverage."

Naomi snickered. "Are you serious? What the hell is wrong with people?"

"I don't know—they can't read, apparently," Chris scoffed. "Nobody wants to read anymore. They just want to waste away on the Internet, be on their phones, and binge-watch their brains out on Netflix. Slobs. They couldn't even get her name right in the obituary, called her, 'Marguetta.' Damned putzes." He sighed. "That's been my life, though. I'm either too much of this...."

"Or not enough of that," Naomi said solemnly. "I know exactly the feeling you're talking about. As far as others were concerned, I wasn't white enough for the system...and then I had people in my neighborhood, these gangster wannabes who thought they were blacker than the other black people, ostracizing me because my mom's white, calling me 'Milky' and all that. I'd be like, 'What's wrong with you? You lactose-intolerant? Milk make you shit blood?' I know precisely what you're talking about, Chris. We're neither good enough or bad enough to fit in anywhere. Society still wants to be ignorant and look at us like we're 'halfbreeds' or something."

"People are shitty," Chris said. "Race is just an illusion."

"It is," Naomi muttered. "It's the twenty-first century, and still these immature douchebags want to cling to that stupid prehistoric mindset, that someone's skin color somehow makes them a different species or something. Dumbasses."

"Or they turn to dust at the sound of the 'F' word," Chris scoffed. "You're just speaking Dutch is all. I don't why people gotta bleep it out. It's no different than saying 'fornicators' or 'fornicate that' or something."

"Well," Naomi said, looking away. "I don't like cussing. I mean, I know I do it, so I guess I'm a hypocrite like that. I shouldn't cuss. But I do get what you're saying. It's just language. Words can hurt, but only if you let it. People gotta grow up. People gotta have a tough skin, even though we don't enjoy it. Callin' somebody a shithead ain't any different from callin' 'em a moron. Same principle." She huffed and shrugged. "I don't know. Society's weird like that." She eyed her goblet. "Oh, no."

"What?" Chris asked.

"My ice cream melted," Naomi said, then she giggled at the remaining chunk of vanilla steadily integrating into the root beer like a shrinking iceberg, shifting to a caramel color. "It's not a float anymore."

"Mine, either," Chris said, picking up his goblet. "That was quick."

She examined hers closer. "It's more like a..."

"Cream soda."

Naomi peered up at him and smirked again. "Yeah. Kinda like...you and me, a new mixture." She picked hers up. "What should we toast to?"

Chris smiled. "To...survival, I guess."

"And...to being just the right mixture."

Chris nodded. "Yeah."

Naomi grinned as they clinked glasses, then each of them took a sip of their new beverages. She made yummy sounds, then took a gulp, then licked the foam from her upper lip.

"Tastes better than Oreos," Chris joked.

"Mm-hmm," Naomi concurred.

The waitress returned to the table. "Is it going to be together or separate?"

Chris looked at Naomi. "You sure you don't want me to get it? I don't mind, now."

Naomi hesitated, then looked up at their server. "Separate."

Chris shrugged at the waitress. "I tried."

The waitress laughed. "I'll come back with the checks."

Naomi looked at him. "I said we'd do separate checks."

"I know, I know," Chris said. "I just...."

"You're a very sweet man, Chris," Naomi complimented with a smirk, getting her wallet out of her purse. "And you may need to look for something smaller than just a gig with a salary, maybe...stock shelves at a grocery store. You don't have to do it for the rest of your life. I mean...if they're threatening to evict you...I don't want you to wind up homeless." She looked at him. "Do you have any family you can ask for help?"

Chris shook his head. He peered with gloomy eyes at his cream soda, the drink no longer seeming appetizing. He just wanted to get the hell out of there, just vanish in the wilderness. Alone. This whole thing was a mistake. Now, he was fully emasculated in front of the very one he had feelings for. And she didn't love him back. Nobody could, apparently. He was the scum of the earth, after all. Though Naomi meant well, each of her words were daggers puncturing his heart. She didn't realize how much damage she had done. Grocery store? Really? He, with a bachelor's degree in English, after all that college and tuition money, all that experience on his resume, the once-ambitious published author with so much promise, with such a bright future.

All reduced to ashes. Just for the amusement of a sociopathic world.

And he couldn't wait for the Apocalypse any longer.

"Chris?" Naomi said.

"I'll...think of something," Chris grumbled, getting his wallet out. "Don't worry about me. They haven't killed me yet."

"Speaking of killing," Naomi said, "I didn't wanna mention this earlier, but...have you heard about the Vulture, that serial killer."

"Yeah," Chris said. "The guy who was killing in Seattle, Portland, all over California." He cleared his throat. "And now he's over here?"

"He killed Stanley Pfeiffer, I heard."

"The judge?"

"Yeah. He's dead."

"Well," Chris scoffed. "Whatever. He targets pigs of the government most of the time, from what it sounds like, so I'm not all that worried. Neither should you."

Naomi stared at him like a deer in the headlights, unnerved by his callous response.

Chris raised an eyebrow at her.

The waitress returned, giving them each their respective bills.

"Uh, can I get a to-go cup for my float, please?" Naomi requested.

"Certainly," the waitress replied, then turned to Chris. "Would you like one as well, sir?"

"No, ma'am."

"I'll get that for you," the server said, strutting back to the kitchen. "Be right back."

Naomi pursed her lips. "So, how long have you been sober now?"

"Just a few days."

"Well, keep up the good work."

"What are you doing now? You still a receptionist at the hospital?"

"Part-time," Naomi said. "I actually got another gig lined up. I start tomorrow."

"Doing what?"

She smiled. "I'm gonna be a nanny. Pays much better, too. I'm only at the hospital until twelve, then I go and take care of this little girl while the mom goes to work, then I'm gonna stay there until six in the evening. Got the weekends off. She's homeschooled, which is weird for someone so young, but whatever."

"Alright, good. Awesome!" Chris congratulated.

"I just hope I can do it," Naomi said. "You know...be like a mommy."

"You gonna do great, Naomi." Chris sighed. "You gonna do great."

"Remember what I told you," Naomi scolded. "Okay? Don't you wind up on the streets—I mean it! Hey, you hear me?"

"Yeah, I hear you, Mom."

"Boy, I'm being serious! Do you understand me?"

"Yeah, I do! Loud and clear." Chris got his debit card out. "Guess we'll half the tip too, huh?"

"Yeah," Naomi agreed. "Sounds good." She looked up at the woman at the register. "Hey, do we go up there to pay, or...?"

"Yes, ma'am, I'm ready for you," the cashier said, waving them forward.

Both of them rose up as the waitress returned with a tall Styrofoam cup. Naomi thanked her and poured the rest of her cream soda into the container and sealed it with its plastic lid, piercing it with a straw. Chris went ahead up to the register, with Naomi following behind.

Naomi noted his posture: like a zombie. He might have been trying to get better, but he wasn't trying hard enough. At this rate, he wasn't going to be okay.

At all.

And it bothered the shit out of her.

But there was nothing she could about it. She could not offer him what he sought. The last thing they both needed right then was a relationship. Even more so, she couldn't dare let him know who it was she was going to be a nanny to.

A certain five-year-old little girl. With Chris Sullivan's brown eyes.

The fruit of his loins.

VIII: The Nest

Early afternoon came as Naomi clocked out of work at the hospital and drove to a nearby gas station to refuel and get a bottle of water and a chef salad, still unsettled by Chris's predicament the other day. He was going to be evicted? She couldn't let that happen. If only he was more motivated. But it was hard to blame him, considering the circumstances. She didn't want him becoming a vagabond, but she also didn't want yet another worthless, shitty codependent relationship either.

Regardless, she didn't want to lose him.

She already knew he had feelings for her…and she found it kind of hot. Chris was a pathetic, grungy, scrappy underdog, one of her many weaknesses. That face, those broad shoulders. And more importantly, he was a daddy, one who actually cared about his child. Such guys with that quality were getting harder and harder to find, and as far as she was concerned, he wasn't the worst-looking person in the world. She fancied true good looks, the real deal, not some airbrushed phony façade. And besides, having Chris just a tad bit insecure would only keep him around longer; if her man thought himself a real-life Adonis, he would just be more prone to being unfaithful to her.

Dogs thought themselves too sexy to handle.

Still, it was painfully obvious the whole thing was a bad idea. How many times had she indulged such nonsense? How many times had it blown up in her face, costing her so much? Then again, life was too short. If she did not let love back into her life now, she may never get another chance. It wasn't like any of them were getting any younger. Her thirties were just around the corner, and so were his. She couldn't wait forever. Chris Sullivan had become her new guilty pleasure—but she couldn't dare let him know that! Even more so, she couldn't confide to him who she was playing nanny to.

His little Melanie.

Under Evelyn Whitaker's thumbnail.

Naomi wasn't exactly sanguine about it, quite nauseated today, with barely an appetite under the hazy afternoon sun, trying to pierce the thin gossamer clouds above La Sombra. But she had to eat something, even if it was some cheap gas station salad. She was also on a budget too, living paycheck to paycheck, and if she didn't watch out, she also wouldn't be able to pay rent and would be evicted herself. But she had to know. Evelyn said that Chris abused her. Chris claimed that Evelyn fabricated the whole case.

One of them was lying.

But who?

What sort of ungodly mess had she subjected herself to?

She was still garbed in her sea-green scrubs, tennis shoes, and a zip-up hoodie as she shivered in the brisk mountain winds, pumping gas into her gray sedan. She didn't have time to go back and change; she was already running late, trying to brace herself for the ass-chewing conversation from her new employer on the first day. Not good. And she needed this gig, the receptionist thing alone was not cutting the mustard. She was so sick of limiting herself, all because of some bogus criminal record the system slapped on her had restricted her and Chris Sullivan both, pigeonholing them as crooks.

But the irony of judging one by a criminal record...is that, at one time...they *didn't* have a record. At all. They were as clean as a whistle. Therefore, it stood to reason that those who didn't have past charges just hadn't been caught yet. Having no record did not automatically make someone a law-abiding citizen. Nobody was without fault. All of them were guilty of something. Why should some people have more privilege than those who have been arrested before, guilty or not? And permanently hindering individuals through such bureaucratic ostracization only tempted the crooks into more unsavory activities, producing a downward spiral rather than allowing one to redeem one's self.

If they were not permitted to be a part of society, why should they care about its system? The system had no problem cheating them. Why not cheat the system back?

That was the overall mentality of the criminal; they had little choice but to make a career of being an outlaw, nothing more than a survival instinct. They had just as much of a right to exist as the corrupt rich assholes, or as Chris had lovingly called them, the "CRAPs" of civilization. Even rats will fight back if put into a corner. Misfits like Naomi and Chris were seen as such...and were forced to follow suit; sooner or later, they would have to rise up against the tyrannical elitists and so-called "high-profile" figures in society. And contrary to popular opinion, high society wasn't all that composed of just old, bitter white males.

It was a lot more diverse than what people liked to think.

And they were all causing catastrophes left and right.

Just what, exactly, was sanity?

She couldn't agree more with Chris; she also blamed society and the corruption polluting it, the money-grabbers, the voracious misers, the profiteers, causing all the world's suffering. As pitiful and morose as he was, his impassioned speech managed to pluck a rusty harp string within her the other night at the AA meeting.

But she was getting ahead of herself.

What if he *was* truly guilty?

Had she not actually taken into account the grim possibility, being swept away by her careless emotions once again? Was she being just as biased as the ones who had accused him? One thing she *did* know, she certainly despised the age-old butterflies exacerbating her queasy stomach, having been dormant for so long. She felt like a teenage girl all over again, both loving and loathing the tumultuous sensation brewing inside her.

She was actually falling for Chris.

That is…if he was, in fact, innocent as he claimed.

Time to stop guessing…and conduct her own investigation.

She finished refueling her vehicle, then scurried into the store, snatching a one-liter of bottled water, then took a bag of M & M's, then grabbed a chef salad from a refrigerated shelf, then got in line at the register, with a few people in front of her. Behind her, she failed to notice a stranger in a fedora and a brown coat lined with a red and black plaid design. He took a bottle of tea from the freezer, then strolled and joined her in line. He smirked at her.

"My, what healthy habits you have," the man's smooth, gravelly voice commented.

Naomi turned to him. "I'm sorry?"

"You're getting a salad instead of a greasy hamburger."

"Oh, yeah," Naomi replied, smiling. "Trying to be good…even though I got a bag of candy."

"That's all right. Nothing wrong with treating yourself here and there," the man told her. "You doctors and nurses are a great asset to the world. I commend you for your service."

"Oh, I'm just a receptionist—but thank you." Naomi said, her smile growing more difficult to maintain.

"St. James Memorial?"

"Uh…at a clinic," Naomi lied.

"Down the street?"

"I'd rather not say, sir."

"My apologies," the man said.

The line moved. Only two more people ahead of her.

"I don't mean to be rude, but—"

"No, you have a right to your privacy," the man said, amused by her defiance. "You have such beautiful fall colors here in Colorado. The trees are so majestic this time of year."

"Only the finest," Naomi agreed, her eyes darting around.

Who was this creep? Why wasn't the line moving faster?

It was like having a buzzard loom over her shoulder and….

Her heart skipped a beat as a cold chill ran over her. Buzzard. She gulped, her throat growing dry. Surely it wasn't him. Surely it wasn't the Vulture they had been talking about. Something seemed to emanate from the stranger, as if he were some entity in disguise, mocking mortality, a grim reaper wearing human flesh.

"Where are you from, if I may ask?" Naomi asked.

"From out of state," the man told her. "On vacation."

She gulped again as the line moved again. Only one more person in front of her.

"Have you ever been on…the West Coast?" Naomi questioned, testing him. "I've heard it's beautiful out there too."

The man nodded. "I go from time to time. Sometimes I visit family out there." He gazed at her. "The name's Andrew. And you are…?"

"Connie," Naomi lied again.

"I can take who's next in line," another cashier said, appearing at another register.

Naomi dashed with the items as "Andrew" studied her with his watchful blue eyes; his smirk widened as she hastily checked out. He could taste her fear, entertained by her unease. He could almost feel the goosebumps rising on her succulent caramel skin and the vibrations of her trepidation.

"Enjoy your lunch," Andrew told her.

Naomi nodded at him, taking her plastic bag of groceries. "Enjoy the sights."

"I will," Andrew assured her, waving at her.

With that, Naomi almost jogged out the sliding doors, frantically fishing for her car keys in her pocket. She unlocked and entered her vehicle, cranking the engine, then took one last look at Andrew, his piercing gaze fixed on her. Then he finally turned around and greeted the cashier, placing the bottle of tea on the counter. She almost peeled out from the gas pump and into the street, her heart fluttering in her chest. She looked at her phone on the car seat. It would do no good to call 911; damned pigs wouldn't do anything. And maybe it wasn't even him. Why was she being so neurotic? It wasn't like it was the first time a stranger had struck up a conversation at a checkout line. She was quite a social butterfly, rather extroverted. She shook her head, glancing at the clock, reading 1:47 p. m.

Evelyn was going to have her ass.

So much for the nanny gig.

And so much for Melanie.

Naomi pulled into Evelyn's driveway, her heart still churning in her rib cage, but more because she was beyond late. Already, she was rehearsing an excuse for being behind schedule. She couldn't keep her diva of an employer waiting much longer, lest she miss her next interview; the paparazzi was still in town, and they still couldn't get enough of Evelyn's newfound stardom. This time, the TV show, *48 Hours: Hard Evidence,* was craving a scoop for a new episode. It would supposedly feature her "survival story" and how the uncertainty of the limited evidence and the testimony created much division amongst the masses. And the fact that Chris Sullivan was an author of apocalyptic fiction somehow made the account juicier and all the more sensational, despite the fact that her ex-husband's novels were ultimately pulled. Nobody wanted to financially enable someone who was seen as a "wife-beater," no matter how shady the whole case was overall. It was true what Naomi had said to Chris; not every woman was thrilled about the outcome of the trial. Evelyn was not the empress of females. Neither was Bianca Sterling. Rather than flying Evelyn out to Los Angeles for the umpteenth time, the schmucks came to her, staying in La Sombra on this occasion, as she had claimed that her family life lately had left her temporarily grounded.

Sure it did.

Naomi huffed and exited her car, with the bag of groceries in hand, then she slammed and locked the door to her vehicle, her eyes surveying the neighborhood. She just couldn't shake the feeling that someone was watching her. A cool wind whipped between the houses and trees, then she shivered and approached the front porch. Upstairs, she could hear the muffled crying of a five-year-old girl.

"Shit," Naomi whispered to herself, then she took a breath, then exhaled, then reached up to knock.

But the door opened.

Revealing Evelyn's bruised face.

"I am so sorry I'm late," Naomi blurted. "Traffic was awful, the lunch rush and all—I promise it won't happen again—I am so—!"

"It's fine, it's fine—get in," Evelyn said, unusually calm and gloomy. "It's freezing out here."

Naomi stepped in to the well-furnished living room as Evelyn strutted to the kitchen. The lavish home was something akin to the cover of a *Southern Living* magazine. Evelyn was clad in a beige sweater and dark-blue jeans, her blonde hair tied into a ponytail. Naomi noted a fresh scar down her cheek and neck, resembling something like a bad cat scratch. One of her bruises showed an imprint of some kind, yet she failed to make out what. On the second floor, Melanie continued to wail in a furious tantrum from behind a bedroom door…and something else.

"I should have called you earlier," Evelyn told her, stirring something in a pot on the stove. "I made some lunch for you and Melanie. It's some chili, just in case that salad doesn't hold you."

"Thank you," Naomi replied. "What happened to your face?"

"Oh," Evelyn gasped, then turned, her pale-blue eyes wide. "I, uh…was outside trying to do something in the backyard and I tripped on the water hose, and I fell on a tree limb lying on the ground." She feigned a giggle. "Looks…a lot worse than what it is."

"You didn't go to the hospital?"

Evelyn shook her head. "Nah. It's not…it's not that bad."

"Where's Melanie? Is she okay?"

"Oh, yeah, she's fine," Evelyn said, peering up at the ceiling with arms akimbo. "She's been acting out here lately. She's in timeout right now. If she gives you any trouble, just give me a call, and I'll handle it when I get back." She washed a few dishes in the sink. "They called earlier and moved my interview to three o'clock, so you're fine."

"You have such a nice house," Naomi complimented.

"Thank you," Evelyn said. "Newton has such a promising career working with the tech company…unlike somebody *else* I know." She dried her hands on a towel. "And the royalties I'm making from *my* career are doing quite well, too, so…everything's working out much better now. Much…much better."

"Right," Naomi said, squinting at her, then she perused the living room.

"Make yourself at home," Evelyn told her, then sighed and strode up the staircase. "Need to go check on her, I guess."

Naomi sat down on a cushioned wicker chair, then watched Evelyn's lithe form vanish down a hall upstairs, then she heard a bedroom door open. Melanie had quieted down; not even the noise of sniffling was heard. Then Naomi heard another door open. She raised an eyebrow.

A closet?

"Are you going to behave now?" Evelyn scolded. "Or do you need more timeout?"

"No," Melanie whimpered. "It's dark in there."

Naomi's eyes bulged, then she put her hand over her mouth, appalled by what she had just heard. Surely, that wasn't Evelyn's twisted version of "timeout."

Was it?

"So, you're going to behave now?" Evelyn asked. "You're gonna be a good girl?"

Melanie said nothing.

"Good," Evelyn huffed. "Come down stairs and get something to eat, then. Come on, I want you to meet your new nanny."

"I don't want a nanny!" Melanie squealed. "I want Daddy!"

Naomi shed a tear, feeling her heart shatter inside of her.

"I've told you before…and I'll tell you again," Evelyn said firmly. "Newton is your daddy now. Your other one is gone…okay? Do you hear me? Do you—hey!"

Melanie darted down the hall and made it halfway down the stairs, then froze, locking eyes with Naomi.

"Hey, sweetie," Naomi cooed, grinning and waving. "My goodness, what a pretty little girl you are! You're just a little baby doll."

"She *is* that," Evelyn agreed, appearing at the top of the steps with a smirk, crossing her arms. She looked down at her daughter. "Say, 'Thank you.'"

"Thank you," Melanie reluctantly muttered, slowly stepping down to the first floor, still hesitant to approach her nanny, yet another anomaly in her hellacious environment.

Naomi took a step toward her. Melanie Whitaker was nothing like her mother. Her long, wavy dark-brown hair draped her shoulders and the top of her blue denim skirt and long-sleeve shirt of pink and black stripes. White stockings and black dress shoes adorned her thin, short legs and tiny feet. She really did look like a baby doll. Even more so, she had her father's brown eyes and facial features—even his skin tone! Naomi's heart ached, realizing how similar she was to Chris Sullivan. No wonder he wanted her back.

She truly was a piece of him.

And Evelyn couldn't stand it!

"My name's Naomi," she said, rising up from the chair. "What's yours?"

"Melanie."

"That's a pretty name. Are you hungry?"

Someone banged on the door. Naomi looked and peered outside the blinds at a black SUV. She gulped. Chills ran down her spine. She knew from her harrowing past experiences that there was only one kind of person in the world who bludgeoned a door like that.

And they could all go to hell.

"I'll get it," Evelyn said, rushing down the stairs.

She reached the front door and opened it. Naomi pursed her lips, her suspicions confirmed: two FBI agents, a bald black man and a younger white guy, standing on the porch. Their eyes instantly shifted to Naomi, causing her blood to boil. Let the pigs get a good look, then. Immediately, Melanie instinctively retreated to Naomi, a complete stranger, rather than to own mother. Her nanny held her.

"It's okay, baby, shh," Naomi calmed.

"Ms. Whitaker?" one of the cops asked.

"Hello, officers," Evelyn said, producing a fake smile. "Can I help you?"

"Yes, I'm Agent Vince Redman," one of them said. "This is my partner, Agent Theo Nash. I don't know if you remember us, but—"

"Yes—you were the ones who handled the case with my ex-husband," Evelyn chimed.

"That's right," Redman confirmed, noting Evelyn's wounds. "What happened to your—?"

"Gardening accident outside," Evelyn stammered, faking another giggle. "Just clumsy, that's all. Tripped on a tree limb and fell. Looks worse than what it is."

Naomi raised an eyebrow. Didn't she just say it was a water hose she tripped over? What was this peculiar duress that had settled into her? And why was it so contagious?

Nash stepped to the side near a rocking chair on the porch, getting his phone out and noticing Evelyn's abrasions, readying his camera app, with her attention still fixed on Redman.

"That looks like it may need stitches, Evelyn," Redman observed.

"Oh, it's fine, trust me," Evelyn claimed. "Would you like to come in?"

"Actually, we can't," Redman told her. "We're on our way back to Denver on a case…and we were passing through the area and decided to check on you and see how you and your husband were doing. Didn't mean to alarm you or anything."

"Oh, not at all, that's very sweet of you!" Evelyn said.

Redman looked at the other woman. "And you are…?"

"Naomi," she replied.

"Last name?"

"Monroe. I'm the nanny."

"Okay, that's fine." Redman nodded, then smiled down at Melanie. "That your little girl?"

"Oh, yeah," Evelyn said, turning to her daughter. "She's growing like a weed."

"She certainly is," Redman chuckled, taking a knee on the threshold. "Hey, sweetheart. You're gettin' so big. How old are you now?"

Melanie just stared at him.

"Tell the nice policeman how old you are," Evelyn commanded.

Cautiously, Melanie held up five fingers. "This many."

"Oh, wow!" Redman said. "You're five already? You're a big girl."

"Say, we're in kindergarten, aren't we?" Evelyn said to Melanie, then turned back at Redman. "She's just shy."

"Oh, that's all right," Redman smiled, then he groaned, rising up. "You haven't had any...contact with Chris Sullivan or anything, have you?"

"No," Evelyn said, shaking her head. "Not at all."

"You...you got remarried," Nash said, approaching the door. "Right?"

"Yes—well...no. Not yet," Evelyn said. "He and I are just...dating right now."

"And his name?"

"Newton. Newton Malcolm." She toyed with her ponytail. "He's at work right now. He'll be home this evening."

"Okay, well that's fine." Nash carefully studied her scar. "Sure you don't need to—"

"Well, actually," Evelyn cut him off. "I don't mean to sound rude, but I have to get ready to go to an interview in town very soon. I have to do...an episode for *48 Hours: Hard Evidence*. They're expecting me soon."

Naomi glanced back and forth at the three. Should she tell them about "Andrew" at the gas station just now? Like they'd do anything, anyway. They would just regard her as just another paranoid bitch; they wouldn't take her seriously, not with her bogus record. Maybe it was nothing. Maybe she had just overreacted.

Hopefully.

"That's fine. We need to be going too," Redman said, then he glanced at his partner.

Damned right you do, Naomi thought. *Damned pigs.*

"Congratulations, once again," Nash said.

"Thank you," Evelyn replied.

Nash looked at Naomi. "Ma'am."

Naomi nodded at him.

"Did we ever give you one of our business cards?"

"On the fridge," Evelyn told him.

"Okay, well...you take care," Nash said with a grin.

"Have a nice day," Redman farewelled.

Evelyn smiled back, then gently eased the door shut. Both agents walked back and entered their cruiser, with Redman on the driver's side. The senior officer scowled at his subordinate.

"Why are you taking pictures of her face?" Redman snapped.

"You and I both know those bruises were no accident," Nash said, sending the photos via text to Curtis Tully. "She's full of shit...and maybe I'm remembering wrong, but her abrasions looked much different from the Chris Sullivan case. I want to make sure."

"It's inadmissible evidence," Redman rebuked.

"It's not for the court—it's for us and our guys in forensics," Nash said, calling Tully. "Hey, it's Nash. I need you to analyze something for me. I need a side-by-side comparison to the photos I just sent you alongside the one from the Chris Sullivan file. I want you to pay close attention to that indentation on her left cheek. It looks like it was made by a piece of jewelry, but I'm not entirely sure. There was a similar abrasion around her temple when Sullivan was tried. I just want to make sure." He nodded. "Okay. Thanks, bud."

He hung up, then looked at Redman, his partner visibly annoyed.

"Hey, this was your idea to open up this can of worms again," Nash defended. "Leave no stone unturned. Remember?"

"Yeah, yeah, alright," Redman conceded, rubbing his face. "She *did* seem like she was dodging us…and she did not hesitate at all to press charges against Sullivan. Why now?"

"I think your gut is tellin' you what mine is tellin' me," Nash said, peering at Naomi, who was unable to see through the tinted windows of their SUV through the blinds of the living room.

"Might need to do twenty-four-hour surveillance," Redman said, cranking the engine.

"And bring Malcolm in for questioning," Nash added.

"Not yet. I want to see what Tully and them say about those photos first," Redman said, driving off. "You're right, though. Something stinks about it. And having the Vulture loose doesn't make it any better, especially after what happened to Bianca. DNA results say she wasn't raped. And I had no idea there were that many cases with the name 'Sam' in it. He might have used an alias."

"And the plot thickens," Nash groaned.

Redman sighed. "So it does."

Back at the house, Evelyn grabbed her purse, making sure her wallet was there.

"Okay, Naomi," she said. "I'll be back sometime after six. I'll call you if I'm running late." She knelt down and hugged Melanie and kissed her on the cheek. "You be a good girl while I'm gone, okay? Love you."

"Love you, too." Melanie nodded. "Bye, Mommy."

She looked up at Naomi. "Just in case you get locked out, there's a spare key underneath the doormat out here on the porch."

"Okay, thanks." Naomi nodded.

"Good luck!"

"Same to you."

With that, Evelyn left and entered her white sedan. Naomi watched as she pulled out of the driveway and sped off down the street. She looked down at Melanie, yet the child's eyes suddenly seemed so…oblivious, gazing up at her new caretaker with such a blank demeanor that invoked the sensation of the uncanny valley, briefly tempting Naomi to think Melanie *was* a plastic baby doll that ran on batteries.

"Are you my new mommy?" she asked.

"Oh, no, no, no, no, sweetie!" Naomi laughed, bending over with her hands on her thighs. "I'm just your nanny. Your mommy's gonna be back this evening, then I'll go home."

"Why can't you stay?"

"Because, baby, Nanny has to go back and sleep at her house." She tilted her head. "Have you eaten yet?"

Melanie shook her head. "Mommy makes me eat spicy stuff."

"Oh," Naomi said. "Burns your tongue?"

Melanie nodded.

"I'm sorry." Naomi reached into her bag and pulled out the M & M's. "I'm not supposed to do this, but...it being the first day...I'll share my candy with you. Okay? Just don't tell Mommy, or we'll both get in trouble."

"No! No more timeout!" Melanie screamed.

"Okay, okay, I know," Naomi assuaged, opening the bag and sitting on the couch. "Come here. Come sit with me."

Melanie obeyed and snuggled with her as Naomi poured a few pieces of chocolate on her small hand. Gleefully, she popped them in her mouth as Naomi ate a couple more.

"Mmm," Naomi hummed, hugging Melanie.

Melanie took a few more pieces.

"Maybe...later," Naomi said, "we'll go get some chicken nuggets. I'm kinda craving some myself. And Mommy doesn't have to know. Okay? It'll be our little secret." She extended her little finger. "Pinky promise?"

"What's a pinky promise?"

"Well...see," Naomi told her. "That's what best friends do when they say they're gonna do something, and so they can trust each other, they grab each other's pinky...and they make a promise. That way, they know they're telling the truth. Here, I'll show you. Poke out your pinky like I'm doing."

Melanie complied, then Naomi wrapped her finger around hers and shook.

"There," Naomi said.

Melanie smiled. "I like you."

"Oh, that's so sweet!" Naomi said. "I like you too, Melanie."

"Daddy used to give me candy sometimes."

"Your old daddy?"

Melanie glared at her. "My *real* daddy."

"Oh, okay. I'm sorry," Naomi apologized, debating about whether or not to admit to her she knew Chris.

"The policemen took my daddy away, and I don't know why," Melanie pouted. "Mommy puts me in timeout for it. I just want Daddy back." She looked up at Naomi. "Did I make my daddy go away? Does he hate me?"

"Oh, baby," Naomi said, on the verge of crying, holding her tightly with both arms as if she were her own child. "No. Your daddy doesn't hate you, okay? In fact…I truly believe that you will see your daddy again…very soon. But you have to be patient."

"Why can't I see him now?" Melanie whined.

"Because, baby," Naomi said, another tear rolling down her cheek. "Life isn't always fair, not even to us grown-ups." She looked up at the bedrooms upstairs. "Now…when Mommy puts you in timeout, does she—?"

"No, I don't want to go! It's too dark in there!"

"Dark where?"

"The closet."

Naomi's lips fell ajar. Her blood boiled, then she rubbed Melanie's back. "You listen to me. No one—and I mean no one—is going to put you in 'timeout' while I'm around. Do you hear me? Do you hear me?"

Melanie nodded.

"But I *do* want you to listen to me…and behave yourself," Naomi added. "I'm your nanny, but I'm also your friend, and I want you to trust me. Pinky promise?"

"Pinky promise!" Melanie squeaked.

They extended and shook their little fingers again.

"I'll tell you what let's do," Naomi suggested. "Why don't you go get some warm clothes on…and you and I will go get some chicken nuggets…and we'll go to the park. Okay? If there's still some snow left on the ground, maybe you and I can build a snowman. How's that sound?"

"Can we have a tea party with my dollies when we get back?"

"Of course, honey."

"Okay," Melanie said. "I'll show you my room."

"Okay."

The five-year-old girl led her by the hand up the stairs. Naomi's blood continued to fume inside her. To think that this is what the "legal system" had done. And that pretentious, abusive harlot that Chris called his "ex-wife." Who could ever fall for such a woman? She tried not to scowl, not wanting to unnerve Melanie. This had to change.

She had to fix this. She and Chris both.

Or something far worse was going to happen on top of it.

As if a serial killer running amok wasn't enough shit to deal with.

Night had fallen on the other side of the neighborhood as Naomi sat on the couch in her house, watching TV, trying to take her mind off all that had happened earlier that day. The blinds were closed and the curtains pulled to, lest "Andrew" try to peek through the windows. Outside, the winds besieged the walls, its disconcerting moaning undulating with each gust bending around the edifice. Her home was little more than just a glorified apartment, nowhere near as posh as Newton Malcolm's house, but it would have to do. On the cushion, she kept a pocket knife handy, should the Vulture come for her as well, though she would prefer a gun to defend herself. She ended up eating the chef salad and a sandwich for her dinner, having followed through with what she had promised Melanie: chicken nuggets for lunch, and they did manage to find a patch of icy powder at the park, having made a stocky snow-lady they named "Matilda." Evelyn had returned, exasperated and petulant about the interview. Just like a spoiled prima donna. Nothing seemed to be good enough for her. Naomi had sampled the chili in order to appease her new high-maintenance employer and claimed that Melanie had some as well. It *was* rather unappetizing...and over-seasoned. She rubbed her forehead, anticipating her return tomorrow, not knowing what they would do. Already, she had grown attached to Melanie, as if she were her own daughter...and it broke her heart, realizing what Evelyn was doing to her own flesh and blood.

Was there absolutely nothing that could be done?

There had to be something!

If only Naomi's parents could see how well she was with Melanie. Would they be willing to relinquish custody of Aeriel? Would Aeriel even know or care about her biological mother?

Her doorbell ranged, causing her heart to lunge up in her throat.

"Shit," Naomi cursed under her breath.

She turned and rose up, slipping the knife in her pocket as she warily approached the front door. She could still see Andrew's piercing gaze...and that eerie, infuriating smirk, a ghastly parody of charm. With a sigh, she peeked through the peephole in the door.

"Chris?"

"Yeah," he said.

She unlatched the door and opened it, revealing Chris's unkempt visage.

"What're you doing here?" Naomi asked. "It's cold, and it's after ten."

"I've been thinking about what you said," Chris told her. "And I'm gonna start getting my shit together again. I don't know how, but...I don't know. I've got a long drive ahead of me, so—"

"Wait, what are you talking about?" Naomi chirped. "Here, get up in here—it's cold as hell out there."

"Naomi...they evicted me today," Chris confessed.

"What?"

"I went into town today, trying to look for work and all that," Chris sighed, "then the bastards at the leasing office said they put my furniture out, told me to turn in my keys. Yet my furniture was gone—I don't know if somebody stole it, or the garbage man just hauled it off. It's gone, it's all gone. I came over here to say...goodbye."

She shook her head. "No, you're not...you're not leaving."

"Naomi—"

"Shh—get in here before somebody calls the cops!" she rasped, pulling him inside. "Neighbors get cranky about shit like that." She flicked her curly hair out of her face. "Where are...where you plannin' on going?"

"I don't know. Utah, maybe?" Chris groaned. "I hear there's a lot of public land out there. I'll camp or sleep in my truck while I'm trying to find work or some—"

"I'm not letting you turn into some vagrant!"

"Look—"

"No, *you* look! What about AA?"

"Fuck AA! I'll find another group out there somewhere…if it's that damned important."

Naomi shook her head again, crossing her arms. "So…you just gonna leave? Just like that?"

"What am I supposed to do?" Chris snapped. "I'm homeless!"

"You can stay with me for a few days," Naomi offered, stroking a lock of hair behind one of her ears. "Or a few weeks, just long enough for you to get back on your—"

"No, I'm not gonna impose on you like that—I don't do that! I don't like being beholden to—"

"If I thought you were gonna do that, I wouldn't have offered!"

"It would get…weird."

She did her best not to let her lips quiver. "A little late for that…isn't it, Chris?"

"Naomi…."

Both of them averted their eyes, an awkward silence barring them from each other as goosebumps roiled their skin in prickling waves. Somewhere, a dog barked in the distance as another brisk wind assailed the corners of the house again, soughing through the nearby trees, howling in a wraithlike voice.

"I can't," Chris said. "I'm sorry, but I just can't. I refuse to burden you, especially like that."

He turned back to the door, twisting the knob.

"Evelyn's hurting Melanie," Naomi blurted.

He stopped, then turned back to her.

"How do you know?"

Naomi sighed. "I'm…her nanny now."

"Oh, shit, Naomi!"

"I didn't want to tell you—I didn't want to upset you!" Naomi stammered. "I caught her."

"A nann—wait, wha—how the fu—you…you didn't call the police?"

"What the hell are those pigs gonna do, other than treat me the same shitty way they did you?"

"What's she doing to her *now*?" Chris's voice grated. "Tell me!"

Naomi raised an eyebrow. "What do you mean 'now?'"

Chris stepped back to her. "A few weeks before I was arrested, I caught her one evening having locked Melanie in the closet. Evelyn called it 'timeout,' because she claimed she didn't want to spank her." He scoffed. "Like imprisoning her in there is any healthier. I chewed her ass out so bad that I drove her to tears in nothing flat, threatening to call social services and press charges if she ever did it again." He slammed his hand on the wall. "And I should have then and there—but, no! I had to be the 'merciful nice guy.' And it cost me everything." He glared at the hardwood floor. "Not too long after that…she filed for that life insurance thing. I got paranoid, because I suspected she was gonna take me out for the money. We got into another argument, then that night, she afflicted herself somewhere outside, then called her daddy, a retired FBI agent. He told her to press charges for assault and attempted murder with the bureau in Denver." He huffed. "I don't have to tell you what happened from there."

"So, why did you come here to La Sombra where she was?" Naomi asked.

"I didn't!" Chris barked. "She and her stupid evil Mr. Rogers clone of a boyfriend evidently found out I was over here, trying to get out of Denver and away from her, then they moved here…I guess to taunt me, trying to make it seem like *I'm* the one violating that bullshit restraining order they slapped on me." He slammed the wall again. "If I had gotten camera footage of what Evelyn was doing…it would've made all the difference in the world."

"Wait!" Naomi said. "That's it!"

"What?"

"Nanny cams," Naomi told him. "I'll get a few nanny cams. They disguise 'em like…teddy bears, you know? I'll put some in the house, put 'em where nobody'll notice, one where the closet is. We'll catch her in the act, Chris."

"Do what?"

"You can get your life back! Get Melanie back!"

"You honestly think it's that simple?" Chris clenched his teeth. "The court doesn't care! I can't get an appeal for that."

"Your constitutional rights were violated, Chris Sullivan," Naomi said sternly. "And even more so, Melanie's rights were as well. She's also a U. S. citizen. She never got to testify. She was on the witness list, and Bianca Sterling violated her freedom of speech by taking her out of the equation."

Chris exhaled a heated breath through his nostrils. "Bianca kept shootin' down each argument we had, objecting to Evelyn's motivations and the abuse she was doing to Melanie, claiming it was 'irrelevant' to the case, and Pfeiffer just let her." He sighed louder. "And of course, Evelyn lied through her damned teeth."

"That's perjury," Naomi said. "And Pfeiffer's dead."

"Tell that to the court."

"And they discriminated you for race. So did the media. That's illegal! It's a violation of the Civil Rights Movement! You and I both know that!"

"So, what about *you*, Naomi?" Chris protested. "What about Aeriel? Why aren't you trying to get her back?"

"Who says I'm not?" Naomi fired back. "Ever heard of Dave Rodriguez?"

"Rings a bell. Advertises on the local channels." Chris shook his head. "Never really knew what to make of the guy."

"Neither did I until I gave him a call a few days ago," Naomi said as she made her way to the cramped kitchen.

Chris followed her to the refrigerator door, then she removed the magnet with Dave Rodriguez's somber figure and his phone number and slogan in all caps in gilded letters.

"'You have the right to fight back,'" Chris mocked the magnet's slogan dryly. "Boy, we sure do got this shit figured out, don't we?"

"Chris," Naomi sighed.

"You honestly think this clown's gonna help?"

"Promise me you'll call him," Naomi persisted.

Chris scoffed.

"Promise me!"

"Yeah, alright. I promise." Chris shook his head. "If it'll make you happy."

"Don't do it for *me*," Naomi scolded. "You know who to do it for."

Chris exhaled a heated breath through his nostrils.

"And she needs you," Naomi told him.

Chris nodded at her.

"Keep that. Don't lose it," she said. "I already got Dave's number on my phone. I think I got it written down somewhere, too."

"So...what does he specialize in? Car accidents?"

Naomi looked at him with her earnest green eyes. "He represents...us."

"Us?"

"He's primarily an immigration lawyer, but he does so much more too." Naomi sighed. "He fights for people who are marginalized. In fact...he actually has had a few cases similar to ours...and he won."

"What about the cases he lost?" Chris asked.

"Why do you have to be so negative?" Naomi groaned. "If you won't do it for you or me...at least do it for Melanie. I can't bear for Evelyn to do what she's doing to that poor child."

Chris only looked at her.

"Does that mean nothing to you?"

"Fine. I guess I'll give him a call...if he answers," Chris pocketed the magnet. "Lawyers tend to be shitty about phone calls and emails."

"No, he's different," Naomi said, stroking her hair again. "I got a good feeling about him...and I can be quite cynical myself."

"You want to audition for one of his commercials?" Chris said with a sarcastic twinkle in his eye. "I think you'd be perfect for the role."

"Well...I *am* a non-attorney spokesperson."

Chris managed to snicker. Naomi grinned.

Then both of them immediately sobered up.

"I still don't know about this, Naomi."

"You have to trust me," she said. "I trust you."

"Yeah?" he said, leaning in.

"Yeah."

He drew closer. "Prove it."

Their lips met as they closed their eyes, their tongues exploring each other's mouths. The weight of the world and the chill of winter burned away as they embraced, his hands on her hips, with her wrists locked behind his neck. They released each other, then wandered to the bedroom. She undid his belt, unzipping his pants and almost clawing his jacket and shirt off, showing his gaunt torso, seeing the outline of his ribs and scars in the dim light. Their breathing quickened. He tasted her lips again as he slipped her pajama bottoms and her lacy black panties down. He pulled her shirt off, revealing her petite, perky bosoms, nestled in a black bra, then he unhooked it, flinging it away. She lay down on the bed, her lips open, waiting for him, their mouths meeting again as he crawled on top of her, kissing her neck. Then he entered her womanhood. She gasped, arching her back, as he caressed her breasts. He could feel her hips gyrate under him as he thrust himself in fluid motions. Both of them melted away, indulging the flesh, feeling so alive, as they tossed and turned in their wild love-making. Naomi lost herself, intoxicated by him, and he by her. She knew this was a bad idea. She knew this would ruin them both. They had crossed the forbidden threshold.

Yet, she couldn't stop.

And neither could he.

There was no going back now.

But right then, they could care less...about anything.

Not even considering that the house was being watched...by a man sitting in a forest-green SUV down the street, veiled in the shadows of the glacial night. He peered at the closed windows with blue eyes...his smirk widening.

Rolling a gravelly, hyena-like laughter in his throat.

IX: Retaliation

Chris Sullivan pulled up into the dark driveway of the small one-story home of the church pastor, Hugh Altaha, wearily surveying the streets lined with spruce and cottonwood trees now thickly blanketed with night. Dusk's last light shone with ethereal blue light beyond the distant alpine peaks, the looming jaws of La Sombra. Parts of the cracked pavement were bathed in fluorescent streetlights and the glow of a nearby traffic signal, shifting from green…to yellow…to red. The brisk mountain wind waylaid into the side of his pickup, causing the vehicle to rock and creak on its wheels, blowing yellow leaves from an adjacent aspen tree across the cramped lawn of short, desiccated grass. Reluctantly, he cut the engine off and removed the key from the ignition, then breathed out a long sigh.

He didn't want to do this. He just wanted to disappear into the wilderness, escape society's cruel, ignorant grasp, and just live off the grid with Naomi, just leave civilization to rot away in its own stupidity. But he couldn't. Not yet. He had to make sure his little Melanie was safe. But regaining any custody of her would be beyond arduous, if not outright impossible.

Naomi had followed through with purchasing a few nanny cams, planting them around Evelyn's house, especially in Melanie's room, facing the closet, making sure they were inconspicuous enough to avoid detection. It had been days since he and Naomi had first made love, and he was still putting in applications at various ragtag establishments in town, much to his infinite chagrin, ranging from fast food restaurants to grocery stores and everything in between. He wasn't expecting them to reply back; he was only doing it to placate Naomi, being an unofficial roommate without her landlady knowing. He had made a new tally sheet to track his days of sobriety on Naomi's fridge, yet he hated losing Melanie's crayon drawing to those thugs who took his furniture

But there was nothing he could do about it.

Days earlier, he and Naomi both had called and met with Dave Rodriguez during his lunch break. The Hispanic attorney's refined personality was composed of dry wit and an impressive knowledge of the law, yet he had just enough empathy to deal justly with his clients. Rodriguez was no stranger to the filthy corruption of the criminal justice system, for he was once an immigrant persecuted and wrongly accused of being an illegal alien, prompting him to go to law school and pursue his career. He was no fan of Bianca Sterling, as the two had constantly butted heads in and outside of court with multiple cases throughout the years. He was her legal nemesis, and she his. A level-headed crusader for the marginalized and politically disadvantaged, Rodriguez was the only lawyer in the area who instilled genuine fear in the prosecutor's cold-blooded heart.

Yet, just as Chris had grudgingly suspected, Rodriguez could not simply wave some magic wand and procure his five-year-old daughter for him. An appeal was a tall order…and there was a lot of heavy-lifting to do even before court. But it was possible.

So he claimed.

Nevertheless, it would be one hell of a delicate situation, with absolutely no room for even the slightest screw-ups or any faux pas. While Naomi told him that she had witnessed Melanie being abused by her mother, this perked Dave's curiosity, not to mention how Chris's constitutional rights had, in fact, been violated, along with Melanie's freedom of speech. Even so…it was dicey, and the nanny cams could very well be disregarded as inadmissible evidence and even misconstrued as invasion of privacy. It would also be a direct violation of the tyrannical restraining order placed upon Chris, warranting a scathing lawsuit from both Evelyn and Newton, even *if* Evelyn had moved to La Sombra knowing that Chris had.

But all three agreed that something had to be done, for Melanie's sake.

Before it was too late.

And according to Rodriguez, the key to the case's success was for Chris to keep cool.

No matter what.

A list of relevant witnesses of Chris's character would have to be compiled, and according to Chris, Hugh Altaha was at the top. Rodriguez had called Hugh and informed him of the situation yet insisted he speak with Chris face-to-face first, sounding disgruntled over the phone. Chris made an appointment that evening to converse with the pastor, thinking that Hugh was simply annoyed by Chris's absence in his dwindling congregation. He had no reason to doubt the preacher's cooperation. After all, Reverend Altaha had seen on numerous occasions Chris's loving attentiveness to Melanie in the church's nursery, rarely ever seeing Evelyn's conduct come even close. Some had blamed it on the "baby blues," and while Chris did not condemn Evelyn for having post-partem depression from childbirth, it was still no reason to take it out on Melanie; it wasn't her fault she was born. Why should she have to suffer from her mother's chemical imbalance? More importantly, Evelyn had a mean streak even *before* she and Chris married. But Chris had ignored it, trying to be "open-minded," trying to give her the benefit of a doubt.

And every time he gave someone the benefit of a doubt, it always came back to bite him right in the ass. In fact, so many things in his life had come back to sink their fangs into his backside, it was a miracle he could sit down. He had been out of ass cheeks for a good, long time. But he was the "nice guy," the lowly, burned-out empath, always trying to care about people.

Caring way too much.

And they didn't care whether he lived or died.

Like a frenzy of mindless sharks, all they did was take, take, and take.

And they never gave anything back in return.

He glared through his grungy truck's windshield, studying the curving fractures snaking across the glass from stray rocks callously slung at him daily on the road. Such was the nature of spoiled, ungrateful, sedentary America, always throwing their relentless salvos of shit at him for their own cowardly, sociopathic amusement, always from a good, safe distance. The rest of the world was no better. The whole world would eventually crumble, and the end wouldn't come soon enough. There was no saving it, not one miserable piece of it.

He glanced at his reflection in the rear-view mirror, seeing his tired brown eyes.

The nice guy was dead and gone.

Time to fight back. Time for liberation. Time to cash in all those good deeds.

Up ahead at the intersection, the traffic light flashed from red…to green.

He opened the truck door and exited, locking it and slamming it shut, embracing autumn's fierce, icy kiss lashing across his face…then he trudged to the front porch.

"I may not be a saint," he muttered, "but I'm not the worst person in the world."

As he approached the door, a security light flickered on, then the front door clacked, unlocking. The doorknob turned. Chris stopped as the door opened, revealing Hugh's visage, clad in blue jeans, hiking boots, and a blue button-up shirt with a leather vest over his torso. His long, straight black hair blew around his middle-aged clean-shaven face in the wind with a turquoise pendant hanging around his neck.

"Get in here," Hugh almost growled, waving him in.

He strode down the narrow hall with Chris shutting the door and following him. A few lights were on in the house, producing a lethargic glow, with an old corduroy couch in the living room draped with a shawl and rustic chairs crafted with planks and logs of pine. A gas heater with a brass lattice burned where a fireplace hearth once lay, its azure flames lapping the artificial wood within like fingers of ghostly hellfire. They ventured into his cramped morose office where a few trinkets of his indigenous culture adorned the walls. A dreamcatcher with a Christian cross woven into its strands dangled near the left of the window of closed blinds behind his rolling office chair; a crucifix of wood and bronze was positioned on the window's right. Church mail and papers lay haphazardly stacked on his desk illumined by a vintage green lamp, with only a square of clean space cleared off to examine an opened pamphlet for a charity helping the Apache reservation. On another table near the wall perpendicular to the desk, a laptop lay open, with a sermon partially finished showing on the screen. Above that, Hugh's diploma from seminary hung framed, along with two other college degrees.

"Sorry about the mess," Hugh groaned, sinking back into his chair. "Have a seat."

Chris sat in a dining room chair in front of the desk, his eyes darting around the masses of paperwork and envelopes.

"Attorney Rodriguez tells me you seek to remedy the custody stipulations concerning Melanie," Hugh asked. "Is that right?"

"Why don't we spare each other the bullshit theatrics and just tell me why you don't wanna help my little girl?" Chris snapped.

"Help *her*?" Hugh said firmly, then he pointed at him. "Or *you*?"

Chris sighed again. "The one time I ask the church to do something, and you—"

"What do you care about the church?"

Chris clenched his teeth. "What do *you* care, Hugh?"

"Probably way too much!" Hugh slammed his fist on the desk, causing some of the papers to cascade to the carpeted floor. "Our congregation is diminishing. We have several people on our prayer list dying from cancer with others struggling to help family members with addiction and those who've lost their jobs. We even had a pack of skinheads, those Trump fetishists, spray-painting swastikas on the outside of the church recently. Change, yes we can? Make America great again? Hah! The American government is just as shitty as it was when everybody and their mother first came over here and took everything, if not far worse! Don't even get me started on how many people living in poverty, even small children, are starving in the reservations right now! And to top it all off, we have a serial killer, this terrorist, on the loose picking people off one by one!" He scowled, showing the wrinkles of his coppery face in the dim light. "What do *I* care? How dare you! I don't like being manipulated for personal gain any more than you do! I may be the pastor of this church, but I'm a flawed human being just like you! I'm not perfect. Neither are you. If I didn't care, you wouldn't be in this house right now, so show some gratitude."

"Yeah, the 'care' part, I get," Chris said. "What I meant was…*why* do you care?"

Hugh shook his head. "Sometimes…I don't even know. I force myself to believe that everything is working for a plan for good."

Chris erupted from his seat. "A plan for good? All the problems you just listed going on, and you think it's good?"

"God is testing you and me and a lot of other people right now," Hugh sighed. "Count it pure joy when you face trials of many—"

"Fuck the test! Chris shouted. "I didn't come for a fucking sermon! How dare you try to push Bible verses on me, especially after the hell on earth I've been through! You can take all that 'count it pure joy' rhetoric and the rest of your Bible-thumping bullshit and shove it right up your ass! A test? A test, he says. Why? So I can be a 'better person?' I must be talking to Charles Dickens over here—hey, are three ghosts gonna visit me like Ebenezer Scrooge or something?"

"Sit down!"

"Fuck you!" Chris flashed his teeth. "That's all the church is, just a bunch of superficial shitheads like my Jezebel ex-wife, just there to make an appearance, then they get their whitewashed sermon and leave, thinking they can go back to being little fuckfaces for the rest of the week, and rinse and repeat! Then I get put on the backburner all because somebody's suffering more than I am, so I get ignored and forgotten about! I guess I'm not a priority to an omnipotent God. But heaven forbid He actually fix any of this shit!" He aimed a finger at the reverend. "All this stupid 'test' is doing is making me hate God—if He even exists—which I highly doubt it now! I'm a living, fucking person, a human being just like you! We're not metal to be thrown in the fire! We think! We feel! We die! All this 'test' is doing is making me hate people! It's making me hate you!"

"Sit! Down!"

"What for?" Chris fulminated further. "All it's doing is making me grow colder and sicker inside! I already knew that I'm a worthless piece of shit who deserves to die—I don't need a fucking test to indicate the fucked-up reality! I don't need to suffer and bleed while the damned, bigoted atheists get fat and happy off of our misery! Maybe *He* should beg for *my* forgiveness! A plan for good? Are you fucking kidding me?" He knocked the papers off the desk and onto the floor. "How about that, preacher man? Is *that* a 'plan for good?' Is that 'working out' now? What if I break all *your* shit, take it all away and ruin *your* life—is that evidence that there is a God, Who actually knows what he's fucking—?"

"That *right* there is why you won't get Melanie back!" Hugh blared. "Sit your ass back down!"

Chris plopped back down in the chair and huffed.

"If people saw how you were acting right now, you'd be completely done for!" Hugh hissed. "You honestly think…if I go up there in that courtroom and tell everyone how you pampered your daughter every Sunday morning that they'll just be like, 'Oh, what a loving father he is! Let's give him his little girl back,' and then you'll live happily ever after?"

"Don't you remember me coming to you that day and telling you what Evelyn was doing to Melanie?" Chris pleaded. "Locking her in the closet? That's child abuse!"

"Do you have evidence, Chris?"

"Not yet."

"Then why the hell do you need me?" Hugh rubbed the bridge of his nose. "Why didn't you call the police?"

"I *did* report it," Chris snapped. "The pigs did nothing. Pretty much told me the same thing you just did: they need evidence; otherwise, there's nothing they can do." He crossed his arms. "And Bianca just kept shooting that argument down in court years ago, saying it was 'irrelevant.' My little girl is not irrelevant!"

"Well, that's the government for you," Hugh said. "It's shit. I, of all people, should know."

"They've always been like that," Chris grumbled. "Especially in Mississippi and Florida. Back when I lived in Orlando, some crazy white-trash douchebag smashed my car window and broke my taillights with a screwdriver or icepick—on Mother's Day, of all things! Called the cops. They did nothing, didn't even conduct an investigation, saying they 'didn't have time for me.' Meanwhile, that guy was taunting me all day long at the apartment complex, driving around. And in Mississippi, I grew up living next to some inbred dipshit Neo-Nazi and his schizophrenic family who always bragged about running some dog-fighting ring, and I don't know what other bad shit he was in to. He'd have 'em in kennels, barking day and night. They'd get loose and shit in the yard, tear stuff up, chase us around—vicious bastards. I fucking hate dogs now because of it! I called the cops three times. They did absolutely nothing. Said they needed evidence. I went over there to try and talk to him. Then thirty minutes later, *I* was arrested for 'trespassing.' Damned cops sexually harassed me at the jail and everything. One day, I finally *did* film him trying to get one of his dogs out of my yard. *He* was the one trespassing! After we told him, he agreed to dropped the trespassing charge, but did those hicks at the sheriff's department arrest him for anything? Hell, no! Then he threatens me with his deer rifle, claiming I better 'watch my back.' Called the cops again about that, and all they did was pull the Second Amendment on me. I don't have a problem with guns, but I *do* have a problem with idiots. Damned lawyers and cops are licking each other's assholes over there, in bed with each other. They think they're a bunch of damned cowboys. I would not be surprised if they were in league with his crooked dog-fighting operation, and no telling what else. Couldn't sue or anything, because everybody knows everybody over there—it creeps me the fuck out! Whole damned state must be rife with incest and corruption—and people thought *I* was like that simply because I lived over there, stereotyping me and all. Not everybody is like that in the South, but the stereotype exists. I'm not one of them, though. It's those racist hicks, those brainless Trump fuckers, who give the South a bad name, and the individuals like me who actually try to give a damn about what is right, we're the ones who suffer for it."

A brief silence lingered in the air between them as Chris huffed in and out, catching his breath.

"You want proof," Chris griped, "I'll get you proof."

Hugh sighed. "I still don't know if that's going to help you regain custody of Melanie, Chris."

"Look, if I'm *that* unworthy to be a father, let responsible foster parents adopt her—something, man—God, please help me already! I don't want my little girl to die! I don't want her to suffer!"

Hugh only looked at him.

"If you won't do it for me," Chris almost whimpered, "do it for Melanie."

He hung his head, his face contorting in grief.

The pastor only stared unblinkingly at him.

"That's very big of you," Hugh finally commended. "I know you love her." He sighed. "But I need the ocular proof, Chris. So does the jury. Do you understand?"

"I wish I had cameras all up in my house that night," Chris said, massaging his forehead. "None of this would've happened. It would've been Evelyn, not me, who went to jail."

"Get me the proof," Hugh said, "and we'll see what can be done. I can't promise you anything, though." He rose up from his seat and stared up at the crucifix. "You asked me why I care?"

Chris peered up at him.

"So many people think us naïve for being Christian," Hugh went on, "even people in my own tribe. I had a falling-out with my family, so I left the reservation and came up here to La Sombra." He sighed. "I don't normally share this with people, but…I've encountered things you would not believe."

"Like what?" Chris rolled his eyes. "Miracles?"

"Like death."

Chris scrunched his forehead.

"You see…I was baptized when I was in elementary school," Hugh continued. "I don't know. My parents saw it as a formality. We were pretty much agnostic; we didn't know what to think about the supernatural, if it existed or not." He picked up a copy of the Bible. "And this can seem very farfetched when you read it." He set it back down on the desk and turned back to Chris. "People coming back from the dead? Talking donkeys? A voice coming out of a burning bush? Pulling fish and bread from out of thin air? Rivers turning to blood? Angels? Demons? People suddenly becoming multilingual all because some mysterious flames appeared over their heads? It sounds like a fairytale, doesn't it, invented by a bunch of eccentric blue-collar fishermen thousands of years ago? Is Christianity not an ass-backwards religion?"

Chris's eyes widened.

"I don't know about you, but such a religion would not have even made it past the first century A. D. if it were manmade, especially when it has to compete with pagan beliefs and worldly philosophies that are more appealing to the flesh. Are we not allowed to scrutinize and question the faith? I'll tell you this much: I would never have attempted to invent such a wild, grueling religion that says that people are worthless and undeserving, a religion that relentlessly demands one brutal sacrifice after another every day, enduring hardship, grief, persecution, and death in martyrdom, walking in a faith that is virtually blind. There is no understanding it with our three-dimensional minds." He sighed again. "There must be something else at work in order for it to have prevailed this far in time. Yes, it should have died a long time ago…if it were manmade, but that's not to say that something seemingly nonsensical can survive merely based on that principle. That's not even scratching the surface. Like I said…there has to be this Almighty God empowering the Judeo-Christian faith. Otherwise, it would not stand. At all." He glared at the Bible on his desk. "If only the damned secularists were strong enough to genuinely question *their* beliefs for a change instead of constantly discriminating and attacking us in their fevered Christophobia and anti-Semitism."

Chris cocked his head. He had never heard his pastor speak like this before.

Hugh shook his head. "Growing up, we never went to church, not as a family, at least. A few friends would invite me here and there around Christmas and Easter, but not often. My family clung to the old ways, not that they believed in it or anything, but…sometimes I wondered. I wanted to believe…that there was a reason for everything, that it wasn't all just random chaos. Then one night, I got in a bad car accident. Everything went black at first…then I felt part of myself levitate upward into the sky, and I saw a white light flowing far above me. I drew closer and closer to it. Then immediately, I found myself gasping for breath in the back of an ambulance, having been resuscitated."

"Why didn't you tell me this before?"

"Because it's not something you just tell anyone, okay?" Hugh barked. "It *still* weirds me out! And the few times I *have* told someone, people either think I'm a lunatic or they're more likely to gravitate towards occultism for their morbid amusement. A few people even committed suicide. So I keep it to myself, mostly. Whether it was a near-death experience or some divine intervention, I don't really know. It was spiritual and profound, I know that. But then you have people who claim something called 'false memory syndrome,' claiming that we hallucinate when the brain loses oxygen when we're incapacitated. I guess they coined that phrase as just another way to show displeasure for us telling them what they don't want to hear. I could just as easily argue that their childhood memories are a product of false memory syndrome. If we can't trust our own five senses, what can we trust? I mean…if the brain loses oxygen, then the brain dies and the body with it, so it stands to reason to believe that it *was* a temporary clinical death…followed by resurrection. I've passed out before; this was different. Far different." He looked back at the crucifix. "That's when I officially converted. I do my best to preach from the Word, not from my strange experiences. But these experiences, these revelations, were for the benefit of my faith, granting me more understanding of the truth. Had it not been for that, I would've left the faith a long time ago. I appreciate cold, hard evidence just as much as the next person. I don't shun science. I'm not naïve. I can see for myself what's going on in the world. If people want to find out the hard way, that's their problem—and they will, one way or another."

"What if we're wrong?" Chris groaned. "What if you *did* just pass out? What if it does just go black in the end?"

"Well, you know what? I've thought about that, too," Hugh countered. "That 'Bible-thumping' you seem so fond of talks about having 'eyes that see' and 'ears that hear.' If one encounters only eternal blackness when they die, wouldn't that be them sinking into the darkest part of hell?"

Chris furrowed his brows.

"And if the eyes and ears of the soul cannot see and hear," Hugh went on, "then they are blind and deaf in the afterlife, so it should be no surprise that nonbelievers claim it only goes black in the end." He lifted a finger at Chris. "But their souls will not be numb, and they will not be annihilated, only imprisoned in eternal torment."

"What would other religions have to say about that, then?"

Hugh squinted at him. "When the day comes when *you* die…you will see who was lying…and who was telling the truth. I have already tasted death. One day, this body shall taste it again." He squinted at Chris. "And another thing, don't you dare go killing yourself, Chris Sullivan! You can't cheat your way into heaven. Otherwise…we'd all have done it by now."

"Alright," Chris muttered. "If that's the case, why does God allow all this shit?"

Hugh sat back down in his chair. "We're soldiers, you and I, and we've enlisted into the good fight. You don't become a Christian for comfort, just like people don't enlist in the military to get free ice cream or wallow in a bed of roses. If people want cheap comfort, the brothel's right down the road. As for us, our Drill Sergeant kicks our ass in boot camp, training us, conditioning us for war, then we're deployed to combat the enemy. All this hardship, all this misery…it's a training exercise, whether we like it or not. It's meant to toughen us up for what lies ahead. It changes us. Makes us stronger, wiser. More alive. And He wants to fight the enemy *through* us. This is how He wants to accomplish that: fellowship with Him. So many people want to blame God for all the shit that's going on, never taking any responsibility for the evil *they* do. People always want to compare themselves to Job when they go through crap in their lives. Yet when they compare themselves to him, it's most likely an indictment of their own self-righteousness, and God is in the process of extracting that poison out of them, and it hurts like hell when He does. Just like now, you were yelling and screaming, puking out the misery. All God is doing right now is, in a manner of speaking, 'pumping your stomach' of poison, purging you soul of the toxins plaguing you. He knew it was there long before you did, and it had to come out. He is the Great Physician already working inside you and others. It's all part of the healing process; you can't get better until you start letting it out. You can't just bottle up your emotions every single day. You've got to talk to somebody, learn to let people back into your life."

Chris averted his gaze, feeling bristling shame wash over him.

And the sickness curdling within him.

"I'm no better than you are or anybody else," Hugh continued. "I've done plenty of 'spiritual puking' myself, and I still do. We're not supposed to judge, but we do it. It's not good, but it happens. I struggle trying not to blame God for what's happening in the world, even though He allows it. I blame the government. I blame society. I blame the Vulture. I blame people screwing everything up. And God allows it to show just how wrong society is to try and live without Him. If civilization could get it right on its own, it would've done so by now. But all civilization does is keep messing itself up more and more, slowing destroying itself. I know that's not what you want to hear, and a lot of times, I hate the way God does things too, but them's the breaks. There's nothing we can do about it but grit our teeth and hold on for dear life." He frowned. "But you didn't come for a sermon this evening."

"Why don't you preach like *this* on Sunday, instead of all the contrived, rehearsed, mechanical crap you usually do, reading in unison out of the bulletin and what not?" Chris flashed a wry grin. "You...you sound like a mystic right now, like you're truly...imbued with something. Maybe I'm going completely crazy, I don't know. Like...is that Hugh Altaha talking...or...?"

Hugh shrugged. "Guess seminary took the piss out of me."

Chris snorted.

Hugh looked down at Chris's right wrist. "I never noticed *that* before."

"What?"

"Your tattoo," he said, pointing at his wrist and rolling up his shirt sleeve. "It's just like mine."

Chris rolled up his jacket sleeve, fully revealing an ink pattern drawn to resemble a beaded bracelet. Hugh put his hand on the desk; the tattoos were identical. Goosebumps formed on Chris's skin.

"I got that when I was...drunk one night," Chris claimed. "I was joyriding with some friends one night and we stopped at a tattoo parlor...and they did this." He rolled up his left sleeve, revealing a barbed tribal mark running along his radius and ulna bones. "And this...I don't know. I just...thought it was cool."

"Cedar berries."

"Huh?"

"The one on your right wrist," Hugh indicated. "It's a good luck charm."

Chris snorted again. "Is it, now?"

"People sell the actual bracelets on the side of the road in Arizona and Utah, out in the middle of nowhere. I'll go by sometimes and buy something, help them out. I got mine at a parlor in the reservation years ago."

"Like I said," Chris told him, lowering his coat sleeves. "I got 'em both when I was drunk."

Hugh shrugged again. "Could've been a lot worse."

"Yeah."

The preacher managed a pained smirk. "You sure about...Melanie going into foster care?"

"Hell, no," Chris admitted. "But something has to be done, whether I'm in her life or not." He got up and walked to the office door. "Sorry about the mess."

Hugh rose up and escorted Chris down the hall to the front door. "Just be careful about *how* you obtain the evidence. You can get into a lot of—"

"If I get sued or jailed for it, so be it," Chris said, grabbing the doorknob. "If that's what it takes to expose Evelyn Whitaker...so be it. I'm willing to make that sacrifice."

"What is love without sacrifice?"

Chris stopped, then looked back at Hugh.

Hugh sighed again. "I'll give Dave Rodriguez a call in the morning. Get home safe. I think it's supposed to snow again tonight."

Chris said nothing and opened the door, walking to the truck.

"I'll say a prayer for you and your family," Hugh told him.

"Yeah," Chris replied, unlocking his truck.

With that, Hugh entered his house and closed the door as Chris cranked the sputtering engine of the pickup, then he watched him through the blinds as Chris drove off through the streets toward the intersection, out of sight.

"I wish I *didn't* have to care so damned much," the pastor muttered.

Smash!

Hugh jerked as glass shattered from the living room. He darted to see the shards lying on the hardwood flooring and the blinds bent and disheveled, swaying in the wind outside. On the couch, a brick lay there, with a note tied to it by a string. He dashed back and peeked out the previous window to see where Chris had driven off.

It couldn't have been him. He couldn't have doubled back *that* quick.

Hugh's heart drummed in his chest. He bared his teeth as he cautiously picked up the brick, taking the note. Letters had been cut out from magazines and crudely pasted to the paper, spelling out a single threat:

STAY OUT OF THIS!

X: Living Paradox

Bianca slowly pulled into the dark of her driveway. The headlights of her car seemed dimmer than usual, as if the shadows of dusk's last light were alive and resisting their synthetic beams. She put the sedan in park, unbuckled her seatbelt, and killed the engine and the lights. Her eyes ventured up to her front porch to the right of the driveway. Yellow crime scene tape fluttered in the howling wind, along with the ominous rattling of tree limbs above. She turned right and squinted westward, at the incoming squall line of shredded clouds skirting across the distant mountain summits and descending down their black slopes like an avalanche of ghosts.

Another storm approached.

Far colder than the last.

In the dark of her car, she leaned over and cautiously opened the glove compartment and removed the silver Beretta, gleaming in the sickly dim luminance of nearby streetlights. She ejected the clip already inside the handle and examined the bullets quizzically. Fully loaded. She slid the magazine back into the gun and chambered a bullet with a smooth, metallic click, then placed the pistol into her purse. Quietly, she closed her glove compartment, then her eyes ventured back up to the front porch of her modern cube-like suburban home and at the black of her windows.

She scoffed. Only now on this night could she notice how much her "chic" volumetric house resembled nothing more than a blocky deformed skull, hollow and dead inside. Goosebumps roiled across her flesh. The proud warrior fire that once blazed within her soul had been reduced to crumbling dying coals, crackling with a new appetite, borne of the abject consequences wrought by her routine lecherous escapades.

Time to be rekindled.

Bianca opened her car door, once again bombarded by the icy wind of the encroaching cold front. The gale seemed to shriek around the sides of houses, perturbing the leftover Halloween decorations swinging madly in the breeze, casting more shadows. She glared at the ragged plastic wraiths and skeletons swaying around from the eaves of nearby homes. One neighbor had gotten way too into the season, an attempt at a "zombie apocalypse" right in their front yard, a flamboyant eyesore, complete with artificial ghoul hands reaching up from the ground near fake tombstones. Some of the headstones had already blown down from the harsh wind. Red handprints of mock blood stained the neighbor's front door, painted with more imitation gore reeking of the stench of latex and marijuana.

Imbeciles. They seemed determined to leave all that crass shit up past Christmas and onward, whether out of cannabis-induced lethargy or the fact that they simply didn't give a damn either way about marring the image of her domain. But that was a far cry compared to what Sam Conroy had done.

Bianca huffed. They didn't know what living a *real* nightmare was.

She shut the door as the wind blew her long straight jet-black everywhere, then she made her way up the steps to her front door, with one hand in her purse fingering her Beretta. With her other, she unlocked the door and crept into the darkness of her house and flipped on the light. Her eyes shifted to the left, then to the right, then she stepped over the threshold and shut the door.

This place felt so foreign to her now.

Slowly, she made her way past her living room to the adjacent kitchen, passing her black leather couch and abstract paintings hanging on the beige walls. She sighed and sat her purse on the counter, then opened the stainless-steel wine cooler. With a jerk, she took out an unopened bottle of aged wine and uncorked the vessel. She guzzled a third of the booze before finally removing the bottle from her lips with an exasperated breath, then wiped a trickling drop from the corner of her mouth. She no longer cared. She was a fucking mess, as was everything else. All those years of being the arrogant, prissy female lawyer, feigning strength, pretending to be prim and proper, struggling to keep up some showy poised appearance everywhere she went, in all that she did.

Right down the shitter.

To top it all off, the rape kit had come up negative. Either Sam hadn't raped her, or he was that damned good at covering his tracks. Nonetheless, she was violated, with her piece of mind shattered. Now, she knew fully the extent of Mina Rosenthal's angst, her soul crippled with perpetual paranoia and shame deep inside.

And for what?

Just what the hell was success? What was she doing with her miserable short life? What was she *supposed* to do with it? What was anyone supposed to do? A tear rolled down Bianca's smooth cheek. Everyone was flung into the world just to be prepared to die, driven by an instinct to survive for nothing, one vain endeavor after another to try and escape the inevitability of death.

And death always got its way. Every single time.

Fuck the future.

Something creaked upstairs. Bianca's brown eyes widened and looked.

She heard it again.

Footsteps.

In her bedroom.

In one fluid motion, she snatched the Beretta from her purse and aimed it up the steps with both hands. Her heart pummeled the inside of her sternum as she crept to the staircase. Slowly, she advanced to the second floor, then flipped on another light. She peeked through the doorway of her bedroom and stopped. The lamp on the nightstand was on, where it had been dark earlier.

She glared harder, doing her best to stymie her nervous breath—then she burst into the bedroom, pointing the gun everywhere, then checked behind the door. Nothing. She moved to the bathroom and flipped on another light. No one was there. Not in the shower, not in the closets.

Nowhere.

She stepped back into the bedroom and turned…then froze. On her desk, her laptop sat there, open with files from the Chris Sullivan case pulled up in various windows…along with a profile picture of Sam Conroy. She stepped toward the screen and squinted as she compared the two portraits.

They both looked all too similar.

Other articles showed on windows, data about mercenaries, images of ritualistic murders in Russia, on the West Coast. One window showed a foreign news article. One of the words stuck out like a sore thumb, a German word.

Abendstern.

"I hope you didn't mind me borrowing it," a smooth, gravelly male voice said to Bianca's left.

Bianca whirled around and beheld Sam's smirking visage looming in the doorway, dressed all in black. His blue eyes taunted her, seeming to molest her brain. She clenched her teeth again, tighter than ever, and aimed the Beretta at Sam's forehead. Sam stepped forward.

"Don't move, fucker!" Bianca growled.

"Why so very angry?" Sam mocked. "It was with your consent, was it not?"

"Fuck you!"

"Ah, but it was not I who fucked *you*, though," Sam touted. "That's what you wanted though. That's what you were looking for the other day anyway, wasn't it?" He took another step forward. "A good…time?" His smirk relaxed temporarily as he squinted at Bianca's pistol. "Beretta…92FS Inox, semi-auto. Good taste."

"Wanna taste it?" Bianca's voice quivered.

"It suits you," Sam said, his smirk returning. "But how many innocent lives have you taken in the court rooms, Ms. Sterling? One bogus verdict after another. You're quite the killer yourself. We have far too much in common, you and I."

"What the fuck did you do?" Bianca said, then looked back and forth from Sam and her laptop. "What is this shit?"

Sam took another step forward. The muzzle of the Beretta was right at his forehead. Bianca tried to squeeze the trigger, yet her fingers somehow seemed boneless in his presence.

"But you and I don't *nearly* have anywhere near as much in common as *I* do with *another*, Bianca," Sam claimed, then he glanced at the laptop.

Bianca followed his gaze, her eyes bulging at Chris Sullivan's mugshot on the laptop screen, then she turned and tightened her face so hard at Sam that her forehead throbbed.

"What do you want?" Bianca screamed.

Sam peered into Bianca's eyes. Her ears rang.

"What the fuck are you?" Bianca squeaked.

"A blur between realities," Sam told her.

"What?"

"A living paradox, two and one simultaneously. I am a hole in the universe, an inversion of existence, the shadow of one's light…and the radiance casting another's darkness. Every light casts a shadow…." Sam reached out his gloved hand and stroked Bianca's face. "I am a walker of dreams, treading…in a sleeping nightmare unraveling, on the verge of waking."

Bianca slowly squeezed the trigger.

"Will you wake with me, Bianca?"

Blam! Blam-blam-blam!

The gun fired…and hit nothing but air and her bedroom wall. Bianca gawked. Sam had vanished. She lowered the smoking Beretta, shuddering in her hands—then the loud clack of her front door flinging open resounded. Bianca turned and ran down the staircase, then snatched her purse from the counter. The slam of a car door echoed from across the street. She jerked around and darted outside and saw Sam crank up a forest-green SUV a few yards away. He turned and smirked at her through the dark window.

"Fucker!" Bianca snarled, aiming the gun at him.

Sam revved the engine and peeled out, headed west. Bianca dashed to her sedan and thrust open the driver's side door. Her shaking hands struggled to jam the key into the ignition. The car came to life. She turned and watched Sam slow down.

The audacious bastard was actually waiting for her!

"You fucker!" she barked.

She put the sedan in reverse, then the car lurched backward into the street. Sam gunned his engine again, starting again. With a vicious push, she placed the car in drive, steering wheel in one hand and the pistol in the other, as she rocketed after Sam. Tires squealed like banshees into the night. Sam turned right down another street, then left down another avenue.

Bianca looked at her phone in a pocket on the side of her purse. Did she have time to call Nash? Would it do any good? Her mind reeled. How could Sam have moved so quickly? A blur between realities? Two and one? What the hell did that mean? Why was he so obsessed with Chris Sullivan?

A car horn blared to her right. Bianca jerked her head up and turned left, narrowly missing another vehicle, then she looked up and slammed on breaks. Her tires screeched to a halt as she looked back and forth in all directions.

The green SUV had vanished. Without a trace.

Like a phantom.

"Damn it!" Bianca yelled, beating the steering wheel with her fist.

She heaved through clenched teeth, then put the car back in reverse and revved madly around, then jabbed the gears back in drive as she sped back to her house. As she returned to her driveway, she put the Beretta down and snatched her phone up and dialed Nash's number. Her eyes ventured up at her bedroom window, still aglow with the lamplight.

116

"This is Nash," Nash's voice sounded over the phone.

"Theo?" Bianca's voice quivered.

"Bianca?" Nash said. "What's wrong?"

Bianca paused, eyeing her house again, too damned terrified to go back inside. Was Sam in there again? And what the hell had he put on her laptop? What was *Abendstern*? And why here? Why now?

She scanned the streets. No sign of Sam's SUV.

Like that meant shit.

"Bianca?"

"It's Sam," she finally uttered. "He's back."

Nash sighed over the phone. "Don't worry, we'll be right over."

"Hurry," she whispered, then hung up.

She put the phone away and grabbed her Beretta again, aiming it upward, holding it just out of view. Her wide eyes glanced westward again, at the cold front's haunting squall line.

Drawing closer.

The wind barraged her car with another violent gale, swaying the vehicle around with almost hurricane force. She huffed as she glanced around the yards. Damn the Halloween decorations, the perfect camouflage for serial killers. But this was different. It was inhuman! And to think she wanted to sleep with him the other day. Her whimpering breath quavered as another tear rolled down her face.

Demons *were* real. A real-life boogeyman.

He had to be close by.

Far too damned close.

XI: Ignition

Evelyn Whitaker held Melanie's hand, hastily leading her down the sidewalk in Denver, her heart beating faster, unable to shake off the neurotic feeling of being watched by someone from afar. November had finally graced them with its seasonal presence as yellow, orange, and red leaves danced down the streets in the strong gusts. The scents of pumpkin spices, pecan desserts, and savory holiday entrées permeated the district, tantalizing Evelyn despite her and her daughter having just partaken of ice cream cones. Christmas decorations were already up, with lights adorning the spruce trees and store awnings…melding with late Halloween decorations…still up due to the collective laziness of Yuppies hellbent on leaving their horror fetishes up for all to see, all year long. Alas, America had once again bypassed Thanksgiving, unsurprisingly. And dogs. So many dogs. Too many dogs. More dogs than people. Dogs everywhere. Dogs on leashes. Dogs not on leashes.

Dogs standing upright and clothed…holding their girlfriends' hands.

Like Chris used to do with hers and Melanie's.

She could no longer tell the hipster jackasses apart, they were so hopelessly homogenized with that weird, banal pompadour buzzcut bullshit, some with beards, some without. Walking travesties. They thought themselves so trendy and unique. She scoffed. It was as if they all came off an assembly line in a douchebag factory somewhere.

Yet the cheer of the bustling section of town did little to assuage Evelyn's strange paranoia; there was a serial killer loose, after all. As the two walked past pedestrians and their leashed "fur babies," the afternoon sun managed to pierce the pellucid veil of clouds high above with the glacial wind raging from the distant Rockies blowing her blonde hair around her face. Newton was with his buddies skiing in Breckenridge for a few days—thank goodness!

She had to get out of that house…and away from him. Altogether.

But she couldn't right now. She was trapped.

And so was Melanie.

She was well in over her head. She knew the feds suspected foul play from her domineering, two-faced boyfriend, and she finally did don a bandage on her face and a small gauze on her neck where the scar was, at Naomi's request. Her new nanny exuded quite a responsible work ethic, even though she did spoil Melanie a little. And even a little was way too much. Naomi had been the one to take Melanie in town for Halloween to shops during the day; with the Vulture loose, a curfew had been placed on La Sombra and several other areas. It had been only two weeks, and Melanie already seemed to favor her supplemental caretaker over her birth mother…for obvious reasons.

But two could play at that game.

No one would take her little girl from her.

Evelyn was determined to bond with her daughter and make her forget about Chris, whether Melanie liked it or not. She could be fun too, contrary to popular belief, and she was hellbent to prove that. She couldn't bear to not be in control of everything, especially her own flesh and blood. She would raise her right, without her ex-husband's coddling or Naomi's "big sister" rhetoric.

"Mommy, slow down!" Melanie complained, holding a red balloon.

Evelyn turned and started to rebuke her…but then her face relaxed.

Maybe she *was* walking too fast. Why couldn't the day be fun for her as well?

"I'm sorry, baby," Evelyn said. "Did you enjoy your ice cream?"

"My feet hurt," Melanie told her.

Evelyn examined her daughter's tiny tennis shoes. "Are your shoes too tight?"

Melanie nodded.

"Probably time for you some new ones," Evelyn replied. "You're growing like a weed, kiddo. How time flies." She scanned the stores. "Let's go get some new shoes. I think I might get a new pair myself. Don't you want some pretty ones?"

Melanie nodded. "Mommy?"

"Yes, baby?"

"I'm scared."

"Scared?" Evelyn scoffed playfully, smiling. "Honey, there's nothing to be—"

"I'm scared of Newton."

Evelyn sighed with a rare display of empathy and knelt down. "I know, honey. But there's nothing to be scared of. Sometimes, mommies and daddies get into arguments and let their tempers get the better of them." She hugged Melanie. "And I'm sorry you had to…."

Melanie hugged her back as the two embraced each other. Evelyn did her best not to cry in front of everyone; she might ruin her mascara, and it would burn her eyes like hell.

"I love you, Mommy," Melanie said.

Evelyn breathed in through her buried nostrils, then exhaled. "I love you too, baby." She looked at her five-year-old's cute face, stroking the blonde locks out of her own face. "Do you love me more than Naomi?"

Melanie hesitated, then reluctantly nodded.

Evelyn grinned.

"Don't tell Naomi," Melanie whispered.

"Oh, baby, I won't!" Evelyn giggled. "It'll be our little secret. Okay?"

"Do you like Naomi?"

"Of course, I do!" Evelyn teased. "If I didn't like her,I would let her anywhere near you or in our house." She rose back up. "I think she's a good nanny…and a big sister."

"I wish Naomi could have come," Melanie lamented.

"Oh, me too, honey," Evelyn lied. "But Naomi was busy today and had some grown-up things to do. I know she wanted to come too. Maybe next time, okay?"

"All three of us?"

"All three of us. That sound good?"

Melanie nodded, then raised her arms up. Evelyn groaned as she picked her daughter up, wrapping her arms around her orange jacket as Melanie clung to her mother's neck.

"I do believe you're getting heavier," Evelyn grunted.

"I'm not fat!"

"No, that's what I meant," Evelyn laughed. "You just…growing taller, getting to be a big girl." She looked out to the street sloping before her. "You'll be in elementary school in no…."

She trailed off as she noticed police cruisers amassing at a nearby intersection, with the clamor of angry voices. Blue and red strobe lights flashed on top of the cops' SUVs, then an armored van pulled up, with a SWAT team pooling out of the back; each officer was armed with shields and teargas grenades.

"Oh, don't tell me they're doing *this* today," Evelyn's voice grated.

"Mommy," Melanie pointed. "Mommy, look! The magic man!"

"Shh!" Evelyn hushed. "What are y…?"

She froze, seeing where she pointed. Across the street seated at the patio of a bistro, a familiar bald man with blue eyes smirked at them, sipping on a paper cup of coffee. The man lifted his beverage, acknowledging them. Evelyn waved back, managing an unnerved grin. Was it him? The strange man from La Sombra in the restaurant the other day? Bianca Sterling had gone with him for some bizarre reason. She had forgotten his name.

Who was he? What was he?

The crowd encroached as the SWAT team advanced in an echelon towards the vociferous protesters, now coming into view down the street, many holding banners and picket signs. A firebomb detonated, followed by water bottles flung at the police. Evelyn and the others fled, trying to escape the impending riot.

"Where are we going, Mommy?" Melanie said, innocently oblivious to the mayhem.

"Let's go somewhere else, baby," Evelyn said, jogging and huffing, her panicked mind whirling in a murky spiral of duress.

"Who are those people?" Melanie said, eyeing the protesters and waving. "Hi, people!"

"Shh! Melanie!"

"Who are they? Why can't I say 'hi' to them?"

"I don't know, baby, but they're not nice," Evelyn rasped, then she skidded to a halt. "Shit!"

Another throng of demonstrators emerged from a street before them, many of them wearing ski masks, flanking the pedestrians, beating cars with baseball bats and throwing rocks through windows. Without thinking, she put Melanie down as one came at her.

He swung.

She ducked, then kicked him in the groin. He grunted and fell.

"Didn't know you had any balls to kick!" Evelyn snarled.

"Fuck you!" he growled. "Crazy bitch!"

She spit on him, then looked as more officers arrived to the furious bedlam, then she backed away and whipped around. Her pale-blue eyes bulged.

Her daughter was gone.

"Melanie?" Evelyn called out. "Melanie!"

Two more rioters came at her, grabbing and carrying her through the window of a nearby store, yet a young man with a beard and plaid shirt punched one, sending him into an adjacent rack of clothing. Evelyn wrung herself free and bashed the other into the wall, then she faced the bearded man, meeting his shocked gaze.

"Have you seen my daughter?" she asked.

"What?" he shouted over the noise.

"Have you seen a little girl pass through here?"

"What's she look like?"

Smash!

Evelyn yelped as the two shielded themselves from broken glass. The rabble hurled more bricks and garbage through the shop's remaining windows. More firebombs exploded as rivers of rioters stormed the streets, wreaking havoc; some were bludgeoned by cops equipped with bulletproof vests, helmets, and nightsticks. She scanned the streets, already pluming with teargas, trying to locate Melanie, her red balloon, her orange coat, any sign of her.

"Melanie!" Evelyn shrieked, then retched from the fumes. "Melanie!"

Further down the street, out of sight, the five-year-old brunette girl ran, yet she was more awestruck than terrified of the pandemonium. A police cruiser conflagrated down the road; the vicious wind fanned the flames and black smoke everywhere.

"Whoa!" Melanie breathed.

The mob drew closer up the streets. She darted into a coffee shop, the building recently evacuated, and scampered into the kitchen, lured by the scent of freshly-baked cookies. A pan rested on the counter, wafting with the rich aroma of pumpkin, chocolate chips, and cinnamon confections. Standing on her tiny tippytoes, she snatched one and bit into the warm dough and walked around, curiously studying the rear of the establishment, taking another bite of the treat.

Bang!

The back door burst open as a few rioters rushed in; three were in black, their faces covered. They bashed and knocked out the other protesters, then the three remaining ones circled her, their forms bulky, out of shape.

"Is this her?" one said.

"Yeah," a second replied.

The third bent down. "You need to come with us."

"No!" Melanie squeaked, then ran past them, hiding in the office.

Bang! Bong!

A bald man appeared from the back door, sending pots and pans to the floor, then he artfully flipped one of the crooks down, then broke the arm of another—then stabbed the third in the neck with a hunting knife. Blood gushed out from the slashed jugular veins as the man gurgled and collapsed.

"You!" the thug on the floor blared.

"Yes," Sam Conroy, the bald man said, smirking. "It's me."

With a hasty jab, the assassin flung his blade into the masked rioter, then he turned to the man with the snapped arm and kicked him to the floor as he passed out from the pain.

Sam's smirk faded. "Hmm. Tempting. Very tempting." He took a butcher knife from the counter and slipped it into the unconscious criminal's hand. "I doubt they buy it. Some of my sloppiest work, if I must say so myself."

He scowled facetiously down at the three. He wasn't one to appreciate competition. This was *his* preserve, *his* hunting grounds! He didn't fancy sharing it with anyone, especially amateurs. And he hadn't time to question them. Like they would tell him anything anyway, and such effective torture would take time and finesse in order to yield any information.

Outside, the fulminations were drawing nearer.

Melanie stepped out of the office with mouth agape, gazing at the carnage. "Whoa!"

Sam looked at her. "Hello again, sweetheart."

"You're the magic man!" she said, smiling.

Sam furrowed his eyebrows, astonished by her disregard for the gore of the slain around her. His smirk returned and bent down. "Yes...I'm the magic man. Wait. Hold still."

She obeyed as Sam reached behind her ear, performing another sleight of hand with another quarter. She gasped with excitement as he placed the coin in her small hand.

"You're a very valuable little girl," Sam joked. "Just have money coming right out of your ears, don't you."

"Yeah!" Melanie gushed. She looked at the masked thugs. "You killed the bad guys!" She peered back up at Sam. "Are you a superhero?"

"Well," Sam said, hesitating. "Something like that."

"You're a hero!" Melanie said, jumping up and down with the balloon bobbing with her. "Just like on TV!"

"My, what a darling little girl you are," Sam said, feigning pity. "You poor child."

Melanie took another bite of her cookie, staring at him so bright-eyed like a lifeless baby doll, adorable and disturbing all at once. Sam studied her; already some sort of disorder was sinking its tendrils into her, making her devoid of genuine emotion. Most people would mistake it for immaturity. But Sam knew better, especially after what the five-year-old had been through.

She was becoming his reflection, sharing the same sociopathic fascination with blood.

Just as he did at that age...and onward.

Incurable. Almost...incurable.

His eye twitched, feeling a peculiar incentive take hold of him. Could he stop it in time? Could he bring her back from her unsettling dissociative behavior? Did he care enough to do so? This wasn't just about dominance. This wasn't like him. At all.

Were they truly alike?

His ears perked up. The rioters were coming closer, as were the police.

"Can you teach me to be a hero like you?" Melanie asked.

Sam opened his mouth, then sighed through his nostrils, his brilliant mind floundering for something to say. "I...you know, I have something even better, Melanie."

"You do?"

"You see," Sam told her. "I'm...actually good friends with your daddy...and he misses you very much. He asked me to bring you to him."

Melanie gasped, her eyes lighting up with excitement. "My real daddy?"

"That's right," Sam said. "But we have a long drive ahead of us." He tilted his head. "I'll show you more magic along the way."

"Yeah!" Melanie said, hopping up and down. "I'm gonna see Daddy! I'm gonna see Daddy!"

"Okay," Sam said. "But I need to do something right quick, then we can go."

"Can I have another cookie?"

Sam looked at the pan, then snatched up a few and put them in paper bag, then he rushed into the office and crushed the surveillance servers and the computer's hard drive. Sparks sprayed, then he eyed one of the cameras. That should do the trick.

Keep the pigs guessing.

Leaving Bianca alive was a fluke.

But it did put some extra sport into the game.

"Whoa!" Melanie gasped, watching the machines flash and sputter.

"Take this," Sam said.

He handed her the bag of cookies and picked her up. They exited through the back door and into the alley, passing numerous mutilated bodies of Sam Conroy's handiwork; too many rioters had been in his way to his target. But even they had played their part, producing just enough of a distraction...with someone *else* igniting their full rage earlier. Those schmucks. They were too easy. His smirk widened as they neared a forest-green SUV. As Melanie reached for another cookie, she accidentally released her balloon into the wind.

"Uh-oh," Melanie said.

"Uh-oh," Sam mimicked campily, unlocking the car. "We'll get you a new one, okay?"

"Okay," Melanie agreed as he placed her in the front seat and buckled her in.

Far down the street, Evelyn and other pedestrians continued to brawl with protesters.

"Melanie!" she screeched. "Melanie!"

She turned, looking up…and spotted a solitary red balloon hovering sideways over the buildings. Terror's icy claws finally took complete hold of her as she staggered in the direction where the balloon had ascended from. She whimpered, nauseated, dreading the worst, realizing her infernal nightmare had come true at last.

Her Melanie. Her baby.

She was gone.

XII: Severed

"What do mean you just put her down?" Newton snarled at Evelyn in the living room. "Why didn't you just get the hell outta there? Those damned protesters are crazy! You could've gotten yourself killed! What the hell were you—?"

"I tried to get us both out of there—they flanked us—there were too many of them!" Evelyn cried. "Don't yell at me—I'm already sick enough about it as it is!"

Newton turned and aimed his finger at Naomi. "And you! Where the hell were you? Why didn't you go with them?"

"I asked to!" Naomi fired back. "Evelyn just wanted it to be the two of them that day!"

"Shit." Newton stomped out to the kitchen, rubbing his face. "Leave it to women to—"

"Wha—what'd you say?" Naomi barked, following him. "Hey!"

"I don't know why I'm even talking to you!" Newton seethed, pouring himself a glass of water from the kitchen sink. "This is *my* house, not yours! *I* paid for it! *I'll* say whatever the hell *I* want to inside it! With Melanie kidnapped, you're outta of a job, missy!" He took a gulp. "I oughta sue your ass for negligence—probably press charges for child neglect, and—!"

"It's not her fault, either!" Evelyn defended. "And where the fuck were you, Newton? Nobody twisted your arm into going to Breckenridge with your little friends!"

"I work hard! I deserve a hobby!" he shouted back.

"Oh, and we don't?" Naomi growled.

Newton's razor-sharp gaze cut into her, yet she resisted him, shaking her head.

"You *are* like an evil Mr. Rogers," Naomi hissed.

Newton pointed at the front door. "Get the fuck outta my house before I call the police. Again. Now!" He took another slug of water. "And take those baby toys, those damned teddy bears, with you!"

"So charming," Naomi taunted, collecting her two nanny cams from the kitchen and living room, then she ventured up the stairs to Melanie's room to retrieve the third. "You found yourself a real peach, Evelyn."

"Speak for yourself, you little skank!" Newton blared.

"What'd you call me?" Naomi fumed.

A few seconds passed, then she appeared and rushed down the steps with a third nanny cam in hand. As she scowled, an acidic smirk slowly curled on Newton's face.

"You think I don't know?" Newton told her.

Naomi's blood turned to ice.

"I've seen Chris Sullivan at your house, stalking us, violating his restraining order, being in this neighborhood, and you're enabling it!"

"What?" Evelyn snapped.

"Yeah, no one told you to move in right next to him and harass him like that!" Naomi yelled back, heading for the door. "He tried to get away from her getting out of Denver!"

"How could you?" Evelyn accused.

"What do *you* care, you greedy cow?" Naomi growled. "You never truly loved him. You dumped his ass and ruined his life! You have no idea what you threw away!"

"Oh, no, my dear," Evelyn uttered a biting laugh. "It is *you* who doesn't know just what kind of worthless snake you're sleeping with, just letting him coil up right next to you in bed. But by all means, find out the hard way…that is if you survive to tell the tale like I did. Slut!"

"Oh, you are one piece of work—you spineless cunt!" Naomi derided.

Evelyn's jaw dropped. "How dare you and your filthy mouth!"

"I would *not* be surprised in the *slightest* if you two kidnapped Melanie!" Newton indicted.

"You're crazy!" Naomi deflected. "And if you call the police on me, I'll tell 'em that you and Evelyn have been abusing Melanie!"

Newton scoffed. "You don't have any—!"

"I *do* have proof!" Naomi scorned. "If *I* go down, we *all* go down together, so what's it gonna be, Newton?"

He stared the three nanny cams cradled in her arms, noticing the lens apertures camouflaged as plush toy eyes, realizing what they truly were. "Give me those, you little—!"

"Have a nice night!" Naomi blared at him, opening the front door. "Bitch!"

With that, she exited and slammed the door, scurrying to her sedan, then she opened the driver's side. Her breathing quickened, her heart drumming in her chest. As she entered and cranked the engine, Newton appeared and lunged down the front porch steps, rampaging across the yard.

"You get back here, you tramp!" he cried out.

Naomi peeled out of the driveway, then rolled her car window down, flipping him off with her middle finger as she gunned the engine down the street, tires screeching on the icy pavement.

"Damn it!" Newton raged.

Mina stumbled out of her bathroom, hearing the sounds of garbled voices through radios and people in her living room. She stepped in, seeing a crime scene photographer taking snapshots of something lying on the couch. Multiple FBI agents with latex gloves examined the house, dusting for prints, taking samples with tweezers. Over the couch, Vince Redman, Theo Nash, and Lucy, her weeping sister, loomed over the sofa.

"She was so young," Nash commented.

Lucy buried her face in her hands, shaking her head. "This can't be happening—it can't be!"

"Lucy!" Mina tried to yell, yet her voice was rendered mute.

"It always makes me sick when I see cases like this," Redman said.

Dread swelled in Mina as she forced herself to gaze upon the female corpse lying on the couch.

Her corpse. Gray, eyeless, and mummified with mouth agape.

Somewhere, a ghastly, ongoing shriek echoed from the distance, closing in. Mina turned...and saw him, his shadowy, bloated visage standing just beyond the window.

Her rapist. The crooked cop from Indiana.

He had broken out of jail!

She tried to get the agents' attention, yet they ignored her. The corpulent wraithlike form bashed through the window and plowed her into the bathroom with uncanny strength, ripping her pajama bottoms off, tugging at her panties. She yelled, her voice slowly returning as the ethereal racket of police sirens rang out all around her.

"No!" Mina shrieked awake on the couch.

She rose up in the dark of her house, gasping for air, trying to recover from the nightmare. Trembling, she fumbled for a light switch of a lamp on the end table, then checked her clothes. They were still intact. No stains. Nothing was torn.

"Fuck off!" a woman shouted distantly from a car outside, revving her engine down the street.

Mina jerked to attention, her breath shuddering, and snatched her revolver from the table, then waited. Listening.

Several minutes passed, seeming like hours.

She flinched again as police sirens abruptly sounded and rushed by her house, their blue and red strobe lights trying to breach the closed blinds as they screamed down the neighborhood into the night. She gripped her handgun with both hands, hyperventilating. The Vulture was here.

Everybody was here. After her.

There was no solace.

Tears flowed from her face as her expression wrenched in grief, whimpering, sobbing, then collapsing back onto the sofa cushions. She hated this! She was dying in here! In this house!

In La Sombra.

The past had trapped her within its jaws, this maddening agoraphobia holding her captive, suffocating her, depriving her of life, severing her from the world. Paranoia was her prison...and every day, she gave it power over her, feeding the monster she thought would protect her. She didn't want this anymore. She despised the fear, loathing the wretched loss of her peace of mind.

Fear had become her existence...as just another stereotype.

Just another victim. Robbed of her individuality.

She wailed, dropping the gun to the floor, halfway tempted to spend a bullet on her head, just one squeeze of the trigger away from the end of pain.

She couldn't do this anymore. She didn't want to be this anymore, this de-filed flower withering in the darkness of permanent sorrow, steadily drowning in shame and disgrace.

Her rapist may be in jail…but he had somehow won.

He would never suffer enough for what he did to her.

And men would never know what this feels like.

As she calmed, the epiphany washed over her.

If she didn't die or get raped out there…it would happen in her house.

She glanced at the walls, at the windows. None of it would shield her. It didn't keep crooks at bay. It was only impeding her, hindering her life, and she let it. Every single day. She wiped her face, stroking her dark-brown locks from her face, then picked up the revolver, staring at the shimmering barrel.

It would do no good to waste a bullet on herself. No one would miss her. She had been to funerals of close friends, people who were beloved by so many, friends who had committed suicide…and everyone's grief seemed to evaporate only days later. It was as if they never existed at all. Self-infliction was not the way.

But she knew what she had to do.

She glanced at the front door…and made her decision. She had to venture out and escape the event horizon of the black hole of terror, no matter how much it made her sick. She had to do something. Slowly, she rose up and approached the front door, weapon in hand, her shaking hand grasping the knob. If she were going to die, she would not do it in here.

Not without a fight.

"Shit, shit, shit!" Naomi cursed, bursting through her front door and rushing to the kitchen.

With quivering hands, she placed the nanny cams on the table and hooked one of them up to her laptop by a USB cable, uploading the most recent footage and saving it to a folder labeled, WHITAKER_LIVING ROOM. Other video files were listed on the screen, evidence of Evelyn's child abuse, as well as Newton slapping Evelyn. As she copied the data, she examined the footage hours earlier, right after Melanie was kidnapped. She surfed through the police and news crew interrogating the two, their answers spotty, then she passed the point right when the police and reporters left.

Newton's hands were on his hips as Evelyn dried her crocodile tears.

"What were you thinking? We don't have a hundred grand for reward money just lying around!" Evelyn snapped.

"No," Newton concurred, turning to her. "The bureau does, though. It'll help encourage the others to search for her. And they'll also provide the…."

He muttered something, then stopped himself and cleared his throat.

"What?" Evelyn squinted. "Wait, *what*?"

"What?" Newton griped, aiming an icy gaze at her, perturbed by his slip of the tongue.

"You," she breathed in shock. "Did you…?"

"I didn't say anything."

"You did! *You* took her!" Evelyn shouted.

"Do what?"

"You in on it, aren't you?"

"You're insane."

"You are! You're holding her ransom for—!"

Smack!

Newton punched her in the face, then grabbed her by the arms.

Naomi covered her mouth as she watched the footage, eyes wide.

"You know nothing. You think it's cheap trying to get your little career set up and provide for you and Melanie at the same time?" Newton barked. "This whole thing with your book deal has been slower than molasses, and what happened to all that money you made from TV? That lawsuit money from suing Chris? Where'd all that go? Did I get a dime of that? All the lavish vacations, cosmetics, and other needless shit you've squandered on! There are queens, celebrities, and drug dealers who are more frugal!"

"Things cost in Colorado, Newton!"

"*You* damned sure do, you glorified Pomeranian!" Newton growled. "Your spendthrift habits are wringing me dry! What the hell have you been buying, Princess Gold-Digger?"

"Oh, fuck you, you—!"

"You conniving black widow!" Newton condemned, shaking her. "If you don't cool it with the money…I'm gonna tell everyone about *your* dirty little secret!"

"And I'll tell them about *you*! I'm not afraid of you!"

"And I'll just stick to my story about the Vulture taking Melanie!" Newton sneered. "They won't believe you this time! Daddy's not here to fix every-thing, remember? Ralph is dead. I've got friends in high places, too, way higher than yours are! I know how to pull strings! I also have known the sheriff since elementary school. And those thickskulled feds probably sus-pect Chris Sullivan is the killer by now, and *he's* the only one with the motive to kidnap Melanie and murder Stanley Pfeiffer. He doesn't have an alibi—I do! I was in Breckenridge! And unlike you, at least I'm better at making gen-uine abuse wounds." He snorted. "Seriously, you don't even know how to fabricate a convincing wife-beating, do you? Are you *that* stupid and useless? Just a trophy wife bimbo, pretty to look at with your new boob job and not much else, huh? Nothing to offer society. No life skills whatsoever. Can't even raise and protect your own daughter."

"Go to hell!" Evelyn whined.

"You women, I swear…." He shook his head. "You're lucky the press was gullible enough to buy into your fake story all because of your candy ass and that pansy ex-husband of yours was too grody to believe!"

"You…bastards!" Naomi choked, tears streaming down her face.

Newton scoffed. "I guess 'feminism' has its perks after all."

"Fuck you!" Evelyn sobbed.

Bash!

Newton knocked her against the wall. "Call that damned nanny up. I wanna chew *her* ass out now." He squinted down at her. "Get up, you big faker! But I guess you *are* capable of genuine tears, huh, as long as I beat them out of you? Huh?"

Naomi pushed the pause button and closed her laptop, sniffling from the grim revelation and no longer able to bear Newton's ruthless misogynistic demeanor, feeding off Evelyn's anguish like a vampire. A sociopath. A parasite. All this time, he had concealed his true toxic nature under the cheap veneer of class and pleasantries.

He knew the sheriff? And no telling who else.

Just how many crooked cops were there in La Sombra? In Colorado?

And everywhere else?

"Chris," she whimpered, leaning back in her chair. "Oh, Chris…you were right. You were so right. I'm sorry. I'm so sorry!"

She looked up, realizing how quiet the house was, eyes darting around.

"Chris?" she called. "Chris!"

She checked every room. No sign of him. As she returned to the kitchen, she spotted a note on the refrigerator. Her lips became ajar as she read the words scribbled in pencil:

> *I've gone to find my daughter. I saw the amber alert on my phone.*
> *They think I took her.*
> *Thank you for everything.*

> *Love, Chris*

"Oh, no you didn't," Naomi snapped, ripping the note from the fridge door, then dashed and checked out the windows. "I *know* you didn't just…."

She scanned the driveway. His truck was gone.

Then she eyed an object on the dining room table: his phone.

With a shrill amber alert ringing loudly.

"Damn it! He ain't gonna get anywhere in that old clunker!" Naomi hissed, reaching for a backpack and stuffing the note and her laptop in it. "Everybody's lost their minds. They probably already caught him and…."

She trailed off, hearing the whir of distant police sirens drawing closer. She squinted. Newton. She glanced at the backdoor, then the front. She couldn't trust the pigs. They most likely suspected her of being Chris's accomplice. There was no time to get to the car, and they would stop her with a roadblock if they didn't catch her first.

The blue and red strobe lights flashed from down the streets, slowing down.

Preparing to converge at her home.

Naomi slung the backpack behind her, then she made for the backdoor, silently slipping out into the yard in the shadows. Always having to run from cops, all because of their prejudice, always "profiling" people, always catering to the elitists of society.

The CRAPs.

As Chris had lovingly put it the other night.

She went through the back gate of her picket fence, quietly shutting it behind her, then skulked down the sidewalk behind her house, down another street, trying to avoid the streetlights. The windchill tore into her like knives, as she was clothed only in one of her thin hoodies. She grunted through clenched teeth, pulling her hood over her head, doing her best to withstand the freezing gusts. She skittered from trees to azalea bushes, rushing through unfenced yards. Up ahead, another distant shriek of sirens blared. She looked right…at a gloomy pale-green house, then impetuously ventured to the backyard. To her surprise, a window was open, the curtains billowing ominously in the wind. Without thinking, she heaved herself through, plopping on a bedroom floor, gasping for breath.

Then she heard it.

The click of a revolver.

She froze.

"Don't move!" a female voice's grated in the dark.

Naomi gawked at a petite woman's outline looming over her, both hands aiming a handgun down at her. The tenant reached over and flipped the switch on a lamp, revealing her pale Asian form, glaring down at her intruder.

Instinctively, Naomi held her hands up in the air.

"Look, I'm not a burglar!" she rasped. "Just—"

"Shut up!" she growled. "Get up! Slowly!"

Naomi complied, gradually rising to her feet, her breath shuddering.

She squinted, tilting her head. "Wait…I know you."

"No. You don't."

"You're Mina. Mina Rosenthal."

"You don't know me," Mina seethed. "You're the Vulture, aren't you? Wasn't expecting it to be a woman. Clever bitch. I guess you couldn't resist an open window, could you…especially at this hour?"

"That's…bait?" Naomi looked behind her at the glass, then back at her. "You're trying to bait a serial killer with—wha—are…are you crazy?"

"I can't call the cops!" Mina snarled, trembling. "They do nothing!"

"Well, great minds think alike."

"Oh, spare me!" Mina scoffed, combing her locks out of her face with her fingers.

"Look, I'm not the Vulture."

"Yeah, right."

"I'm just looking for my friend, okay?" Naomi said, taking a step towards her, calling her bluff. "He's missing, and I thought—"

"You come any closer, and I—!"

Boom!

Mina fired—and missed, the bullet puncturing the wall. Naomi grabbed her and wrestled her into the bathroom, the gun slid from her hands. She finally managed to pin Mina down, both gritting their teeth at each other.

"What do you want?" Mina fumed.

"Chris Sullivan!" Naomi barked. "Someone kidnapped his little girl, and now they think he did it! He's on the lam, looking for his daughter, and I need to find him!"

"Well, he's not here!" Mina retorted. "And it's just as well they arrest the little shit!"

"He didn't do it—he's innocent!" Naomi shouted.

"Yeah," Mina chuckled sardonically. "How do you know?"

"Because I'm that little girl's nanny, and I have evidence that Evelyn Whitaker is a fraud!"

"What evidence?"

"I'll show you…if you promise not to shoot me."

Naomi released her and pulled the laptop from her backpack, opening it up to the video. As Mina watched, her furious expression melted into disgust and horror. Naomi closed the computer, then slipped it back into her bag.

"I can't go to the police, because they've already threatened to press charges," Naomi griped. "They think I'm his accomplice to a crime he did not commit."

"So, who has her?" Mina asked. "This…piece of shit, this Newton guy?"

Naomi shook his head, sitting and leaning against the bathroom wall. "I don't know. It's all a bunch of bad shit."

"Yeah, well," Mina said, rising up. "Good luck with that. Get out of my house."

"Just like that, huh?" Naomi sniped.

"It doesn't concern me," Mina replied, retrieving her revolver.

"But it does."

"Yeah?" Mina glared at her. "How so?"

Naomi licked her lips. "Because when word gets out about Evelyn Whitaker's fraudulent abuse scandal, you and many other women will be affected by it. You talk about one screwed-up political controversy—and if you think shit's bad *now* for you, just wait until people second-guess you and start thinking *you* faked your rape case."

"I didn't fake it!" Mina roared.

"Tell that to the masses when they come to scrutinize your ass. You'll be sullied, along with so many others. *I* might even be affected by it!"

"What if I take you out now?" Mina heaved. "There won't be a controversy."

"Do you hear yourself?" Naomi criticized, standing up. "A five-year-old has been kidnapped and is probably going to be raped and murdered. An innocent human being is going to go to prison—possibly death row—for something he didn't do, while losing his daughter to a group of psychopaths conspiring against him. And to top it all off, the *real* wife-beater is going to

134

go free. You really want that on your conscience, along with the hell on earth *you've* been through?" She stretched her arms out. "Pull the trigger, bitch. I'm waiting."

Someone banged on the door. "Sheriff's department—open up!"

They looked down the hall at the front door, seeing blue and red lights filtering through the closed blinds, then they looked at each other. Mina peered down at the floor, lowering her handgun.

"Hello?" the officer's muffled voice shouted. "Police!"

"Stay here," Mina commanded. "Don't even think about going out the window."

"Trust me, I'm not," Naomi agreed, seeing the glow of more police strobe lights shining on the spruce trees.

The fist beat on the door again, then Mina put her revolver in her blue jeans pocket, then she backed away to the living room to the door, watching Naomi creep low into the bedroom. Her mind became a murky maelstrom of disorganized thoughts and emotions, too traumatized to fully discern what to do. She turned the knob, then faced the door and opened it.

Revealing three police officers in bulletproof vests, Lieutenant Terry Nelson, Rita Carlson, and Harry Brown, with voices garbling through the radios clipped on their uniforms.

"Evening," Nelson said, chewing gum. "You doin' okay tonight?"

"I was asleep," Mina lied, feigning grogginess and rubbing her eyes.

"Sorry to wake you," the lieutenant smacked with the gum in his mouth. "We got a call just now that there are two fugitives on the loose in the area: one male, one female." He took a step forward. "Have you…seen or heard anything suspicious tonight?"

"No, sir."

"Okay," Nelson said, unblinking, his moving mouth reminding Mina of a cow's jaws as a message crackled through his radio's speaker. He pressed his fingers on his device. "Ten-four," he replied. He looked down and took another step forward, then looked to the houses on his left. "Well…we also got a call about a gunshot. Someone discharged a firearm nearby." He looked at her. "Is that what woke you up."

Mina shook her head. "No. Your police sirens did."

"Right," the lieutenant said, gazing past her toward the bedroom. "Mind if we come in and take a look around?"

"You got a warrant?"

The lieutenant turned to Carlson and Brown, then looked back at her. "No, we don't…but we would really appreciate your cooperation."

"I am cooperating, sir," Mina said. "I didn't hear any gunshots. You sure it wasn't a car backfiring? Someone…slamming a screen door?"

Nelson squinted at her. "Possibly."

"We're just trying to make sure everyone's safe, ma'am," Carlson told her.

"I understand that. I haven't seen or heard any fugitives." Mina squinted back and leaned into Nelson's face. "And I know my rights."

135

"Yes, ma'am," Nelson said firmly.

"Let us know if you see anything," Brown added.

"I sure will," Mina said. "Now, if you excuse me...I'd like to get back to sleep."

Nelson nodded. "Sorry to disturb you, ma'am. Have a nice night. Stay safe."

"Yes, sir," Mina retorted.

With that, the other two officers left the porch. Nelson and Mina continued to stare at each other, then the lieutenant finally turned and followed his colleagues back to their vehicles. She stood at the threshold for several minutes, watching them eventually drive off into the night. Chills wracked her flesh as she reentered her house, shutting the door and striding back to the bedroom. She eyed Naomi, hiding under her bed.

"Are they gone?"

"Yeah," Mina said. "Get up from under there!"

Naomi squirmed out and lumbered back to her feet, panting.

Mina sighed. "Do you have any idea where Chris might be?"

"Not exactly," Naomi said. "But I know what his truck looks like."

"Alright," Mina moaned, running her fingers through her dark-brown hair again. "Tomorrow, we'll look for him, I guess."

"No, we need to go tonight!"

"*Tonight*? Why tonight?"

"Time is of the essence, Mina!" Naomi griped. "Every second counts! It could be the matter of life and death for Melanie!"

"Who?"

"His little girl!" Naomi crossed her arms, her eyes downcast as she shed another tear. "I've bonded with her in such a short time. She's almost like...*my* daughter. I can't bear to think what's happening to her right now—I can't sleep!"

Mina huffed. "Well, you know what? I can't sleep, either. I'm too pissed off and freaked out right now. I could stand to drive around a little bit, so long as we don't run into the pigs again." She got her keys from her nightstand. "I don't even know why I'm doing this—it's ludicrous! I must be going insane."

"Join the club, honey," Naomi smarted, stepping out into the hallway, surveying the dimly-lit house. "You got a backdoor to this place?"

"Get out of my head," Mina quipped dryly. "C'mon, this way."

Naomi's phone went off, whirring with an earsplitting tone. She checked the screen, reading, AMBER ALERT, featuring information about her, Melanie, and Chris.

"This shit." Naomi shook her head at her phone's screen.

"Ditch the phone," Mina said.

"What?" Naomi argued.

Mina scoffed. "They can track us with your phone."

"What about *your* phone?"

Mina turned off the amber alert on her device. "They're not looking for me. And if we're going to avoid roadblocks, I'm the safest one to have a phone." She squinted. "Pitch it somewhere on the road, not here. Not in my house."

"Fine," Naomi said.

"What about the laptop?"

"No! That's our ace in the hole!" Naomi griped. "Besides, I turned the tracking thing off on it awhile back. I don't want scumbags stalking me."

"That doesn't mean that it's—ugh!" Mina growled.

"Sooner or later, the pigs are gonna put two and two together and track *your* phone!" Naomi said. "But by the time they do, we'll be long gone."

"Gone where?"

"I don't know right now—somewhere out west! We gotta find Chris first." Naomi rasped. "I know a few places he might be."

"Fine, whatever." Mina rolled her eyes. "Let's go!"

They slinked out the back and to Mina's dark-blue SUV, covered in sticks and leaves. Both of them were discombobulated beyond words, feeling as if wandering in a fevered dream. None of this seemed real. Naomi looked at the distant mountains, the skyline of the prominent evergreens jutting like black teeth in the haze illumined by La Sombra's light pollution. Everything seemed so wraithlike and terrible, waiting to swallow them whole in the creeping delirium of the early hours. As Mina unlocked and opened the driver's side, Naomi recoiled at the derelict condition of the vehicle.

"When's the last time you drove this thing?" she complained, getting into the front seat of the passenger's side.

"Relax," Mina said, hopping in and cranking the engine. "It's only been two weeks. Sometimes, I just try to make the block, then I come right back home. I'm just…you know, paranoid because of…."

Naomi sighed. "Are you okay to drive?"

Mina glowered at her, then backed out of the driveway.

"Oh, shit," Naomi muttered.

Mina reached the road, then proceeded down the street, then down another stretch of pavement, steadily arriving in the eerie isolation of downtown, with both of them searching for cops. Naomi looked at the car clock, reading 12:07 a. m. It was going to be a long night.

"What's his truck look like?" Mina inquired.

"It's, uh…I think a '90s Chevrolet Silverado, red and kinda rusty," Naomi told her. "There's a…a green panel near the front passenger's side where something was replaced. It's got some dents in it around the driver's side— I don't remember what the license plate number is."

"That's fine," Mina breathed, pulling the revolver out of her pocket and placing it below the console. "Something like that shouldn't be hard to spot."

"You'd be surprised," Naomi said.

An hour went by, scouring the entire town, every area where Naomi might think Chris would have gone to; she thought he might be hiding, waiting for the heat to die down before resuming his hunt for Melanie. Police cruisers passed by here and there, yet they paid Mina's SUV little mind, with the wind having blown most of the leaves off the vehicle.

"Let's try outside of town," Naomi said as they waited at a red light.

"Where?" Mina asked. "Wait…I think I see something."

She pointed up ahead at La Sombra's outskirts. Naomi followed where she indicated…and saw the inert shape of a pickup truck. The light turned green, and Mina proceeded. As they approached, Naomi noticed the familiar brownish-red color of the vehicle, its hood fastened by bungee cables.

"That's him—that's the truck!" Naomi said.

"Roll your window down," Mina replied.

Naomi did so as the glass slid down the door, studying the truck. Yet it was empty. No sign of Chris. He had even left his red gas tank in the bed.

"Damn it!" Naomi cursed. "Those bastards must've got 'im."

Mina looked up ahead, seeing the towering sign of a filling station off an exit on the highway.

"I need more gas," she said.

Naomi remained quiet, rolling her window back up as Mina made her way off the road and down the ramp, trying to bury her false hope that maybe he ventured down this far, that maybe his truck just ran out of fuel.

Hope. Hope was a damned joke.

She was jobless *and* homeless now. They had nothing to go back to, and she had just dragged a random person into this mess. Why? Why did all this have to happen? Why were people punished for doing the right thing? And why did Melanie have to suffer? What did she do to deserve this? Her face twisted as another tear fell down her face; it was like losing Aeriel all over again. Did she truly love Chris this much? Was he even worth it?

The image of Newton beating Evelyn jabbed her mind like a dagger of cold lightning.

Pigs. Both of them.

And the fact that she couldn't just tell the cops, what did that say about society? How many of them did Newton have leashed? Was Newton the Vulture? This whole time? What the hell was really going on? How she just wanted to rip the whole world down! She felt so sick. The grief made her very bones ache. She looked at Mina, then at the revolver beneath the console. Had she made herself a hostage too? What the hell had she gotten herself into?

She sobbed. It was a living nightmare.

And there was no getting out of it.

"Ugh!" Mina grunted, pulling into a gas pump.

"What?" Naomi moaned.

"See that homeless guy over there?" Mina said, nodding at the sidewalk.

Naomi looked. She saw a scrawny man in a brown jacket, blue jeans, and a gray beanie sitting on the concrete with his head hung and his arms crossed over his knees, veiling his face. She pursed her lips, adding a bittersweet combination of pity and revulsion to the soundless hurricane brewing in her soul.

"I need to use the bathroom," Naomi said.

"Here," Mina said, handing her a beanie. "Make sure nobody recognizes you. And pay cash."

Naomi rolled her eyes and opened the door. "Yes, boss lady."

She donned the headwear then walked into the store, feeling the biting mountain gusts assail her again. She shivered, wrapping her arms around her. That windchill had to be below zero! After doing her business in the ladies' room, she went and got pumpkin-spiced coffee for her and Mina, seeing her refuel outside and clean the remaining debris from the SUV. Then she looked at the gaunt vagabond again. He wasn't asking for any money. He might freeze to death tonight. She shook her head; he was probably a junkie contemplating an elaborate lie that was eccentric enough to believe. She normally didn't care about such people, wasting their lives with addiction.

Then again…that's how people saw her: an irresponsible alcoholic who was "unfit" to raise her own child, a daughter whom had most likely dismissed her biological mother's existence as folklore.

A strange instinct took hold of her, a benevolence that seemed entirely separate of her, then she turned…and ordered a third coffee. She paid for the goods, then headed back out to the car and handed Mina her caffeine.

"Geez, girl!" Mina remarked, seeing the three cups. "Must've been running on empty too."

"This other one's for him," Naomi said, eyeing the hobo.

"Naomi—"

"I know, I know!" Naomi said. "I don't really…."

She sighed and brought the coffee to the man, her heart pounding even more. With the bottom of the cup, she nudged his knee. Without looking up, he took the beverage.

"Thank you," he said.

"You're welcome," Naomi said, then she turned and walked away.

"Wait, Naomi?"

She froze, then twirled around. "Chris?"

He rose up as they finally recognized each other. The two embraced and kissed, then they beheld each other's faces.

"What're you doing running away?" Naomi scolded.

"I ain't runnin' away!" Chris defended. "My little girl is missing! I'm looking for her. I ran out of gas and came down here. I can't just do nothi—wha—what're *you* doing out here?"

"Ahem." Mina cleared her throat. "Shall we go, then…before trouble shows up?" She scowled at Chris. "You! In the back. I want you where I can see you!"

Naomi shuddered again from the cold.

"Here," Chris said, offering her his jacket.

"Chris, no!" she rebuffed. "I'm fine!"

"No, you're not! Shut up, and take it—you're freezing!"

Naomi growled and reluctantly slipped his coat on.

"It's the least I can do," Chris stated.

"Thanks," Naomi said flatly.

All three of them entered the SUV as Mina cranked the vehicle and drove off into the night.

"You know how you were talking about…going to Utah a few days ago?" Naomi said to Chris.

"Yeah?"

Naomi nodded. "I think you might have something there."

"Utah?" Mina grumbled. "Really?" She shook her head. "And then what? Become Mormons?"

"Do *what*?" Chris snapped.

"I don't know what to do right now, okay?" Naomi sighed. "My head's swimming. Damned crooked cops."

"We'll think of something," Chris assured, cradling his coffee. "Let's just…lie low for now." He glanced at Mina. "And…thank you."

"Shut the fuck up!" Mina scourged. "If we all live through this shit, you both owe me big time—I mean it—you have no idea!"

"Just drive," Chris scoffed.

"Phones! Both of you!" Mina demanded.

"Left mine at the house," Chris said.

"Yeah, yeah," Naomi grumbled, slinging her device out the window.

Mina said nothing more, getting her phone out, tapping the touchscreen and looking up maps, seeing where roadblocks and any congestion were. They drove out of La Sombra, heading west, winding through the isolated jaws of the mountains, soon to reach the interstate. Their hearts pounded madly within them, a triad of renegades, traversing the fraying road of uncertain fates suddenly splaying in so many precarious directions. Above, the mist gradually parted, revealing the stars in the clearing night sky. They shone on them amidst the dark unknown, gazing like indifferent eyes, far off and aloof.

Witnesses. Detached. Pure. Free.

Just like they were.

Severed from the restrictive murk of the superficial corrupt world.

As they traveled, they failed to notice a lone vehicle following them. They didn't see him parked at the filling station earlier. Neither did they see his passenger. But he saw them. He was careful not to tailgate them but kept close enough to faintly luminate them from the rear, wearing a conniving smirk.

And had a five-year-old girl, buckled up and asleep right next to him.

XIII: The Fledgling

Sam Conroy and Melanie traversed the crisp deserts of Utah for days, a seemingly aimless joyride, had it not been for Sam tracking a certain blue SUV and its three naïve occupants from afar. They simply didn't have a clue. Neither did the so-called "law enforcement." He was right underneath their noses the whole time, and they were completely oblivious to his presence. He was a shadow, a master of the hunt, an adept professional with a colorful past seeking his next thrill. Yet, no matter how much sport he put into the game, his adversaries were utterly beside themselves to try and prevail against the one they dubbed the "Vulture."

It was getting…boring.

But he was savoring this next kill, his next victim.

The scum they called…Chris Sullivan.

But his fixation went deeper than that. Sullivan was in the way.

Holding Sam back.

His unwitting five-year-old hostage proved to be extraordinarily peculiar, much to Sam's amusement. He had bought her a new pair of shoes and some additional outfits, only to make her blend in better. She was yearning for blueberry pancakes with ice cream yet again and had also discovered his 9mm, the muzzle equipped with a silencer. And she wanted to learn to shoot it so that she could become a "superhero" like him.

To which Sam obliged.

They drove out to a remote area on a dirt road and stepped out. Sam finished his soda and placed the can on a cluster of boulders, nestling it within a crack to keep the forceful winds from knocking it down. He surveyed the desiccated wasteland, sprawling with patches of sagebrush, dead grass, and igneous rocks, with gnarled, stubby juniper trees growing here and there. A vast gorge yawned in the distance, with a few slender, windswept monoliths jutting along its walls; one would be tempted to think it an extremity of the Grand Canyon carved through the earth by time. The deep ravine was surrounded by plateaus, undulating hills, and steep cliff facings bulwarked with buttresses of eroded stone, displaying various layers of strata, standing like the walls of a primordial fortress wrought by ages of nature's brutality. The sun had reached its daily zenith in the clear azure of the heavens, cresting high above at noon with lofty cirrus clouds spanning the horizon like wispy veins of platinum.

"Such majestic desolation," Sam marveled at Utah's rugged grandeur.

"What's desolation, Mr. Sam?" Melanie asked.

"Well, it's kind of like this, Melanie," Sam replied, his hands on his hips. "You see, some parts of the world aren't as…nice as others, not as green. Some places are…harsher, hotter…and others are colder, freezing. Not much can really…live in such conditions, as you can see." He gestured at the sparse vegetation. "But…some manage. Though some places are not so nice…life

141

becomes stronger in such hardship. It's possible to find beauty in the bad times, if you know where to look. The creatures, in their suffering, find a way to exist in these unforgiving lands."

"Like the prairie dogs?" Melanie squeaked.

Sam smiled. "Prairie dogs, chipmunks, badgers, foxes, lizards, eagles, tarantulas, and—"

"My daddy and mommy and me," Melanie blurted. "We, um, we went out to the desert once camping in Arizona on vacation, and, um...*we* saw a tarantula."

"You did?" Sam feigned enthusiasm. "How big was he?"

"Big!" Melanie exaggerated, grinning with arms wide. "We were camping and, um, one got in the tent. Mommy screamed, but Daddy smooshed his guts out!" Her grin faded. "But he didn't have the red stuff in him like the bad guys do, or when I see a kitty or puppy smooshed on the road. They have the red stuff. How come spiders don't."

"Well, that's because spiders are different, sweetheart," Sam said, growing sober while loading a clip into his pistol.

"Why?"

"That's a very good question," Sam said, aiming at the horizon, checking the gun's sights. "You know how kitties will play with mice?"

"Yeah?"

"And you know how puppies will chase kitties around?"

"Yeah?"

"Well...spiders like to do things differently, especially tarantulas," Sam told her, lowering his weapon, still gazing at the distant western mountains. "You see, many spiders spin webs between trees and houses and things like that."

"Yeah?"

"The tarantula is even different from them," Sam went on. "You see...he makes a hole in the ground, like a prairie dog...and he spins his webs there, coating the walls with his silk." His smirk returned. "And then he waits...for the bugs to come to *him*. Sometimes, he waits a very long time in that lonely dark hole. But when the bugs come...and get too close," he reached out his hand, snatching the air. "*Ssswooch!* Gets them!"

Melanie gasped with wonder.

"He catches them off-guard," Sam continued, "then he bites them with his fangs, poisons them...and spins them into his web, where he slowly sucks the juice out of them."

"Like Dracula?"

Sam nodded. "Like Dracula." He raised his index finger at her. "But...he doesn't want to eat *too* fast. No. He wants to savor his meal, for he might have to wait a while for the next bug to get too close to his nest."

"Wow," Melanie said.

"But if he gets smooshed," Sam warned, "then the tarantula goes 'Bye-bye.'"

"He's dead!" Melanie said gleefully.

"That's right," Sam instructed. "But when something dies…it doesn't come back."

"Like the bad guys?"

Sam nodded again, his smirk vanishing. "Like the bad guys."

"Can I shoot now?"

"Only if you promise to shoot the can over there," Sam said, bending down and pointing at the target. "I'll show you how."

"Pinky promise?" Melanie questioned.

Sam tittered his hyena-like laugh in his throat. "Now, where did you learn to pinky promise?"

"From my nanny," Melanie said. "Naomi. She says if, um, you pinky promise, you can trust people and they keep their promise and, um, they can be best friends."

"Oh," Sam replied. "But you won't break your promise…will you?"

Melanie shook her head.

"Are you sure?"

Melanie nodded.

Sam's smirk became a grin. "Okay." He held out his gloved little finger. "Pinky promise."

"Do you promise that we'll, um, see Daddy soon?"

Sam hesitated, his grin vanishing. She actually missed her abusive father? He stood back up and pensively scanned the barren horizon of snow-capped mountains again, the wind howling in his ears, blowing light cowls of dust around the desert. He had lost their blue SUV over an hour ago…deliberately.

He had no idea where they had gone.

But he could find out.

Putting a little extra sport in the hunt couldn't do much harm. But maybe he was truly pushing his luck this time. If that's what it took to revive the thrill of the game, so be it, lest he risk his existence becoming even duller. He was doomed to chase the sensation of his very first kill, obsessively pursuing it in vain, each murder more mundane than the last. No matter how much elaborate effort he put into his escapades, he grew less and less satisfied with his career as an assassin.

But there was something about this five-year-old girl….

"Pinky promise?" Melanie asked.

Sam leaned back down and extended his little finger once again. "Pinky promise."

They wrapped their fingers and shook, then Sam showed her his gun.

"This is what they call a pistol," he lectured, "a 9mm handgun. You have to be careful with it, okay? It can hurt and kill people. Okay?"

"Okay." Melanie nodded.

"It's already loaded with a clip of bullets," he explained, pressing the release. The gun relinquished the clip with a click as Sam caught it in his other hand, showing her the magazine. "Now, it's unloaded." He slid it back into the handle. "Now, it's loaded again." He cocked the weapon. "This puts a bullet from the clip into the chamber, so it's ready to fire from the barrel and out the muzzle. You pull this trigger to fire." He pointed at the tip. "These are the sights right here. You line them up to aim at the target. I'll show you." He peered down at the firearm. "Now...normally, this gun would make a loud popping sound when you fire it, but this tube right here is called a silencer. It makes the gun quiet when you shoot it. Watch."

He aimed the pistol at the soda can, then squeezed the trigger. A projectile chirped out, the lead clanking through the aluminum. Melanie gasped again, watching the smoking bullet casing ping to the parched gravel below.

"See?" Sam said. "It's not so loud, is it?"

Melanie shook her head.

He indicated a small button around the trigger. "This is called the safety. See the red ring around it?"

"Uh-huh."

"That means the safety's off." Sam pushed the switch. "Now...the safety is on, which means the gun won't fire as long as the safety is on." He tried to pull the trigger, showing her that it wouldn't budge. "See?"

Melanie nodded again.

"Come over here," Sam said, kneeling and handing her the gun. "Hold it tight."

Melanie stepped in front of him, clumsily fondling the weapon.

"Whatever you do," Sam admonished, "never aim it at yourself."

Melanie pointed the barrel at the rocks as Sam helped support the pistol's weight in her tiny hands, putting his chin on her shoulder.

"See how the sights line up?" Sam said.

"Uh-huh."

"Line them up with the can."

Melanie did so the best she could as Sam continued to assist bearing the handgun for her.

"Now...take a deep breath," Sam told her. "Then gently release it through your nose."

Melanie did so, squinting, almost closing her eyes.

"No, no, no, darling," Sam chuckled. "You have to aim with one eye closed."

"Which one?"

"Are you right-handed?"

"Yeah."

"Then close your left eye. Can you do that?"

Melanie did so, contorting her face awkwardly. Sam uttered another creepy laugh in his throat, still caressing the pistol with her.

"Now...aim."

Melanie obeyed, the gun becoming more stable in their embrace.

"Turn the safety off."

Melanie pushed the button.

"And squeeze the trigger, nice and slow."

Steadily, Melanie's fingers constricted tighter.

The firearm chirped out a round, ricocheting off the rocks above.

"Try again," Sam encouraged, inhaling the fresh scent of gun powder. "This time…don't be afraid. It can't hurt you, so long as you don't aim it at yourself."

Melanie nodded, their grip growing taut around the handle. She squeezed the trigger again.

Another bullet yelped out—striking the can off the rocks with a tinny clink.

"You did it!" Sam congratulated, rising up and taking the gun from her.

"I did it! I did it!" Melanie squealed, jumping and twirling around. Then she stopped and looked blankly up at her mentor. "Can we go get some pancakes?"

Sam chuckled. "Aren't you sick of pancakes by now?"

"No!" Melanie squeaked, grinning.

Sam removed the clip from the gun and clinked out the bullet from the chamber, retrieving it from the ground. "I do believe I've turned you into a pancake fiend."

Melanie giggled.

"I'll tell you what," Sam said. "Since you've been a good girl…and you *did* hit the can, we'll go get some more." He opened the car door. "You know…you got me craving them again, you know that?" He smirked at her. "You're a bad influence."

Melanie giggled louder, then waved at the desert, hopping back into the SUV. "Goodbye, desolation! Goodbye, tarantulas!"

Sam shook his head as he entered the driver's side and started the engine. They drove off, meandering back to the bleached, fractured pavement of the highway, his prey long gone. For now. His smirk widened; nothing a little technology couldn't solve.

Along with some mad ingenuity.

But he had to know something first.

And Melanie was the key to the riddle.

One that had been pestering him for quite some time now.

Afternoon rolled around as Sam and Melanie sat in the booth of a dingy roadside diner attached to a gas station. A small dust devil had kicked up about half a mile away in a field of more sagebrush, lazily wandering Utah's sandy wastelands, with the mountains jutting on the horizon. Over the peaks, more cirrus clouds had accumulated in the light-blue sky, the foremost of another cold front soon to arrive; its segmented, cottony spread was already veiling part of the sun, producing a fragment of an iridescent halo in the heavens. As they feasted on their plates of flapjacks, Sam noted a familiar blue SUV pull up to one of the pumps outside, seeing an Asian woman with long dark-brown hair exit the driver's side, with a man and woman obscured by thick clothing emptying out the passenger doors.

He squinted, recognizing the license plate.

That was lucky.

It certainly saved him a lot of trouble. He glanced at Melanie, happily munching on her pancakes, then back at the unaware trio at the filling station. The question now was what to do.

It was far too easy.

But he had to know.

"Did your daddy ever make you pancakes?" Sam inquired, chewing and wiping his mouth.

Melanie nodded, smacking. "Sometimes. Daddy would sometimes, um, put bananas and whipped cream on mine."

Sam swallowed, then sliced another hunk off his stack of flapjacks and skewered it with his fork. "What about Mommy? Did she ever make you pancakes?"

Melanie shook her head.

"What about waffles?"

She shook her head again. "Mommy makes me eat yucky stuff."

"Yucky stuff?"

"Uh-huh."

Sam soaked some of the syrup on his plate into the impaled chunk of pancakes, then popped it into his mouth, chewing contently, working it to the side of his mouth.

"You don't like vegetables?" Sam asked.

Melanie nodded. "I like vegetables." She smacked. "I like broccoli, spinach, carrots, peas. I like how Daddy cooks it. Then Daddy gives me a treat for eating my veggies." Her eyes grew downcast. "Mommy makes it tastes yucky."

"Daddy cooks for you?"

"Mm-hmm," Melanie hummed. "Daddy said it's dinosaur food. He showed me, um, on a movie how the big dinosaurs ate leaves and stuff. He says if I eat dinosaur food and the little broccoli treetops, I'll be big and strong like the dinosaurs."

Sam smirked. "You want to be a dinosaur?"

"Yeah! Rawrr, rawrr!" Melanie growled playfully.

"So, how does Mommy make it tastes yucky?"

Melanie's cheer suddenly vanished. "I don't like Mommy."

Sam raised an eyebrow. "You don't like Mommy?"

"No," Melanie pouted. "Mommy's mean to me. So was the prossapuber."

"You mean…prosecutor? Bianca?"

"Uh-huh."

Sam gulped his food down, then he took a sip of his coffee and cleared his throat. "What about Daddy? Was he ever mean to you?"

"No," Melanie said.

Sam glanced back at the blue SUV outside. "Was Daddy ever mean to Mommy?"

"Mommy and Daddy would yell sometimes," Melanie said, dropping her fork to the plate.

Sam wiped his lips, eyeing his subject. He had struck a nerve in the child. "Did Daddy ever hit Mommy?"

"Mm-mm!" Melanie shook her head. "Mommy hates Daddy! Mommy was mean to him too! Mommy was mean to both of us!"

Sam watched the Asian woman and her two companions reenter the SUV. "So…Daddy never hurt you?"

"I miss Daddy!" Melanie whimpered. "I wanna see Daddy! When can we see Daddy?"

The blue vehicle left the gas pump and drove away. Sam allowed his prey to escape once more. He rested his elbows on the table, grappling his hands by knotting his fingers together beneath his angular chin. The wheels were turning within his bald head with the sheen of the sun gleaming on his contemplative blue eyes. This remarkable little girl was already smart enough to call Sam's cruel bluff. He didn't want to lose control of her…or anything, for that matter. Perhaps he *had* been too reckless with this unusual escapade in Colorado, willfully sparing Bianca Sterling as a loose end for the feds to find.

The time was drawing closer, anyway; he was tiring of the chase at last.

The only question that remained was…how and where.

Sam turned back to her. "Let me give Daddy a call so I can see where he's at, okay?"

"I need to go potty," Melanie declared.

"Can you go by yourself?" Sam questioned.

"Uh-huh," Melanie said, then she scampered down the corridor and looked up at the passing middle-aged waitress. "Hey, where's the potty at?"

"Oh, it's right there, sweetie," she said, pointing at the ladies' room.

"Thank you," Melanie said, venturing into the restroom.

The waitress approached the table as she and Sam exchanged smiles.

"She's a big girl," Sam quipped.

"She's so precious," the waitress commended, shaking her head. "Just a little baby doll."

"She certainly is that," Sam concurred.

"I could just take her home with me," the waitress giggled. "You're such a good daddy to her. It's so sweet." She eyed him up and down. "Handsome fellas like you are so hard to come by in this day and age."

"That's very kind of you."

"No, I mean it," the waitress teased. "Gosh, you're so modest."

Sam smirked and nodded. For the first time in so long, he was somehow vexed by someone's misconception of what he was. Of all the people he had met, this five-year-old girl had left the greatest dent in a heart he had forgotten he even had.

And he knew not what to make of it.

147

The server eyed Melanie's unfinished pancakes. "You need a to-go box?"

"Yes, please," Sam said. "By the way…this is probably a longshot, but you wouldn't, by any chance, have a payphone here, do you?"

"We used to," she sighed. "But they took it down awhile back. Everybody's got smartphones now. Payphones are a thing of the past, I'm afraid. Makes me feel old. You *might* could try up the road, or if you feel like driving to Salt Lake City. I apologize for that, sir."

"I'll…figure something out," Sam told her. "Thank you."

"You need anything else, hun?"

Sam smirked up at her. "Check, please."

Mina, Chris, and Naomi stopped in a sprawling wide-open range at night in the Wah Wah Mountains a few miles from Frisco, the sunbaked husk of an old ghost town with a violent past; all that remained were skeletal wood structures, the caved-in silver mine, and the empty shells of its beehive kilns partially collapsed from an earthquake during the 1800s. The prewinter gusts lashed against the SUV in waves, rocking it on the side of a lone dirt road populated with a few junipers and patches of more sagebrush. The ruts were littered with cow patties and horse feces here and there, having been reduced to oversized, flat dirt clods from the arid climate. Mina vehemently regretted going so far down such a path—if one could actually call it that—with it dipping sharply into bowl-like pits of rocks and ore along the steep hills at times; it was a miracle that her tires were left intact from the trek.

A miracle…inside a living nightmare.

For the most part, the three had kept to themselves during the trip, spending more time hiding than searching for Melanie, as if they had any leads to go on. Mina constantly demanded that Chris be within her sight at all times, berating him simply for having a penis. Her wounded, aching heart was utterly festering and swollen with rabid androphobia the entire trip, thinking Chris would rape her the moment she let her guard down. Then, a day came when Naomi finally had her fill of it and exploded, lambasting Mina for her sexist paranoia, passionately vouching for Chris. Not all men were slobbering sex offenders. And not all women were self-absorbed, conniving bitches. Nevertheless, Mina threatened to shoot him if she even as much suspected him of making the wrong move, which Naomi warned that she would avenge him if Mina did. But they all shared a collective disdain for the police and the government. Though they were extremely leery of all cops, there had to be something they could do other than just mindlessly evade their uniformed adversaries. And they were running lower on money and supplies with each passing day. Soon, they wouldn't be able to even purchase gas.

The clock was ticking.

Time was gradually betraying them.

They quibbled amongst themselves about whether or not to go directly to the press with the evidence Naomi had gathered and expose the corruption of their enemies; Newton couldn't have his tentacles in *everything* in the world. Then again, they weren't all that eager to roll those dice. Even more so, it might force the hand of Melanie's kidnapper…if she were still alive.

Who knew what sort of harrowing consequences that would entail?

Posting the video of Newton abusing Evelyn on social media was also out, considering that featuring something as appalling and reviling as a psychopathic misogynist beating his sobbing girlfriend would be immediately censored or removed altogether. Even if such web platforms *did* tolerate its presence without tampering with its content, the so-called "fact-checkers" would eagerly misconstrue and downplay the validity of the confessions with their errant political biases, especially with it being broadcast from three fugitives. It would also instantly compromise Mina's subtle profile and give away their location in Utah.

But maybe the feds already knew, already closing in on them.

Maybe they were just delaying the inevitable.

"What if we *did* actually take a shot at the press without them knowing it was us?" Chris suggested. "Maybe we can head to Salt Lake City. Isn't there a way we can do it inconspicuously?"

"They *would* know it was us," Naomi corrected. "Who else would do it?"

"And if we *don't* reveal ourselves, it'll look shady either way and be discarded as a fabricated character assassination," Mina argued. "This isn't like Andy Dufresne on *The Shawshank Redemption* getting the warden back for embezzlement. This is real life. It's not that simple."

"And also, Chris," Naomi added. "No offense to you…but they think you're the Vult—"

"Alright, whatever!" Chris conceded. "I'm too tired to think anymore!"

Mina yawned. "I think we all are. It's after one in the morning."

"Look, we're gonna find her," Naomi said, eyeing Chris. "Maybe I'm just crazy and stubborn at this point, but I am determined to find her just as much as you are."

"So am I," Mina admitted. "I'm ass-deep in it with you two, anyway."

"Thanks for the support," Naomi quipped flatly, reaching for the backseat. "Chris, pass me that roll of toilet paper back there. I need to go take care of some business."

"Don't grow an icicle down there when you squat," Mina jested solemnly.

"Oh, ha, ha, ha, ha," Naomi mocked. "*You're* gonna have to go too again."

"Yeah, I know," Mina sighed, crossing her arms.

"I think our bottled water's starting to turn to slush back here," Chris said, holding up one of the beverages.

"Wha—are you serious? Even with the heat on a while ago?" Naomi said. "Damn."

"Don't step in cow shit," Chris warned.

"Or horseshit," Mina said.

"Or any kind of shit," Chris recommended.

"Bit late for that, if you know what I mean." Naomi waved her hand at them. "Always trying to look out for number one…and trying not to step in number two. The story of my life." She shivered, bracing herself for the cold, then she opened the door, the frigid breeze waylaying down into her bones. "*Oooh*—shit!"

With that, she slammed the door and marched as Mina and Chris watched her petite, wiry form vanish through the sagebrush towards a lone juniper tree beneath the starlit sky.

Chris squinted at Mina. "Well, milady...aren't you gonna give me the old 'don't-you-rape-me' spiel yet again?"

"Don't have to," she replied, raising her .357 magnum with her finger on the trigger. "I've got my insurance policy right here."

"Tee-hee," Chris scoffed.

"You men have it so good," Mina teased.

"Don't," Chris snapped. "Just...don't start with me tonight."

"What? You do!" Mina observed. "I'm not blaming you necessarily, but all you gotta do out there is stand up, aim, and piss in the wind. Easy-peasy." She looked at him. "Just be glad you weren't born a woman. It sucks, really."

"So, you want to be a man?" Chris raised an eyebrow.

Mina shook her head. "Not really." She huffed. "I just wish...men didn't treat women like shit so much, always thinking we're lesser and inferior."

"Yeah, well, I'm a man, and I don't do that," Chris groaned.

"I know," Mina confessed, licking her chapped lips. "I don't think Naomi would have blown up the other day and fancy you the way she does if you were. At least...I *think* she fancies you." She nodded at where Naomi had ventured to. "Are you two...kinda...?"

"Yeah," Chris said. "I don't really know what she sees in me, though. I'm balding. I look like grungy shit, so—"

"No, don't do that...pity-party bullcrap," Mina said, flicking her dark-brown bangs out of her face and running her fingers through her silky, wavy locks. "And the thing is...*all* people will eventually look like shit, bimbos and douchebags both. Everyone's gonna get old, wrinkly, and decrepit someday, so people might as well go ahead and look for those with decent internal quantities...because those will last longer than the flesh." She sighed. "We're *all* gonna look like shit when we get old. It's everybody's future—it's coming. There's no running from it, so...there's no since in being shallow about it."

"Well, I guess I *am* shallow," Chris lamented. "Otherwise, I wouldn't have wound up with Evelyn. And I paid for it. I'm being punished for my shallowness. Evelyn seemed so nice when we first met."

"If that's the case," Mina said, "then she took *you* for a ride...along with everybody else, it seems." She uttered a quavering breath. "I just don't want to get punished with her...when all this shit comes to a complete head. We can't run forever."

"Why would *you* get punished because of Evelyn?"

"Because society is stupid like that," Mina explained. "Man-eaters like her tend to manipulate other women to fit their selfish needs, amassing and as-similating them into this...ungodly spaghetti monster of shit. I had women at my…rape trial—and maybe some of them *did* truly mean well for me. But many of them…offered their 'support' for their own self-serving purposes, trying to piggyback on what I went through, trying to use me as some sort of political siege engine all in the name of 'social progress.' But I'm smart enough to see…that I'm just a means to an end to them. I'm a self-aware individual; I don't take credit for the achievements of other individuals—and I also shouldn't be held responsible for the wrong other individuals do. That's the very thing that births stereotypes in the world. I don't want people taking credit for what I do, and I *damned sure* don't want them dragging me down with them." She managed to smirk at him. "I think somebody like you can understand that, considering what all you've been through."

"My mother brought me up to treat women right, may she rest in peace," Chris told her.

"I'm sorry for your loss."

"Thank you," Chris said. "And no matter how much women piss me off or how much they want to hurt me, I try my best to do right by them. But I still tell them how it is, but not to hurt them. We all get told things we don't want to hear. All the constructive criticism we get is done out of tough love, not out of bigotry, or misogyny, or whatever politically-correct label people want to slap on there. I love women." He averted his eyes. "They just…don't love me back."

"Naomi loves you," Mina said. "And from what I've seen on the video and heard from Naomi, Melanie loves you too, apparently."

"That's because they're individuals," Chris debated. "They're exceptional."

"Like you and me." Mina fluttered her eyelids.

Chris looked back at her. "Yeah." He squinted at her. "Why *did* you come? You could have easily handed Naomi over to the cops, with or without seeing that video. What's in it for you, if I may ask, other than making sure Evelyn's perjury doesn't sully you and many others? You could have kept your life."

"Life?" Mina scoffed. "What life? I was leading a meaningless agoraphobic existence after the rape trial—I got to where I couldn't even talk to my own mother or sister over the phone!"

"What about your dad?"

"He passed away shortly after I graduated college years back," Mina told him. "My sister and I were adopted, and we took the last name, Rosenthal; our original surname was Tanaka. I was working for a company in graphics design before I was assaulted by that crooked cop in Indiana. Now, I do freelance gigs from home. Meanwhile, Lucy got married, and now she has a little boy." She showed him photos on her phone of a smiling woman and her husband holding a plump male infant. "His name's Tommy."

"Wait," Chris said. "Your sister's named…Lucy?"

"Yeah," Mina rasped, putting the phone away. "Apparently, my biological father, whoever the hell he was, had a thing for—"

"Bram Stoker's *Dracula*."

"Exactly!" Mina hissed, facing the windshield.

"Damn," Chris sighed, peering down at the floorboard.

"What's even more ironic…is that I was abducted, by a real-life 'vampire,' in a manner of speaking," Mina said, shedding a tear. "A four-hundred-pound, bloated sexual predator in uniform…and he took the life out of me. Monsters *do* exist, just not in the forms we'd expect." She glanced at the passenger's side. "The night Naomi broke into my house just happened to be the night I decided to take charge of my life again. I didn't want terror to slowly kill me. And everything happened so fast that night…I wasn't thinking clearly—nobody was and…I don't know! Here we are, I guess." She raised the revolver again. "I have five rounds left…and I mean to make them count." She eyed him. "And if I recoil or freak out around you…try not to take it personally."

"I can't guarantee that I won't," Chris retorted.

Mina eyed an orange glow just above the mountains in the distance. "Is that…a wildfire?"

"Where?" Chris peered out the windshield.

Something bumped the glass on the right. Both of them jerked, then relaxed as Naomi opened the door, putting the toilet paper roll in the backseat, wearing a grin on her face.

"What's with you?" Chris asked.

"Close the door!" Mina rebuked, shivering.

"Y'all gotta come see this," Naomi said with childlike wonder.

Mina groaned, taking a shawl, as they exited the vehicle and tramped through the brush, the fiery eminence from afar growing more prominent, drowning the starlight. Nearby, cattle and mustangs huddled together around them, trying to keep warm. The pungent scent of raw flesh and fecal matter permeated the wind as they drew closer to where Naomi pointed.

"See the baby horse?" Naomi whispered. "She just gave birth."

Mina gasped as Chris saw it: a pale newborn foal staggering up on its wobbling legs still coated in fresh afterbirth as its mother nuzzled her young, licking its face, then snorted as her young laid down and curled up next to its proud parent. The brown and white mare then turned to the three human spectators, her great belly lying on the ground, gazing at them with her fierce jet-black eyes, daring them to come any nearer to her child.

"I wish I had my phone!" Naomi squeaked quietly. "I wanted to take a picture of the baby."

"I wouldn't get any closer," Chris said, shuddering.

"Yeah…you're probably right," Naomi agreed, her smile fading.

"Mama Horsey doesn't look too happy to see us," Mina said, wrapping the shawl tighter around her. "Ooo-oooff—it's freezing!"

"Don't we have any extra blankets?" Naomi questioned. "For the colt?"

"Are you crazy?" Mina barked. "If that thing freezes to death out here, then it freezes."

"It might," Chris said, eyeing the baby horse. "It might not." He turned and faced eastward. "Oh, wow!"

The women turned…and exhaled a breath of sheer awe.

Over the mountain peaks, a great orange moon slowly ascended, warped by the atmosphere at the horizon, a waning last quarter. The incandescent lower curvature seemed to grin a twisted smile down at the battered lands, as if contemplating the dastardliest of mischief.

Nature was so capricious, with life so splendid and horrifying all at once.

All three of them returned to the SUV, but Chris offered the backseat to Naomi.

"I'm fine, Chris," she said. "I want the front seat this time."

"There's more room to lie down in the back," Chris said with a twinkle in his eye.

"You sure?"

"Yeah."

Naomi looked down. "Alright. Thank you."

They gave each other a goodnight kiss, then he looked to Mina. "What about you?"

"Same thing I've been doing," Mina yawned, entering the driver's side. "I'll sleep in the back tomorrow if I need to. We'll decide whether or not to make for Salt Lake City later." She yawned again. "One of you can drive again if I'm too sleep-deprived."

Naomi crawled into the back, making one of the jackets into a makeshift pillow while draping another shawl and coat over her. Chris slumped into the front seat and closed the door as Mina locked them all inside for the night. He rested his head on the upholstery, watching the moon's wondrous, deranged grimace rise higher over the snow-covered summits, still feeling the chill of the desert. His restless mind drifted into neutral, wondering if they all would freeze to death tonight…or get frostbitten.

Wondering where Melanie was.

Hoping beyond hope that his little girl was still alive.

153

XIV: Vermin

Vince Redman and Theo Nash studied an unsettling man's profile on a computer screen within Denver's daunting bureau headquarters. Forensic specialists, Deanna Gordon and Curtis Tully, read the bizarre background information of their blue-eyed suspect while examining surveillance footage. A video showed a fateful interaction between their subject and the Asian prosecutor that took place outside a bistro in La Sombra on a Saturday afternoon, while another visual recording played of the two at dinner later that same night. They strained to listen to the audio, trying to enhance and isolate the two voices from the restaurant's distorted clamor. Attorneys Bianca Sterling, Dave Rodriguez, and Leah Anderson, the assistant DA, gawked at the suspect's name with bulging eyes.

Sam Conroy.

Leah was a matronly brunette in her mid-forties. She already suffered faint parentheses lines around her mouth and crow's feet around her serious eyes, yet she was quite skilled at airbrushing her aging façade with makeup and blush, causing her to appear ten years younger. Her thick, wavy hair rested on her shoulders, her pink lips stiff and austere to match her cutting brown irises. A gilded crucifix on a fine chain hung around her neck. She sported a suit and matching skirt of burgundy with an ash-gray sweater beneath. Brown pantyhose contoured to her slender legs while she stood on polished black stilettos. She was a respectable veteran in the courtroom's arena and Bianca's mentor, possessing only a trace of her protégé's toxic demeanor. The years of countless cases had psychologically matured her and opened her mind to other aspects of humanity and society, something Bianca still had yet to learn. That said, she was slow to relent to the preferences of men and dunderheaded individuals, but she did her best to be fair and just and had a much sharper eye for details than Bianca. Yet, even that had done little for Chris Sullivan's sake, despite the fact that it was Leah who managed to convince Bianca and Evelyn to drop the attempted murder charge years back.

Which shocked them to their souls.

Leah had done it out of mercy for Chris, finding Evelyn's claims rather hyperbolic at best. Bianca, on the other hand, warped her mentor's recommendation by swindling Evelyn into dropping that particular charge, claiming that convicting her ex-husband merely of assault would bode well for Evelyn's reputation, as an additional publicity stunt. The media would see Evelyn as a "forgiving wife" and "loving mother." Thus, it would bolster her superficial repertoire as a "survivor of domestic violence" and embellish her image all the more as a "strong and independent female." Though there was nothing Leah could do about what Bianca had done with what was intended to be a humble and benevolent suggestion, she greatly frowned upon her young ward's churlish ulterior motives. Somehow, Leah secretly pitied Chris and Melanie, as she, too, was a loving parent, a wife and a mother of two. The thought of someone losing their child was unbearable to Leah, irking her healthy maternal nature...and something about Evelyn's abrasions and melodramatic attitude did seem...manufactured. She always had a lingering feeling that something was horribly amiss about the whole thing. But she could never substantiate that they were. She was never entirely sure...as were a lot of other people all across the nation.

Regardless, that case was over.

Before them lay this cold-blooded atrocity skirring through their beloved Rocky Mountains, this wretched interloper staring back at them with his infuriating smirk...and his hypnotic glassy eyes.

"Conroy. Special Forces," Gordon read Sam's profile aloud. "Enlisted when he was eighteen. Stationed in Germany in 2006, then Japan, Syria, conducted espionage and surveillance in Russia, North Korea, Turkey, Pakistan...and a whole lot of other places. Was given a psychological evaluation and diagnosed with antisocial personality disorder, killed several men in his company, including his commanding officer during a suicide mission. Reported MIA afterwards." She scrolled through the files, sifting through various images of other military delinquents. "He's suspected to be affiliated with a group of terrorists who call themselves the *Abendstern*, the 'Order of the Evening Star' led by Sebastian Hader, a German mercenary who migrated to Russia. He called himself the *Sturmvogel*."

"*Abendstern*?" Leah asked.

"*Sturmvogel*?" Vince inquired.

Rodriguez removed his glasses and wiped the rectangular lenses with a handkerchief. "*Abendstern* is German for 'evening star.' *Sturmvogel* roughly translates to 'stormbird.'"

"So, Hader was the big bird of the flock," Nash scoffed.

"Maybe back in the day," Tully replied. "According to intel, Conroy turned on them for some reason and vanished shortly after. Hader hasn't been seen in years. He's presumed dead." Tully shook his head. "*Abendstern* was a cult, seeing themselves as soldiers of light trying to bring about the Apocalypse to 'cure the world.' Hader was obsessed with the occult and Heinrich Himmler's abominations during World War II. He even began offering human sacrifices all over, including within the forests surrounding Houska Castle in the Czech Republic, starting at the turn of the new millennium. They were trying to coax the '*dunkelheit*' out of its infernal dwelling." He paced around. "The castle's architecture is unconventional, boxlike with ramparts facing inward, as if built to keep something in rather than out. People claim that it's constructed upon a portal to hell deep in the limestone, keeping demons from infiltrating the surface world."

Redman snorted. "Really, now?"

"More psycho nutjobs," Nash commented with a wry smile.

"That's putting it far too mildly," Rodriguez quipped, slipping his glasses back on.

"So, Conroy's a Nazi?" Bianca questioned.

"Possibly," Gordon replied.

"Oh, shit." Bianca cringed. "I actually let that…thing, that…creature in my house."

"Could've happened to any of us, Bianca," Leah told her.

"But why did he spare me?" Bianca asked. "Why didn't he rape me?"

"I'd count my blessings if I were you, Ms. Sterling," Rodriguez admonished.

"No, it's a valid question," Leah defended. "What is Conroy's true MO?"

"And why not use an alias?" Gordon inquired.

"Because he wants to be found," Redman surmised. "And not necessarily by us. He's trying to flush somebody out…and it's not our fugitives. With Stanley Pfeiffer in all the bad shit *he* was in…there's no telling what's really going on."

"He said something to me when he broke into my house the other night," Bianca said. "That he was…a 'blur between realities,' that he was 'two and one.' That's when he put all this crap on my laptop."

"A blur between realities?" Redman asked.

"So, what—he's from a parallel universe?" Nash rolled his eyes.

"Just more crazy nonsense," Gordon scoffed.

"A special kind of crazy," Tully added.

"So, what does a terrorist organization have to do with my two clients?" Rodriguez demanded.

"The answer might be in the question, Rod," Redman said.

"Oh, spare me!" Rodriguez sniped back. "And don't ever call me Rod."

Redman shrugged callously.

"Speaking of 'bad shit,' perhaps someone would like to explain how two sheriff's deputies were found dead in a coffee shop in Denver," Leah prodded, "with a third incapacitated with a broken arm, all three clad in ski masks like burglars?"

Nash raised an eyebrow at Leah.

"Deputies Woodward and Niles were found dead," Gordon said. "But they did not have the Vulture's brand on their foreheads. They were most likely killed in the riot, with Garman dying later."

"Did anybody see who else was in the coffee shop?" Bianca inquired.

Gordon shook her head. "No. Deputy Garman went into shock and died later at the hospital. The cause of death was internal bleeding; his severed ulna bone evidently sliced an artery wide open in his arm. The only coherent thing he managed to sputter out to the EMTs in the ambulance was 'Vulture.'"

"So, Conroy's our guy?" Nash questioned.

"And what connection does he have with Chris Sullivan?" Bianca demanded. "They're in league with each other, aren't they? Old accomplices?"

"Bianca!" Leah scolded.

"Well, what is it, then, Leah?" Bianca sniped back.

"Look, we can either make wild speculations, or we can look at the facts," Rodriguez interjected. "A little girl is missing. A man who is dubbed as the 'Vulture' is loose and has murdered *at least* four people here in Colorado, not counting anywhere else."

"And your 'two clients' are missing, Dave," Bianca hissed.

"All because of hearsay," Rodriguez fired back. "But the media couldn't help themselves and have, once again, given in to racial profiling for the sake of sensationalism, thus driving my clients away to God knows where, endangering their lives!" He glared. "Hugh Altaha was assaulted by an unknown assailant the other night—and it is physically impossible for it to be Chris Sullivan."

"My, my, that's very presumptuous of you," Bianca sneered. "What happened to 'looking at the facts?'"

"*I'm* the one who recommended Chris go over there to ask for the pastor's cooperation in a case I'm compiling," Rodriguez went on. "Seconds after Chris drove off from the house, Altaha received a threatening message on a brick that was thrown through his window. As he tried to phone the police, someone in a ski mask broke into his home and bludgeoned him half to death, warning him not to interfere, then left. He made it look like Chris did it, but Altaha says otherwise, which shows there *is* a conspiracy afoot against my clients."

"Then it's the Vulture," Leah said, looking at the agents. "But why would the Vulture involve himself with Chris?"

"Is it possible that the Vulture took Melanie?" Gordon asked. "If Sam Conroy is, in fact, our Vulture...he might be taking her to...sacrifice somewhere, just like Hader did."

"Old habits die hard," Nash said.

"Oh...." Leah moaned in disgust, holding her hand over her mouth.

"There *is* something else, Bianca," Redman said. "Newton Malcolm may be abusing Evelyn Whitaker, but we're having trouble verifying."

"What?" Bianca blurted.

Nash snapped his fingers as Tully placed two photos from a file and onto a desk before the three attorneys, each showing wounds on Evelyn's face. The image on the left displayed the afflictions from the Chris Sullivan case; the one on the right was taken from Nash's phone a few weeks earlier, the cuts and bruises appearing much more severe than the left picture.

"If you notice the abrasion from the photo Nash took," Tully told them, "is drastically different from the indentation from the photo from the Chris Sullivan case. Upon further inspection and comparing them side by side, the one from the Sullivan case could arguably be one that was stamped on there by force, possibly self-inflicted." He demonstrated with a bottle cap lying on the desk and mashed it harshly on his arm, making a noticeable circular impression on his flesh, virtually identical to the Chris Sullivan case's image. "See?"

"That's preposterous!" Bianca snapped.

"Regardless, we have another potential wife-beater on our hands," Redman said, grabbing his car keys. "We asked about Evelyn's bruises, and she avoided our questions, and it wasn't Chris; otherwise, she would've said so. We brought Newton in for questioning, and he dodged us as well. Something's up."

"Red!" Rick Wellborn rasped, running to them. "We got him! We got the kidnapper on the line! We're running a trace now!"

All of them rushed to a recording room where more FBI agents and a few techs had a man on speaker, his words deep and distorted by a vocal device.

"Where is Melanie?" one of the officers asked.

"The girl is safe," the dark, staticky voice said on the other line, "so long as you do as I say."

"Spare us the clichés!" Nash barked. "What do you want?"

"Ten million in cash in a black duffel bag," the voice replied. "No dye packs in the bag, no bugs, no trackers, no tricks of any kind, or the girl dies! Send only two federal agents to make the drop, no more, no less. Do you understand?"

"Where?" Redman interrogated.

"Almost got his location," one of the techs whispered, tacking away at a keyboard, looking at a computer screen. "Just a few more seconds."

"Where?" Redman growled.

"Tomorrow evening in Utah. Midnight, on the dot," the voice said. "In Torino. There's an old storehouse on the north side of the town. Don't be early. Don't be late, or the girl dies."

The grim voice hung up, then the dial tone tolled.

"Damn it!" the tech griped. "I was so close!"

"Torino?" Gordon asked.

"It's a ghost town several miles southwest of Salt Lake City," Wellborn replied.

"I'll arrange for the ransom money," Redman said.

"I'll go," Nash volunteered.

"We'll talk about this later," Redman rebuked, then looked at Rodriguez. "Altaha's still at St. James Memorial?"

"He finally woke up from his coma early this morning," the attorney replied. "I went to see him on my lunch break today. He's in Room 2247."

Redman sighed. "No offense, counselor, but I'd like to get it straight from the horse's mouth."

"So would I," Leah agreed.

"By all means, be my guest." Rodriguez turned to the women. "Ladies first."

Bianca stormed past him, her high heels clomping briskly like cloven hooves, with Leah following, then Rodriguez and Nash exited through the halls, with Tully, Gordon, and Wellborn examining and scrolling through the files again. Their stomachs felt as if transmuted to leaden knots. Nash turned his head and took one last look at Sam Conroy's face on the computer screen as they walked out, that wretched psychopathic smirk etched into his mind. There was something so disturbing about his eyes. So mesmerizing. Malefic. Unearthly.

Lifeless.

Redman, Nash, Rodriguez stepped out of an elevator at the hospital, with Bianca and Leah accompanying their hasty stride down the hall towards Hugh Altaha's room. As they approached, Lieutenant Terry Nelson and two other deputies, Rita Carlson and Harry Brown, stepped out and shut the door behind him. Nelson's eyes were veiled by his aviator sunglasses, his jaw smacking more gum. He turned to them.

"Agents. Good to see you again," Nelson questioned. He nodded at Bianca and Leah. "Ladies."

"How's Altaha?" Nash asked.

Nelson looked at the floor, then back at Nash. "He's resting right now. Not gonna be able to get anything out of him at the moment."

"We need to speak to him," Redman said.

"No can do," Nelson said. "We have the situation under—"

"Step aside, sir," Nash said firmly.

"I'm gonna have to ask you and your posse to leave," Nelson snapped. "I have my orders from Dan Addison himself. This is the sheriff's department's matter, not for some pompous G-man goons like—*aawgk*!"

Nash slammed and pinned the lieutenant against the wall.

"Theo!" Redman reprimanded.

"You listen to me as hard as you fucking can, you gum-smacking hick!" Nash yelled in Nelson's face. "*You're* the one interfering with a *federal* investigation! A little girl's life is in danger! If she dies, I'm gonna drag Dan Addison's name and his so-called 'ironclad' reputation through the fucking mud, and you and the entire department will be in shambles, do you hear me?"

Nelson grabbed Nash's throat, trying to push him back.

"Theo, let him go!" Redman shouted.

"Sir, let him go!" Carlson said, drawing her Glock.

"Oh, I dare you to pull that trigger!" Nash barked at her.

The medical personnel yelped as doctors, nurses, and patients ducked, running from the ensuing standoff.

"I wouldn't if I were you," Redman growled through clenched teeth, drawing his piece, aiming it at the female officer.

"Want a bloodbath?" Brown said, pulling his firearm. "Hospital's a good place to have it."

"Let him go, Nash," Redman commanded.

"Not with guns aimed at my head," Nash snarled.

"Save 'em, Carlson," Nelson said. "Brown."

"Let. Go. Of the lieutenant," Carlson seethed.

"Go on," Nash taunted. "Bust that cap."

"Rita!" Nelson rasped. "Put it away! That's an order! You too, Harry!"

Reluctantly, Carlson and Brown holstered their weapons, then Redman followed suit as Nash released Nelson. All the medical personal peeked up from the desks, wondering when security was going to save them.

The lieutenant stomped down the hall, spitting his gum on the floor. "Let's go!" He glared at Nash. "I'll see to it that your superiors know what kind of junkyard dog you—!"

"Speak for yourself, lieutenant!" Nash retaliated.

Nelson snorted as he and his other two deputies followed. Redman knocked and entered with Leah and Rodriguez. Bianca approached Nash, stroking his neck.

"You okay?" she asked, caressing his cheek.

"Yeah," Nash coughed, noticing her unusual tender touch.

She immediately recoiled. "Sorry."

"It's fine," Nash said, clearing his throat. "What?"

"Nothing," Bianca cooed. "I'm...not a *complete* bitch, you know?"

Nash smirked. "I know."

Bianca walked past him into the room, flicking her straight, silky black hair as goosebumps roiled her creamy-tan skin in riveting waves. For one fleet moment, she could just feel him undress her with his eyes, simultaneously revolting and arousing her like the nymphomaniacal sex machine she was. Nash followed her, his smirk instantly dissipating; good thing Laura wasn't there to see that awkward encounter. She'd have his head served on a silver platter, garnished with his mutilated manhood. Then again, his wife *had* grown cold and distant here lately.

Regardless, they all had far greater problems at hand.

Which was putting it mildly.

They stood over Hugh Altaha's bed, with parts of his weathered head still bandaged and his long, straight black hair unkempt from bedrest. A tray with a late lunch of meatloaf, mashed potatoes, English peas, and a plastic cup of green Jell-O sat next to him paralleling the window, barely touched; he couldn't have ingested more than five spoonfuls of his hours-old entrée. The pastor peered up at them with a deep, ill melancholy.

"Sorry to bother you, Reverend," Redman told him. "I'm Agent Vince Redman. This is my partner, Agent Theo Nash." He and Nash showed their badges. "We're with the FBI. These are Attorneys Bianca Sterling and Leah Anderson. I see you've already met Mr. Rodriguez."

"What do you...want?" Hugh croaked.

Redman looked at Rodriguez. "The counselor over here already gave us the basic rundown of what happened to you. You're positive it wasn't Chris Sullivan?"

"Yes," Hugh said.

"Was it anyone familiar to you?" Nash inquired.

"Seconds after Chris drove away," Hugh said, "some...idiot threw a brick through my window with a note tellin' me to...stay outta something." He grunted and sat up in the bed. "I went to phone the police...then some guy,

161

toned and bulky, broke through another window in a ski mask and some kind of black military fatigues, tactical gear. He must've taken steroids—he was built like a juggernaut! He caught me off-guard, beat the crap out of me—he knew martial arts, whoever he was. Then, as I lay there, he said something like: 'This is your only warning. Don't...interfere with the great work,' or something like that, I don't...."

"Great work?" Leah asked.

"Is that a reference to the ritual this...*Abendstern* group wants to conduct?" Bianca questioned.

"There was something...wild and evil about his eyes," Hugh wheezed. "For a moment...I could've sworn I saw something like...dying red coals deep in them."

"Brown eyes?" Nash interrogated. "You couldn't recognize his voice?"

"No," Hugh coughed. "He had...blue. Blue eyes. Stormy blue. I can still see them every time I blink. He had a harsh...accent, like...something foreign. Slavic, maybe, I don't know."

Redman and Nash exchanged concerned looks.

"I blacked out shortly after," Hugh rasped. "Evidently, Nancy, the church receptionist, noticed the broken windows the next morning...and found me." He shook his head. "I just now woke up. I had nightmares...visions.... Horrible visions. Blood. Fire. Death. So much death. Desolation. Flaming wings. Bodies...everywhere."

"Look, just rest up, okay?" Redman said. "We're gonna find who did this."

The agent nodded them out of the room, with Nash staying behind.

"If you need anything, just let us know," Nash told him.

"The Vulture," Hugh said. "Be careful...."

"I will. Get some rest."

"You don't understand," Hugh groaned in groggy delirium. "He is not what he seems...."

"I know," Nash said, walking out.

"No," Hugh whispered. "You don't...."

Nash paused, squinting, then he resumed his exit, catching up with the others down the hall and back into the elevator. The leaden feeling in their guts only amplified. Time was running low. Yet the pastor's parting words to Nash only exacerbated his turbulent soul all the more, biting into him with fangs of infernal ice.

He didn't doubt that Sam Conroy wasn't what he seemed. But deep down, he knew what Hugh Altaha had actually alluded to, raking its glacial claws against his ghost deep inside. The Vulture had already proven himself to be no ordinary criminal. Ritualistic killings. The Lady in Gray. Phantom Canyon Road. Denver. And now Torino. What the hell was in that ghost town? It wasn't just cheap, morbid fascination that attracted vermin like Conroy to the paranormal. There was far more to the carefully-wrought mutilations of his victims than what Nash's colleagues would care to admit. The cryptic symbols painted around Stanley Pfeiffer's body. The blood angel patterns in the snow around the triad of drug dealers. It was not just some mere serial killer's signature. Neither was the brand scorched on their foreheads. There was something truly insidious at work here, something malevolent.

Inhuman.

Chris and Naomi sat outside on a bench in Salt Lake City at night, with Mina inside an adjacent burger joint, ordering food for the three. Streetlights bathed the gleaming asphalt with indolent orange and blue fluorescence here and there, showing some of the sparse foliage and the tangled industrial morass of the concrete jungle, a crude oasis in Utah's bitter landscape. The mountain wind was as frigid as ever, lashing at them relentlessly, yet the overpass nearby shielded them from some of the onslaught. Yet, even then, the incoming winter was hellbent on converting all three of them into icicles. Time was growing shorter, and gas and money was dwindling quickly with each passing day. Something had to give.

Chris and Naomi both had phoned a few radio shows, local TV stations, and even a few podcast hosts about their evidence, yet they either couldn't get anyone to answer or were simply told that they were not interested in "defamation" or "conspiracy theories." And not revealing their names did not help their predicament, making the media even less cooperative.

Apparently, invasion of privacy and ruining someone's reputation only mattered when it suited them. They certainly had no problem doing it to Chris Sullivan. Bunch of damned, slobbering pigs. Something was working against them, something dark. Did Newton have connections out here as well? Or was something even more horrid meddling with them?

But some luck was on their side. The cops were at least ignorant to their presence. Multiple cruisers passed right in front of the bench where they sat—and even some officers had stood right next to them in convenient stores and filling stations, way too close for comfort. But their invisibility would only last for so long.

Mina walked to them with takeout bags. "Figured anything else out yet?"

"Is there anybody in Utah we haven't tried?" Chris sighed, taking a bag. "Maybe we should aim for California."

"It'd be a hell of a lot warmer over there," Mina huffed, having a seat and pulling out a burger from one of the bags and taking a bite. "I hope, at least."

"I don't know," Naomi said. "Do we have enough money for gas?"

"If we stay out here, we're gonna freeze to death," Mina complained with a mouthful of food.

"We could just email them the footage," Chris said, then rolled his eyes. "That is…if Hollywood's receptive to the scoop. They ain't gonna listen to me, though."

"Why?" Naomi asked.

"I'm 'Sullied Sullivan,' remember?" he mocked. "I'm the 'crazy wife-beater,' the 'evil, subhuman misogynist' as far as they're concerned. They won't take my word for anything, with or without a damned video."

"Then Naomi's up," Mina said, then swallowed and wiped her mouth with a napkin. "I mean...you *are* the nanny who got the footage, after all."

"Look." Naomi gritted her teeth. "I don't know about just going all the way to—"

"Well, we gotta do something!" Chris retorted, standing up. "I'm beyond ready to attack this shit head-on! I'm sick of running and so are y'all! We'll either die or go to jail, most likely both. Our only hope now is to take Newton and Evelyn down with us."

"What about Melanie?" Naomi squawked. "The kidnappers might—"

"She's probably already dead, Naomi!"

"Chris, don't say that!"

Mina's phone dinged with a text as the couple argued. She stopped chewing and pulled the device out, checking the screen. Her eyes steadily widened at the message, then she timidly surveyed the streets and the buildings.

"Look, I don't like it any more than you do—that's my little girl," Chris said, trying not to whimper. "I'm all out of hope. I'm sorry I dragged you two into this and...." He glared at Mina. "What the hell's with you?"

"It's him," Mina said, her breath quavering.

"Who?"

Chris snatched the phone from her and read the text:

ANSWER YOUR PHONE AT 12:17 AM.

LOVE, V

Chris squinted at the number. "You sure it's him?"

Mina's phone rang!

All three of them jumped a mile. Chris gawked, the number matching the one from the text message. The clock on the righthand corner of the screen read exactly 12:17 a. m. Immediately, he fumbled with the phone and answered the call.

"Who is this?" Chris snarled.

"Ah," the smooth, gravelly voice replied on the other end. "That's a pity. No one answers their phone with a friendly 'Hello' anymore, do they?"

"Who are you? Where's my little girl?"

"Oh, she's fine," the voice assured with eerie charm. "We actually went sightseeing in the desert the other day, then we had pancakes. Your daughter is quite a sweetheart, with a ravenous sweet tooth to go along with her. In fact...here, let me put you on speaker. There's someone who wants to talk to you."

Chris froze as a brush of static sounded in his ear.

"Here's Daddy," the voice muttered.

"Hi, Daddy!" Melanie's voice chimed.

"Melanie?" Chris choked, almost collapsing on the sidewalk with his knees wobbling.

"What?" Naomi squeaked.

"Shit!" Mina rasped.

"Baby, is it really you?" Chris sobbed.

"Daddy, Mr. Sam showed me how to shoot a gun, and, um, I hit a tin can!"

Chris hesitated, not wanting to alarm his daughter. "Th…that's wonderful, baby—I'm so proud of you!"

"She is quite a sharpshooter," Sam said over the phone. "Sweetie, isn't there something you want to ask Daddy?"

"Yeah!" Melanie said. "Daddy, can you, um, have pancakes and, um, come watch cartoons with us tomorrow?"

"Y-yeah, of course, baby! I'd love to!" Chris said, tears flowing from his eyes. "It's so good to hear your voice! Daddy loves you so much, baby!"

"I love you too, Daddy!" Melanie said, then yawned. "I'm getting sleepy."

"I know, baby, I know," Chris said, wiping his eyes.

"It's way past your bedtime," Sam teased.

"Melanie, let me talk to…let me talk to Mr. Sam. I'll see you tomorrow."

"Okay, Daddy! Night-night!"

"Night-night, baby. Love you."

Another brush of static crackled.

"You're off speaker now," Sam told him.

"What do you want?" Chris demanded. "Money?"

"No. Money does not interest me," Sam said. "I want what Melanie wants: I want you. And I trust you will bring your two lovely accomplices with you?"

"What's he saying?" Mina barked.

Chris waved his hand at her, baring his teeth. "What accomplices?"

"Oh, spare me, Sullivan," Sam said. "I know far more about you three and where you are than what you'd like to think. Don't bother looking for us tonight, lest things get ugly. But you and I have a common enemy. I'll relay the details at our meeting. I can't stay on the line much longer. It's way past my bedtime also."

"Where do you want to meet? What time?"

"There's a delightful little hole-in-the-wall place down the road, about a hundred miles south of here. It's called Sandy's Diner. Say…one o'clock sharp? Little Melanie insisted. You owe her much. I can't wait for the family reunion. How long has it been since you heard her voice, I wonder?"

"Where are you?"

"I'll text you the name and address of the place," Sam suggested. "I'll have to tuck her in pretty soon. And don't bother calling back. I use a random-number generator; it won't work on your end. What do you say, Chris? Would you like to have pancakes with us?"

Chris nodded. "We'll be there."

"I look forward to meeting you," Sam breathed. "Night-night…Daddy."

With that, he hung up. Chris's arm fell at his side, his fingers threatening to crush the phone.

"What did he say?" Naomi blubbered.

Chris said nothing, taking his bag of fast food and stomping back to the SUV in the parking lot. The two women followed him.

"Say something!" Mina protested, grabbing her phone from his hands.

"We're gonna get her," Chris managed to utter.

"Where? When?" Naomi questioned.

"Sandy's Diner," he said as if in a trance, entering the vehicle. "One o'clock."

"Get a pen...and paper!" Naomi snapped. "Is that here? Chris?"

He said nothing more as Mina fished around her purse, then in the car's console, as the two women scurried to write down the name and time on the back of the restaurant's grease-stained receipt. Chris only sat there in the backseat, his head reeling from the phone call. It had been at least a year since he heard Melanie's voice, an eternity for a loving parent.

And this...Sam. Who was he?

What was he really doing to her?

He shut his eyes at Mina and Naomi quibbled up front, gradually seeming like background noise, as they read the new text message and looked up the map on the phone. True to his word, Sam sent the name and address of the diner. He was too tired to rest but too fatigued to stay fully awake. As he sat there, he could still hear Sam's voice echo in his weary mind, groaning and murmuring to him like an undead ghoul roused from its tomb. And if Sam knew where they were, then the feds probably did as well. Just as they had feared, those phone calls to the press must have outed them, blowing Mina's cover, giving away their location.

But something had to give sooner or later.

Hell and highwater were coming straight for them.

It was only a matter of time before all the vermin converged on them.

And no telling what other horrors hunting them down.

XV: In His Talons

Chris exited the driver's side, with Naomi and Mina getting out on the right, staring the lone diner down, built in the middle of nowhere right next to the highway. The one o'clock sun shone overhead through the white wisps of feathery cirrus clouds marbling Utah's vast blue sky above. A few tumbleweeds waltzed aimlessly around them in the road as they heard the many grains of sand and pebbles sprinkle across the asphalt from the vehement gusts, rife with the scent of dead earth. They surveyed the desert wilderness, with the range of snow-crested mountains and weathered monoliths in the distance. Miles of sagebrush, rocks, and a few junipers spanned the plains and rolling nearby hills in all directions. Only four other vehicles sat in the gravel parking lot, one of them being a forest-green SUV, with the oxidized signage looming high over them on a solitary pole.

Sandy's Diner.

This was it.

It truly was a hole in the wall, one of the grungiest places on the planet, resembling something out of a horror movie. The glare of the warm afternoon sun prevented them from seeing the interior of the restaurant from outside through the dusty windows. Its architecture was almost a parody of 1950s nostalgia, with rounded corners of tarnished chrome and a corroded metal Coca-Cola logo all shimmering in the solar rays. To the right, a single glass door sat atop three cement steps, fractured by the elements with a blue and red neon "OPEN" sign flashing.

Beckoning them forth.

Only a psychopath would select such a derelict establishment for a showdown.

"You got your gun?" Naomi asked Mina.

Mina patted her pocket. "Let's do this shit."

"You two wait out here," Chris said.

"Uh-uh! No!" Naomi refused. "We *all* go in, and—"

"If all three of us go in, all three of us might die," Chris told her. "I need you two out here for cover, as a failsafe…in case things go south in there." He looked back at the diner. "He's probably already shot up the place."

"Chris," Naomi said, her lips quivering.

"See if you can lure him out and separate him from Melanie," Mina suggested. "If she's even here. I'll blow his friggin' head off!"

Chris took a few steps to the door. "I got a feeling he's smarter than that, but…yeah." He continued to the glass door. "Stay sharp."

"Come on," Mina said, grabbing Naomi's arm.

Reluctantly, she complied as the two vanished on the SUV's right side, crouching for cover. Chris turned and shook his head at their half-baked plan; he should've brought a gun too…if only he knew where to procure one. He took a deep breath, then steadily released it through his nostrils. With sweaty palms, he opened the door, the bell ringing above his head…then he stepped in.

He had taken the plunge.

"Howdy," a rotund woman said from behind a dingy, cramped counter, grabbing a menu from a shelf. Her nametag read: BETTY.

"Hey," Chris greeted.

"How many?" Betty inquired.

"Actually," Chris said. "I'm…just here to meet a…."

He stopped, feeling a strange presence come over him. Something sinister was here. He turned…and he saw him, dressed in black, wearing leather gloves, sitting a few booths down, his blue eyes locked on to Chris.

Smirking.

Right at him.

His elbows rested on the table, his fingers cradling his chin with a morbid facetiousness. Before him sat a plate of syrup and soggy crumbs where pancakes once lay. Chris observed two other patrons further down, dressed like truckers, conversing about some blue-collar nonsense, then back at the menacing customer. This was him. It had to be.

Sam Conroy himself.

Yet, another plate lay there across from him, the stack of pancakes partially eaten.

With the whipped cream still fully intact.

Melanie wasn't here. If it was one thing he knew about his own flesh and blood, she would have eaten the whipped cream first before even touching the flapjacks or even the syrup. Just how badly had they screwed up? Yet another one of his worst fears had come true.

It was a setup.

And they willfully fell for it.

Chris stepped forward to the man. He glanced out the window at the blue SUV, seeing Naomi and Mina peek over the hood, watching. Waiting. How he wanted to dash out the door, telling the two women to save themselves, save the evidence. But something stopped him, barring the way. Something diabolical was in the air. Literally.

He looked back down at his conniving dark adversary.

"Have a seat, Chris," Sam invited, then he looked at Betty and the obscure cook in the kitchen. "Another order of pancakes for our guest, please?"

"Comin' right up, hun," Betty replied. "This your buddy you were talkin' about?"

"Yes," Sam claimed. "He's running a bit late." He winked up at Chris. "But we won't hold that against him."

Chris squinted down at him, then regarded the unfinished pancakes again.

Who else was here? It damned sure wasn't his daughter.

"Come, sit down, sit down," Sam said. "Join us, won't you? Hope you brought an appetite."

Reluctantly, Chris eased into the booth opposite of his unblinking enemy.

Sam observed the worn décor of the janky diner. "Forgive me. I know this is not the best place to meet...but I have such an...eccentricity for such places. Believe it or not, I care much about small business, struggling against the rapacious franchises of the world, constantly trying to drive the little man to extinction."

"Sounds about right," Chris quipped dryly. "So, we meet at last."

"Indeed."

"You're the big, bad Vulture everyone's been talking about, am I right?"

"Call me Sam," he told him, then pointed at a hideous buzzard eating a maggot-ridden armadillo carcass outside. "*There's* your vulture right out there, Sullivan." His smirk faded as he became strangely sober. He knotted his fingers together and lowered his elbows, resting his forearms around his plate. "You know...they get such a bad rap for...being unclean, eating dead things. Scavengers. Scum. But even *they* have a significant function in nature: they cleanse the world of decomposition, taking the necrotic flesh upon themselves so that other life will not be harmed by its languishing taint and miasma. They're cleaners, unsung heroes, eradicating the filth of the world, one useless body at a time."

Chris squinted at him.

"You see, the vultures are raptors," Sam went on, twiddling his thumbs. "Just like eagles, hawks, falcons." He cocked his head. "Did you know that eagles eat carcasses as well?"

"I'm aware."

"Good." Sam nodded. "I thought you might. You're from Mississippi, after all. There are all sorts of dead things in that swamp. You are not a stranger to it. So much death, decay. Roadkill. Very gothic atmosphere. Plenty of vultures over there as well...along with murders of crows, maybe a few eagles, all feasting upon cadavers daily." He squinted out the window. "For wherever the carcass is, there the eagles will be gathered together." He glanced back at Chris. "You know what that's from?"

"The Bible."

"Exactly." Sam leaned in. "Do you know what that means?"

"Where is my daughter?"

"Indulge me...and you'll see her."

Chris glared. "What do *you* claim it means?"

"It's a reference to the Rapture of the Church," Sam said. "The final judgment. The Apocalypse. You see...Jesus had this peculiar knack for using such...macabre imagery and language to convey great truth, to get people's attention. Such a great sense of humor God has. He, the living God...described himself...as a carcass, the One Who died on the cross and rose on the third day to save the world...and ascended. But He didn't rot like a carcass. He did not know corruption." His smirk returned. "They say He's coming again, Chris...and that His chosen will be caught up in the air with Him, the eagles...gathering with Him, the Body still bearing the wounds from the crucifixion." He cocked his head to the other shoulder. "Do you believe that, Chris?"

"I didn't come here to be preached to by anyone!" Chris growled, slamming his hands on the table. "Especially by some psycho shit-eater like you, you hear me?

Sam tittered his deranged laugh deep in his throat with lips closed.

"You have, like, the shittiest laugh in the world," Chris taunted flatly. "Seriously, it sounds like you have a sick hyena with a dying seagull in its mouth, all lodged in your throat, that weird…smoker's voice of yours. What'd you do, eat cigarettes for the past fifty years?"

"I concede that my laugh is not the best in the world." Sam grinned. "And…speaking of eagles, I don't know if you've noticed, but…America has made their national animal…an eagle, an endangered species. How quaint…and ironic." His cheer vanished. "And all other countries surround us like ravenous wolves. America will not last. We like to think that the United States is an eternal nation, that it will always be. But that's what the Ancient Egyptians thought about their dynasties of yore and the Romans about their precious empire. The Babylonians. The Medo-Persians. The Ancient Greeks. They, too, were once the world superpowers. But their end finally came. This country *will* follow suit, along with the rest of the world, sooner or later. Society is a manmade illusion, a cheap, translucent veneer hopelessly unable to conceal the rot that we call 'politics' slowly sundering civilization to pieces. It is excruciatingly obvious. Everything is slowly being vivisected by corrupt governments and totalitarian oligarchies, those fat cats, all orchestrated by its…carcass-eating eagles, gorging themselves on the cadavers of other nations." He squinted. "Or are those vultures in Washington D. C. as well?"

"Look, I've indulged your creepy ass long enough!" Chris snapped. "You tell me where my daughter is right now, or—!"

"Daddy!" a little girl's voice bounded towards him.

Chris turned around as Melanie ran from the bathroom and jumped into his lap. He and his daughter embraced as Sam leaned back, smirking again.

"Oh, baby!" Chris whimpered with a wry smile. "It is really you?"

"Daddy, Daddy!" Melanie said. "This is Mr. Sam. He's a superhero. He knows magic. I told him about how you, um, smooshed the tarantula that one time."

"Tarantula?" Chris asked.

"She said you and your family went camping in Arizona once," Sam reminded.

"Oh, yeah…that nasty thing," Chris admitted, recalling its pale guts on the sleeping bag. He looked at her pancakes. "You didn't finish your pancakes—you didn't even touch the whipped cream. That's your favorite part."

"Mr. Sam says it's always good to save the best for last, Daddy," Melanie replied.

"That's right," Sam said. "It's always good to save the best for last."

"Who are you working for?" Chris questioned him.

"I work alone, Chris," the assassin claimed. "But I'm a sweetheart compared to what's hunting you all out here."

"I know the cops are after us," Chris groaned. "And Newton, maybe."

"No," Sam said solemnly. "There's more. They're an ungodly faction."

Chris raised an eyebrow.

"You and the ladies want to stay alive, I'm sure?"

"Daddy, Mr. Sam says that more bad guys are coming," Melanie squeaked. "He says we need to go to his house so that we'll be safe while he fights 'em."

"Baby, Mr. Sam doesn't know everything," Chris told her. "In fact, I think we need to tell Mr. Sam 'Bye-bye.'"

"No! I wanna go watch cartoons!" Melanie whined.

"We'll watch cartoons somewhere else, okay?" Chris suggested. "I promise."

"Actually, I insist," Sam said. "I'll make it worth your while…unless you want to risk being caught *with* Melanie and making it seem like *you're* the kidnapper, which the FBI and the media are already predisposed to believing. And if *I* can find you out here, what makes you think others can't? I assure you: there are others after your daughter, and as I said: I'm a sweetheart compared to them. I don't think you want to roll those dice." He glanced at Betty and the cook, talking to someone on the phone in the kitchen, eyeing the three. "Better make your decision fast, though. It seems our meeting has attracted some unwarranted attention." He looked back at Chris with a stone poker face. "Your move, Sullivan. What will it be?"

"Please, Daddy?" Melanie begged with her puppy-dog brown eyes. "Pretty, pretty please?"

Chris was beside himself. He looked back at Betty, making out some of the words. It did sound like a 911 call. She and the cook were selling them out. He looked back at Naomi and Mina, now standing up, fully visible, with Mina fingering her .357 magnum in her pocket, ready to shoot to kill. Sam looked at his watch, then at the two women outside. Chris turned back at his adversary.

They were pinned, whether Conroy was bluffing or not.

But it would be just his luck if something else were, in fact, stalking them.

"Where's your safehouse?" Chris queried.

"I'll show you," Sam said, standing up and pulling a hundred dollar bill out of his wallet and leaving it on the table. "But we take *my* vehicle. I'm invisible to the feds. You're not." He strode to the front and gestured him to go first. "Come with?"

Chris stood up as Melanie raised her arms up. He picked her up, cradling her. She was getting heavier. She was growing. And he was missing it all. A year of her life was gone, and he wasn't a single part of it. How it cut him to his heart! Grudgingly, he walked out of the diner, with Sam following them to the two women.

"Freeze!" Mina yelled, drawing her revolver.

"Mina, no!" Naomi shouted, pulling her back.

Melanie hid her face, trembling, as Chris glared at the female gunslinger. Mina slowly lowered her weapon, still gripping it tightly in both hands.

"Ladies," Sam greeted, nodding at them.

Naomi spit at the ground at Sam's feet. She was about to explode.

"Such lovely birds," Sam jested. He pulled out a pair of aviator sunglasses from a pocket in his black coat and slipped them on, then turned to Chris. "I'm so jealous of you, Chris." He nodded at his green SUV. "Shall we, then?"

"What?" Mina snapped.

"We do it his way," Chris told her, then winked at her. "Leave the car here." He turned to Naomi, putting Melanie down. "Get the evidence. Load up any supplies we have left."

"Have you lost your mind?" Naomi growled at him.

"Y-you know what? Yes. Yes, I have," Chris sniped, pointing his finger at them. "Don't argue with me. Just...just don't."

"Ugh!" Naomi moaned. "What the fu—?"

"Naomi!" Melanie cheered, hugging her nanny.

"Hey, baby!" Naomi said, kneeling down and returning the affection. "Oh, I missed you so much! I was so worried!"

"I missed you too!" Melanie giggled. "Will you come watch cartoons with us?"

Naomi glanced at Chris as Sam unlocked the green SUV and hopping in, starting the engine. Her boyfriend only stared at her.

"I...I guess so," Naomi replied sheepishly. "Yes, I'd love to."

"Yay!" Melanie threw her arms up in the air.

Mina approached Chris. "What the hell are you doing? We're supposed to kill this bastard, not lick his asshole! What, you got Stockholm's syndrome *that* quick on us?"

"I have a plan," Chris claimed, looking at Sam, pulling up next to them. "I think there's something else going on here. We need to find out what. We turn in him, we expose Newton and Evelyn, and clear our names, all at once. Okay?"

"You better be right about this, Chris Sullivan," Mina hissed, still holding the handgun.

"Don't do anything to alarm my daughter," Chris retorted.

"She's a big girl," Mina quipped coldly. "She's only been joyriding with a damned serial killer for several days now!" She stomped to Sam's vehicle and opened the front passenger's side door, lurching in. "I think she can handle it...and so can I."

"Get in," Sam commanded the others, peering down the road ahead of them.

Naomi scoffed, then retrieved her backpack from Mina's SUV and placed it in the very back of Sam's car. Then she ushered Melanie into the middle of the backseat, putting her seatbelt on, then she entered on the driver's side, with Chris lumbering in on the right. Sam drove off from the diner's parking lot and down the road towards the winding mountain pass before them, the way populated with thick evergreens and dead trees along steep cliffs and looming rocks, blotting out most of the afternoon sunlight. He had gotten his Melanie back at last, his lively light.

For now.

Yet the reunion was bittersweet.

They all might as well had piled into a hearse.

Driven by a madman, snagged by this infernal creature's talons.

With something far darker at work.

They arrived hours later at dusk in a hilly area veiled by pines and boulders, where a small log cabin and a toolshed sat nestled in the cramped valley. Old snow still infested parts of the ground and some of the tree boughs where the sun could not penetrate earlier. A silver pickup truck was hidden behind the building, covered with sticks, slush, and leaves; it looked as if it hadn't been driven for at least a few weeks. The black outlines of the frost-dusted trees seemed to menace them outside as the wind soughed through the rustling needles as if the woods were alive and hissing at them to depart from their dismal presence.

Such a mysterious and disturbing place, with a pretense of calm and comfort.

A fitting reflection of Sam Conroy.

Inside, the one-story cabin was cozy, rustic, and petite: a two-bedroom, one-bath, all wafting with gamey scents from animal pelts, gunmetal...and a disconcerting musty odor. It was glaringly evident that the home belonged to an obscure couple, to which the Vulture did not divulge on the whereabouts. No one dared prod him about them either, lest their remains be buried just outside in a shallow grave. In the kitchen, Sam prepared for each of them filet mignon with scalloped potatoes and steamed broccoli, having his guests sit at the round dining room table with a chandelier of deer antlers above them. Chris insisted that their host sample the entrées himself first, to which Sam politely obliged. Despite being proven that the steaks and sides were safe to ingest, the two women were still reluctant to eat.

But all three of them were famished and sick of junk food.

Sam had Melanie figured out: chicken nuggets and macaroni and cheese. Yet he and Chris both encouraged her to take some "dinosaur food" as well; only then would she be allowed a thick piece of Sam's delectable devil's food cake. As they ate, Sam had walked outside to the SUV to do something; he was gone for several minutes, possibly burying another body nearby. Yet they were too terrified to make a break for it and jeopardize Melanie's safety, lest the killer have henchmen waiting to ambush them in the woods. After dinner, Naomi agreed to watch a DVD of vintage *Tom and Jerry* episodes with the five-year-old in the living room. Chris told his daughter that the grown-ups needed to discuss some things, then he would join them on the couch that was adorned with quilts. After Sam cleared the table, he proceeded to disassemble his 9mm and clean it, having his tools and oil near him.

"Over the years," Sam said, pensively scrubbing the barrel of his pistol, "I do believe I've manifested…as a gourmet of a certain variety. Life and death have…seasoned me as I gather and reap, harvesting, amassing myself into such an exquisite banquet that both the pure and the evil can resist me no longer." He peeked through the barrel, aiming up at the light fixture. "But your daughter is another story entirely."

"How poetic," Mina mocked. "Did you write that all by yourself?"

"No, actually," Sam admitted.

He eyed her, placing the weapon down, then he glanced at her as she pulled her revolver back out, resting it on the table.

He smirked. "That's a .357 magnum, isn't it?"

"What of it?" she griped.

Sam said nothing, then opened a nearby drawer from the counter and produced a box of bullets. "I once had one, but I had to throw it in a river." He carefully passed her the box of ammunition. "It's all I have left. You'll be needing it more than I will…especially for what's coming."

Mina squinted at him, opening the box, seeing only four rounds rolling within the carton.

"*What's* coming?" Chris demanded.

Sam looked at him. "Ever heard of the *Abendstern*, Sullivan?"

"No."

"It is German for 'evening star.'" He gazed out the window to his right, pointing at a distant, prominent celestial body through the trees. "See there? It shines upon us tonight." He resumed swabbing his firearm. "To make a long story short, I was once in the Special Forces. I grew rather disillusioned with it very quickly. Then I became involved with some rather…unsavory characters, some…ragtag band of mercenaries, deserters, junkies, opium addicts, dabbling in soothsaying, witchcraft, things of that sort. We made…human sacrifices, according to our leader's whims, to bring about the end of the world, supposedly to 'coax the darkness out of its dwellings,' trying to open portals to hell." He glanced at Chris. "Have you ever heard of Cheesman Park? Skinwalker Ranch?" He squinted. "Torino?"

"No—I don't…I don't buy any of this," Mina groaned, loading one of the magnum bullets into her revolver's cylinder magazine. "All those damned Ghostbuster wannabes and their nonsense."

"It *does* seem kinda random for you to kill these people along the West Coast…and now Colorado." Chris turned to him. "And then to just kidnap my little girl out of the blue."

"Who said it was random?" Sam asked, placing the 9mm back down, raising his right sleeve up. "I have my own reasons for killing."

Chris almost leapt out of his chair as he stared at the tattoo around Sam's wrist.

Cedar berries. Just like his.

Sam rolled up his other sleeve, revealing a tribal design of black barbs along his radius and ulna bones…identical to Chris's markings.

"We are one and the same, you and I," Sam claimed. "Two and one."

"No," Chris said, gawking in horror. "I'm not you."

"Wait, what?" Mina snapped.

"We are a blur between two realities," Sam told him. "Converging."

"Chris, what does he mean?" Mina panicked. "How is that even—?"

"I'm not you," Chris muttered. "I'm not you…."

"I am your shadow," Sam said. "You are my light."

Mina's jaw dropped, eyeing the two. "What's going on?"

Chris wanted to vomit. Two and one? Chills wracked his flesh as his ears rang, sensing something like a glacial, intangible hand grasping his forehead, trying to force him to the floor. His head felt as if coming apart. Was he insane? Had he been living a delusion, tuning out a past he only thought happened? Had he fabricated his memories to escape the trauma of bygone things he had committed? A blurry montage of gory scenes and cacophonous voices raged in his mind, a tempest of nightmares. Had he suppressed these things in the recesses of his brain? Dissociating from reality? All this time?

Had he invented Sam Conroy, as a figment of his imagination?

Or had Sam Conroy invented Chris Sullivan…as an alter ego, a scorned family man? But how could they be in two places at once?

Or were they?

A blur between realities? A light casting a shadow? What was this dark, surreal psychosis, this spirit of confusion that had seized him? What the hell was this? How could this be? It made no sense!

Sam's smirk became a grin as he uttered his muffled hyena laugh in his throat.

"Chris?" Mina said, catching him. "Chris!"

Chris's breathing quickened as he staggered up. "One person can't be in two places at once!"

Sam tilted his head to one side. "Can't they?"

Chris glowered at Sam. Yet, the more he stared at Sam, the more he resembled…an older version of Chris. But the eyes. How?

"You've had way too much time on your hands," Sam said, growing sober again, rolling his sleeves back down. "Pfeiffer was very bad to you and me. And Bianca. And Evelyn. And so many others on your list of—"

"Shut up!" Chris snapped.

"Shh," Sam hushed. "You'll wake Melanie."

Chris eyed the two in the living room. Naomi stared at him with concerned eyes as the five-year-old's head lay on a pillow on her lap, fast asleep. He shook his head, feeling so sluggish. Was this real? Or was Sam gaslighting him? But if it was nothing more than that, why couldn't he resist him? Chris knew better than to fall for a sociopath's tricks.

Maybe the filet mignon *was* drugged.

But why wasn't anyone else succumbing?

What was this ghastly power the Vulture had on him? What was he? Man? Hallucination? Or something far worse?

The sensation finally released him. He gagged and stumbled on his knees, wheezing heavily, with one elbow propped on the table. Mina helped him back into his chair.

"Water," Chris gasped. "Water."

Mina snatched a glass from the cupboard and poured some from the faucet, then she handed it to Chris's wobbling hand. He gulped it down and almost flung it down on the table, panting.

Mina glared at Sam. "What did you do to him? What…what are you?"

"Do you see now just what kind of darkness has been awakened here?" Sam claimed, becoming serious. "You cannot best this foe on your own, Chris Sullivan."

Chris steadily recovered from the malefic trance. He was sweating…and it had grown cold in the cabin. He braced himself on the table and beheld the enigma that was Sam Conroy.

"Why do they…need Melanie?" Chris slurred.

"My leader, Sebastian, was seeking out a new spirit to invoke," Sam explained. "He scried in many ways, including meddling with a Ouija board. He claimed he had a vision of a phoenix, then he and all of us 'called upon the spirits' to learn its name, yet it only gave us three consonants of a child: MLN. Either that or Sebastian didn't feel like furthering the hoax by giving us vowels."

Chris's eyes widened, recalling his nightmares of the ghost bird.

"You…defected…from this group, this cult?" Mina asked.

"Yes," Sam confessed.

"Why?" Chris interrogated.

Sam hesitated, then sighed, putting his pistol back together. "I grew…bored with it."

"You lying," Mina said.

"Very well." Sam eyed her sternly. "You want the truth? I *am* a murderous, bloodthirsty wretch. That is no mystery. I will not pretend that I am a saint, no, no. I am a hunter, a survivor, a rogue carnifex pruning society of those just as vile as I am…and those even worse. I detest competition. But I have a rule I abide by: I do not harm or kill women unless they are armed and trying to kill me, and I never harm or kill children. One finds no sport in targeting the prancing does and fawns of this wilderness we call civilization. Only the bucks are worthy of being trophies. I made my way to Colorado…hunting my adversaries." He turned to Chris. "Then I discovered you here. The shadow found its light. I've been watching you for quite some time now, studying you, learning your daily routines, discerning when the right opportunities would present themselves. I researched your case, hacking into your phones and computers, everything: birthdates, browsing history, social security numbers, bank statements, all of it. Melanie, five years of age, was born on the 21st of the fifth month of the year. They believe that she has 'ripened' and is bearing the fully-fledged soul of their so-called 'phoenix.' I intervened in Denver, during a riot the *Abendstern* instigated." He squinted. "Believe it or not, she willfully went with me out here, wanting to learn to be a 'superhero,' when I am the farthest thing from. But in truth, she already *is* a superhero."

"How so?" Chris inquired.

Sam stared at him, unblinkingly. "She testified on your behalf. She saved your life." He stood up. "I added you on my list to kill, along with Pfeiffer and others. I was coming to execute you as well, extinguish you, to be free, untethered. You are my ball-and-chain."

"Well, ain't that a drag?" Chris smarted.

"But your daughter told of your innocence and your love…and how ruthless her mother is to her." He looked down at himself. "If something is not done soon, Melanie will suffer a similar fate. She is ill, Sullivan. She needs your love, and also Naomi's affection, now more than ever."

Chris and Mina averted their eyes, rendered speechless.

"Because of your little girl, though," Sam went on, "I have decided to spare you. For now. You owe Melanie your life." He cocked his head again. "Take good care of her."

Chris sighed. "I would if the system didn't think me the kidnapper…along with all the other shit that's been—"

"I will take the blame, Chris," Sam offered. "I *am* the kidnapper, after all." He squinted. "I am your shadow."

"Will you stop saying weird shit like that?" Chris barked.

"How can we trust you?" Mina scrutinized.

Sam pointed at the box of bullets. "I trust *you* with that ammunition I gave you. I trust that you will not shoot me with it. Can you not grant me the same courtesy? If I had wanted you dead, none of us would be having this conversation right now. I would have fished you out long ago." He glanced at the eagle ring on his bare finger, then peered out the window. "We are in the eye of the storm now, caught in its brief, superficial calm. The game has grown old and is reaching its end…and our opponents are about to make their final move. We must be ready."

"Where are they?" Chris questioned.

"I'm ashamed to say I don't know." Sam looked back at him, smirking again. He finished reassembling his pistol, then loaded and cocked it. "It's like I told Melanie: we must be like the tarantula in the desert, vigilant and patient, waiting in our dark hole of spun silk…and let the spineless vermin come to us."

The lights flickered out.

"Get down!" Sam rasped.

Chris and Mina did so.

"What happened?" Naomi called out.

"Get Melanie in the bedroom!" Chris shouted.

Boom!

177

The green SUV detonated outside, shattering the window. They shielded themselves from flaming debris, igniting the carpet and some of the curtains. Machinegun fire blared from the trees, puncturing the walls and obliterating the doorknob.

"Daddy!" Melanie cried.

Someone kicked the door down, then a bulky masked man in black tactical gear breached the living room, standing like a giant, snarling something in German through the radio clipped to his bulletproof vest. Sam aimed and fired at the man's head, killing him, then two more vaulted through the windows. Mina discharged a few bullets at the arms of one man, causing him to stumble, then he kicked her in the face. Mina yelped, tumbling to the floor, incapacitated. Chris charged him, bashing him unconscious with a frying pan, then he took his weapon: an MP5.

"*Finde das Mädchen!*" one of the German mercenaries barked outside. "*Schnell! Schnell!*"

"Naomi!" Chris yelled, firing out through the window at the veiled soldiers hiding amongst the trees, striking two of them down.

Sam slinked into the living room as the cabin steadily combusted more and more. He gunned down two more of the renegades. The smoke was thickening as the flames cast their harsh red and orange glare on the consumed furniture. Naomi screamed, then a soldier punched her, hauling a wailing Melanie out the door.

"Daddy!" Melanie sobbed.

"Melanie!" Chris blared as a soldier pistol-whipped him from behind.

He blacked out and fell to the floor as three masked assassins ambushed Sam at gunpoint.

"Hello again, Sam," one of the soldiers sneered in a Slavic accent. "It's been too long."

Sam smirked up at him. "Hello…Hector."

The blaze roared around them, lapping to the ceiling as the house bristled like a furnace. Naomi groaned on the floor and shook awake, watching Sam drop his 9mm and haul Chris's body out the door.

"Hands behind your head, comrade," Hector, the Slavic leader soldier, ordered. "Now!"

Reluctantly, Sam complied as another soldier handcuffed him.

Naomi lay still on the floor, glancing at the mercenaries.

Hector pointed his AR-15 out to the door. "*Raus! Schnell!*"

Headlights appeared through the trees as two pickup trucks revved into the driveway. They exited with their two prisoners, leaving the cabin to the inferno. Naomi coughed and crawled to the kitchen, snatching the revolver and the bullets from the table, pocketing them. She shambled up onto one knee, then propped Mina up.

"C'mon, girl—don't die on me!" Naomi said, slapping her face.

"*Sichere das Mädchen!*" Hector commanded. "*Fahrt nach Torino! Sich beeilen!*"

"Fucking bastards," Naomi rasped as the trucks sped away.

Mina coughed awake, wheezing. "What happened?"

"We gotta get outta here!" Naomi said, hoisting her up. "Move!"

Both of them stood up and hobbled out the front door, then Naomi gawked at the conflagrated SUV. Utter horror crept upon her face.

"Shit!" Naomi squawked. "No! The evidence!"

"What?" Mina croaked.

"My laptop was in there!" She faced the driveway. "Damn you!"

"C'mon, we'll take his spare!" Mina said, staggering to the silver pickup behind the toolshed.

Both women jogged to the truck, then Naomi smashed the front window, unlocking the vehicle as Mina hopped into the other side, dizzy. Naomi reached up at the vizor and got the truck keys, then cranked the sputtering engine. She looked over at Mina, still woozy, her face swollen from the boot to the face.

"You okay?" Naomi asked.

"I'm fine—just…drive before we lose 'em," Mina sputtered. "Where's my gun?"

"I got it," Naomi said. "Just stay with me." She looked at a laptop and other equipment in the back of the cab. "The hell's all this shit behind here? A rifle?"

"What?" Mina coughed, then grabbed the laptop from the backseat and opened it. "Look, just drive. Let's go!"

Naomi gunned the engine down the driveway as Mina examined the device. The screen came on with the password already typed in. Mina hit the "return" key as a map showed a red dot traveling just before them.

"He bugged her," Mina said.

"Bugged who?" Naomi asked.

"Sam. He bugged Melanie somehow," Mina replied. "As a failsafe, I guess."

"No," Naomi's voice grated. "I heard what the little shit said in the kitchen." She scowled at Mina. "About the tarantula?"

Mina eyed her.

"He used her as bait to draw out those…Nazis or whatever the hell they are." Naomi clenched her teeth. "This whole thing was a setup. We walked right into his trap."

"Yeah, well the other shitheads are toying with us still," Mina griped. "It's like Sam said: we're just weak, little 'does,' remember? We're the womenfolk. We're not 'sporting enough' to kill. Did you hear him say that?"

"Trust me, we'll be 'sporting enough' for them in a few minutes," Naomi growled, pressing harder on the accelerator. "They wanna play like that? We'll play like that. This 'doe' is packing heat." She looked at the laptop. "I hope we don't lose reception out here."

"I don't think so," Mina said. "This thing has to be run by satellite. They're heading south."

"Everything's heading south," Naomi grumbled as she entered the highway, the tires peeling on the cracked asphalt.

Mina spotted a folder on the screen. She squinted at its title and opened it. Then her eyes widened.

"Uh…Naomi?"

"Not now—look, where…where're they headed now?"

Mina sighed. "Still south. Don't let them see us."

Naomi tensed her face more. "Bit late for that."

Like a bat out of hell, she pursued the cultists from afar as Mina continued pilfering through Sam Conroy's computer, disconcerted and awestruck at the copious cache of data the assassin had collected. Naomi paid her no mind, glowering so hard at the road, she felt able to carve the very pavement to shreds with nothing but her razor-sharp gaze.

She already lost Aeriel. She bitterly refused to lose another baby, especially to these depraved scumbags. She was determined to pry Melanie and Chris both out of their filthy talons.

Even if it killed her.

XVI: Beasts of the Feast

Theo Nash and Rick Wellborn were parked in their black SUV with the engine running on a dirt road a few miles away from the ghost town of Torino, the weak, placid starlight mocking them above. The frigid winds tore around them, lashing through the desert for the past hour, gasping and moaning at them like undead voices blowing in their ears. Yet now…the gusts had all but died down, producing even more unease for the two federal agents. They were both clad in bulletproof vests, standing by for orders from Vince Redman and a squad of FBI officers and military personnel in Humvees and even two Apache helicopters a few miles away, itching to move out. Wellborn had stepped outside and was rummaging in the back, checking the duffel bag of cash. Nash sat in the driver's seat talking with Bianca on a satellite phone as he impatiently looked at his watch, reading 11:52 p. m. It was almost time to make the drop…and the rescue.

Everything seemed darker than normal.

And the darkness seemed…alive.

"Look, everything's gonna be fine," Nash assured. "We're gonna get Melanie. We're gonna get these pricks. Okay?" He gazed out the windshield. "It's nothing we haven't dealt with before."

"I just have this gut-wrenching feeling about this, Theo," Bianca said on the other line. "There is something…truly abominable about Sam Conroy—I don't even think he's human. And these terrorists he's associated with I don't…th-there's something horribly wrong about all of it, something we missed. Something…evil. Please be careful."

"Always," Nash replied.

A few seconds of awkward silence went by.

"That's not the *only* reason why you called," Nash said. "Is it?"

Bianca let out a long sigh. "Am I not allowed to care about someone?"

"Well, it's just the fact that you've called three times today," Nash said, smirking. "Is there something you wanna tell me?"

"We can't just…."

"Can't what?"

"Look, just try not to die—we'll talk later! I have to go," Bianca snapped.

"Alright," Nash told her. "You be careful, too."

"Goodnight, Theo."

"Goodnight," Nash said, then hung up and put the satellite phone away. He looked at his partner. "What are you doing back there, mining for gold?"

"Just…double-checking everything, man," Wellborn said, zipping up the duffel bag, then slammed the back passenger's side door. Then he hopped back in the front. "Everything's in order." He looked at Nash. "Was that the hot prosecutor chick again?"

"Yeah, she's, uh…she's a squirrely broad," Nash scoffed. "It always seems like it's the hot ones who are crazy…high-maintenance. Unappeasable.

They're told they're pretty all throughout their lives and think they can...I don't know."

"Like Laura?" Wellborn said, flashing a grin.

"Don't...don't even get me started on her."

Wellborn laughed.

"She left me a couple of days ago," Nash confessed. "Just picked up and...flew the coop."

Wellborn's smile faded. "Damn. She got divorce papers?"

"Not yet," Nash said, eyeing his wedding band. "'Course, I might die to-night anyway, so what does it matter?"

"Hey, man, don't say that," Wellborn encouraged. "Everything's gonna be okay. I got your back...you got mine," he turned and looked out the win-dow. "And I don't know what the hell happened to Redman. It's almost time."

The ham radio garbled with Redman's voice.

"Nash. Wellborn. You there, over?"

Nash took the speaker. "Nash here. Package is ready."

"My watch has 11:56. Move out."

Nash paused, looking at the dirt road in the headlights, the bulbs some-how struggling to illuminate the perilous way, as if strangled by the darkness itself.

"Do you copy, over?"

"Copy that, Red," Nash replied. "Moving into position. Over and out." He clipped the speaker back on the radio and put the vehicle into gear. "Here's goes some shit."

They drove down the gravel road, the tires juddering beneath the chunks of igneous rocks. Patches of snow still lay beneath the few lone juniper trees as the path wound through hills, the dead sagebrush jutting from the ground like deformed skeletal hands. Outside, the wind picked up again, and Nash could have sworn the brisk air was moaning at him like a mass of ghosts. His heart pounded in his chest as the sunbaked remains of the ghost town came into view.

Then he saw it: a faint orange glow from a window on the far west side of town.

"There," Wellborn pointed. "See the trucks?"

Nash squinted, spotting the vehicles gleaming in the dim light. "Yeah. That's them."

"Park by that old water tower," Wellborn suggested.

Nash raised an eyebrow at him. "You sure?"

Before Wellborn could answer, a team of masked mercenaries appeared, all in black tactical attire and armed with M-16s and AK-47s, aiming and shouting at them.

"Halt! Halt!" one of them yelled.

Nash braked, then parked, cutting the engine off. The terrorists sur-rounded the vehicle.

"*Raus*! *Schnell*!" another soldier barked.

"Show hands!" a third ordered. "Now!"

"Nazi sons of bitches," Nash grumbled, complying.

With hands raised, they both eased out of the car.

"Search them!" one commanded.

They frisked the two agents, confiscating their weapons.

"Hands on your head!" a soldier said. "Come! *Schnell*!"

"Ulrich!" another said, holding the duffel bag, revealing the cash.

Ulrich examined the contents and nodded, then gestured Nash to the storehouse.

Nash eyed Wellborn's Glock. "Why didn't they take yours?"

"Because they can trust me," Wellborn said, drawing his pistol.

Nash chuckled mordantly. "Oh, you gotta be shittin' me."

"Move!" Wellborn snapped. "*Schnell*!"

"Yeah, yeah, *schnell* to you, too," Nash bickered as they kicked him forward into the storehouse.

They kicked him through an open doorway as he stumbled and landed face-first on the cement floor…right next to a large pentagram and strange runes painted with blood and adorned with an array of human bones and skulls brown with decay; numerous vertebrae coiled around the outer circle with ribs and mummified knuckles segmenting the diabolic star's five points. Nearby, a rack of ceremonial bastard swords and flame-bladed daggers hung; their steel edges sharpened so excessively that they looked as if they were able to slice the very wind in twain. An assortment of lit candles permeated the dark building; their white wax already melted and caking the boxes of explosives while illuminating the other terrorists' faces with infernal light…including Terry Nelson and his two deputies, Rita Carlson and Harry Brown.

"Good to see you again, agent," Nelson taunted, his accent drastically different.

"Why am I not surprised?" Nash griped.

"I always considered you cops to be Nazis," a familiar voice said to his right. "But this is fucking ridiculous."

"Many of us have to learn the hard way," a smooth, gravelly voice told him.

Nash turned to his right. "Sullivan? Conroy?"

Both men lay on their stomachs, their faces also to the floor.

Sam smirked at Nash. "I hear tell you brought your friends to the big bash tonight. They're running a little behind, though."

"Says who?" Nash quipped.

"Says me, Theodore," a Slavic male accent rolled from a dark corner. "So glad you could join us on this momentous night."

Nash looked up as a looming figure in a black trench coat strode to them from behind a stack of old crates of dynamite. The grim candlelight illuminated his smiling face.

"Newton?" Nash coughed.

"Yes," he said. "That is what they called me. But alas, Newton Malcolm is a lie…along with the rest of that sick, pitiful charade you call society. Many know me as the *Sturmvogel*." He squinted at the cop. "But you may call me Hector. Did you like my American accent? Good, ya? Those sweaters were getting so very itchy."

"Yeah, well…I think the trench coats went out of style a good while back," Nash sneered. "Sure you're not Dracula?"

"I'll call you a shit-headed pedophile!" Chris snapped, rising up. "Where's my daughter?"

"Patience, Christopher," Hector said, smashing him back down with his boot. "She is not yet ready to take center stage." He pointed at a crude slab of broken cement and rebar in the middle of the pentagram, carved with more hideous markings. "She is a star tonight. She will become so much more." He cocked his head. "You…on the other hand, are nothing. You Americans are always so amusing. So pathetic. But your ex-wife made for such a good fuck toy…when she was not bitching. Such a warm and juicy pussy she has down there. So tight. I was far more of a man to her than what you ever were. If only I had more time, I could tame that shrew; I almost had her broken," he smirked down at Sam, "had not someone interfered with the great work."

"Bold choice to put all these candles around boxes of dynamite," Nash smarted.

"Oh, we're putting on quite a show for you tonight," Hector taunted. "I hope you like big fireworks. We have plenty for everyone."

"How would you like your meat cooked, Theo?" Sam quipped back, surveying the incendiary materials. "I tend to be a medium-rare man myself."

"Fucking psychos," Nash growled, gritting his teeth at him.

Sam only rolled his creepy signature hyena laugh deep in his throat at the agent.

"Tell me something, Hector: do you miss your daddy beating you?" Sam provoked. "Was I not good to you by killing him? You have yet to escape his shadow, don't you?"

"Speak for yourself, you shade!" Hector scorned. "We should never have conjured you!"

Chris gawked at Sam. "Conjured?"

"Samuel died a long time ago," Hector claimed. "Another abides within his flesh, a new kind of super-soldier, at least…he was." He squinted at Sam. "But the ritual had…unwarranted consequences. When we brought him back from the brink, we…opened a door. The two realities blurred. Apparently, there's a whole other dimension to explore, something we wish to further tonight."

"You are not prepared to witness the other side as I have," Sam said.

Hector frowned and paced around the ring of glyphs and candles. "I'm disappointed in you, Samuel. You have lost your edge." He twirled around to him. "I was expecting so much more from our good comrade. But the years have not been kind to you, it seems. You have grown soft…and flaccid." He gestured at the soldiers. "Granted, you were once a respectable warrior. I revered you. After what you've done to our brothers and sisters, I've had to reorganize us, scraping the bottom of the barrel, only to procure the last vestiges of the Third Reich. But a new age is dawning. It begins tonight. We have tapped into the leylines throughout the years, awakening and flushing out the *dunkelheit* in various regions in the world where it can be exposed and destroyed in the blessed light of the *Abendstern*. Tonight, we will release the soul of the Phoenix, and he will ignite the pathways. The door will be opened. The end will wash away the ignorance and corruption from the earth. And all will be reborn, purified."

"You know what? Fuck it," Chris sputtered. "Explain to me, precisely, what my little girl has to do with this imaginary 'Phoenix' of yours." He winked at Nash. "Tell us about this 'great work.' You've got my curiosity up now. You owe us *that* much. Why rush? We have time, don't we?"

"Yeah," Nash agreed, getting the hint. "I'd like to know, too."

"Well, Hector?" Sam asked. "Won't you enlighten us?"

"Gladly," Hector went on, then snapped his fingers. "*Wasser.*"

Carlson passed him a water bottle.

"*Danke,*" Hector thanked her, taking a swig, then he cleared his throat. "Gives the cavalry time to come, ya? I can't wait to see their faces when we surprise them with their 'party favors.'" He smirked again, setting the water down on a nearby box. "The beasts are making their way to the feast. You're in for quite a show. It's going to be spectacular."

Nash's eyes bulged. If Newton, Wellborn, Nelson, Carlson, and Brown had been moles all this time…how many more were there?

"The Phoenix," Chris demanded with clenched teeth.

He glanced at Nash, then at the duffel bag, struggling to hatch an escape plan.

There had to be a way out of this. Naomi and Mina were running into another trap.

And no telling who else.

"Yes. You're so eager to learn, aren't you, Christopher? I'll tell you." Hector clasped his gloved hands together. "In so many words, it goes a little something like this. Years ago, my father, Sebastian, had a vision of a phoenix entwined with the soul of a little girl soaring in the western horizon, mingling with the evening star. He made it our primary endeavor to find this mysterious child as the next step of the great work, the opening of the door. We consulted the spirits through a Ouija board—"

"Oh, you damned crackheads, you." Nash chuckled. "Are you fucking kidd—?"

"Silence!" Hector rebuked.

Ulrich pinned the agent's neck down with his boot.

Nash grunted.

"Anyway," Hector continued. "The spirits gave us only three syllables: MLN. The numbers five, twenty-one, and five were a theme in my father's visions, but we knew not exactly what it was." He slowly meandered back to Chris. "Then came your trial, but that was not what fascinated us, no." He drew closer. "It was your little girl, on the verge of five. Melanie. MLN. Five. Hmm." He scratched his chin. "On a hunch, I did a background check. Sure enough, her birthday is on May 21st, a Gemini, twins…their souls conjoined."

Chris scrunched his forehead. Gemini.

Two and one. Light, casting a shadow.

Hector grinned down at Chris. "Well, we got to work immediately, for she would turn five very soon but then I thought to myself, 'Hector, why not do this as hush-hush as possible, pin it on someone else?' After all, this was supposed to be an espionage mission." He scowled at Sam. "So much for *that*."

Sam uttered his muffled, disturbing hyena laugh up at him.

"They already hate you, Christopher," Hector said. "The media loves a convenient lie. Too bad the policeman here won't be alive to testify about what *really* happened." He eyed the duffel bag. "And why not make a few extra bucks along the way?"

"Yeah, you might wanna count it to make sure it's all there," Chris sneered.

"That's right," Nash said, staring at Wellborn. "He spent a good while in the backseat earlier, pocketing some for himself, no doubt. Don't believe me, go check."

"Hmm?" Hector squinted at Wellborn.

"Don't listen to him," Wellborn retorted. "I made sure there were no dye packs in the bag."

"Wouldn't be the first time you got your hand caught in the cookie jar, you klepto," Sam mocked Wellborn. "I think you're all out of slaps on the wrist this time."

Hector pointed at Wellborn. "*Dummkopf*. If I go out there…and find cash in that—"

Blam—blam-blam-blam-blam!

Wellborn shot Hector in the torso and shoulder, sending him to the floor. Carlson aimed and blew Wellborn's brains out. The crooked agent's body collapsed, knocking over some of the candles and painting the floor red with gore around his skull as his pistol skidded out his limp hand, just out of Chris's reach.

One of the candles rolled dangerously close to an old oil drum.

"Traitor!" Carlson hissed at the corpse.

"We waste time!" Ulrich snarled. "The evening star crests. Bring the girl out! *Schnell!*"

Chris turned his head to the right as they brought Melanie, having dressed her in a white gown with a ball gag fastened to her face. Those monsters. They placed her on the altar as another soldier brought a wad of rope.

"Bind her," Ulrich snapped, then peeked out a window.

Gunfire sounded outside, with the heavy fluttering of helicopter propellers and spotlights approaching. Chris eyed the pistol again, hearing bullets puncture and ricochet off the outer wooden wall of the storehouse. Then the vicious thrum of another engine revved.

Right towards them.

Boom!

A silver pickup plowed through the wall, running over Carlson, Nelson and a few others. Mina gunned down the others with an M-16 from the backseat as Naomi held the revolver in one hand and the steering wheel in the other.

"Get in!" Naomi shouted. "There's more coming!"

Chris snatched the pistol from the ground as he, Nash, and Sam lurched up and removed the ball gag from Melanie's mouth. Bullets suddenly riddled the truck as more *Abendstern* renegades rushed down a hill towards the storehouse...followed by a Hind helicopter, firing rockets.

Boom!

Both Apache aircrafts went down, with one of their tails slicing the building in half, setting everything ablaze, cutting off their path to the pickup. Mina whined as two stray projectiles struck her arm.

"Shit—get outta here!" Chris yelled, firing at the enemy soldiers, taking Melanie's hand. "Go!"

"I'm not leaving you here!" Naomi shouted.

"We'll meet you out there—go!" Chris railed. "Go! Go!"

Mina whimpered through gritted teeth, her arm gushing blood. Reluctantly, Naomi put the truck in gear, with one of the tires already flat, and peeled out of the storehouse's wreckage and out of sight. One of the oil drums were pierced, leaking petroleum everywhere.

Blam!

Nash cried as a bullet landed in his shoulder. Chris looked as Hector rose back up to his feet, with a crazed grin on his face. The leaden rounds lodged in his bulletproof vest beneath his coat gleamed in the firelight like a constellation in the sky. Chris aimed his pistol, yet the gun clicked empty. The *Sturmvogel* grinned.

"Going so soon, Christopher?" Hector said, aiming the gun at Melanie's head.

"Daddy!" Melanie squealed.

Shing!

A blade knocked the gun from Hector's hand. He turned...and beheld Sam brandishing one of the bastard swords near the altar, wearing his smirk across his face.

Hector glared at Sam. Sam only cocked his head to one side.

"Not very sporting of you, Hector," Sam said. "What would Sebastian say?"

"Sebastian is dead!" Hector seethed.

"As am I," Sam claimed.

"Sam!" Chris yelled.

Sam turned to Chris. "Take Melanie and the cop. Get out of here. Save yourselves."

"What about you?" Chris asked.

Sam turned back to Hector. "I have business with the *Sturmvogel*." He looked back at Chris. "It's been a good hunt. Take good care of Melanie. Remember what I said. Go, before the dynamite goes off!"

Chris put Nash's arm over his shoulder and supported him as they and Melanie shuffled out of the inferno around them. Sam turned and faced Hector, his adversary drawing the other sword from the rack. Both of them stared each other down, preparing themselves.

"Still resorting to recruiting Hitler's feeble corpse to do his bidding, I see?" Sam mocked. "Have the years taught you nothing?"

"Times are tough," Hector taunted back. "A man has to make do with whatever cruel hand he is dealt. It is called improvisation. I'm sure a killer like you can appreciate that."

"Can I?" Sam jested.

Hector smiled again. "Why did you forsake us, comrade? We breathed new life into you, did we not? Were my father and I not good to you? We were brothers, you and I."

"Fret not, Hector," Sam teased, taking the hilt in both hands, eyeing Chris, Nash, and Melanie through the roaring flames, vanishing behind a building towards the smoking silver truck. He kissed the eagle emblem on the ring adorning his finger. "A *new* phoenix is about to take flight."

Both rushed and clashed against each other in deft strokes as more of the roof collapsed around them in embers. Steel sang in fierce, clarion rings as the two slashed at each other within the crumbling bonfire of the storehouse, dancing around the satanic altar. Two vultures, battling for dominance. Battling for the right to hunt, the right to soar.

The right to exist.

Over them, the Hind gunship hovered over a hole in the roof, its hull damaged and pummeled with bullets. As their swords clanged, Hector slipped on the water bottle, staggering backwards on top of the altar.

Shing!

Hector gagged up crimson as Sam impaled his opponent above his bulletproof vest, just missing his heart. The *Sturmvogel* grew weaker, dropping his blade, and retched up more gore, his blood spewing on the stone and glyphs.

"The price is paid," Hector wheezed, grinning. "The work is done."

"You're welcome," Sam quipped. "Are you going to spare me the cliché sentiments?"

"Why spoil a good thing?" Hector gurgled, then grew sober. "I've always been…eager to see what hell looks like. You *will* come with me…won't you?"

"Who, me?" Sam smiled. "I wouldn't miss it for the world."

"*Auf wiedersehen*…Samuel."

Sam looked down at him earnestly. "*Auf wiedersehen*."

A rocket shrieked and blasted against the Hind, sending the helicopter whirling down into the blazing ruins. Hector looked up as the airborne gun-ship's tail came down on him and the altar like a manic guillotine.

Boom!

Chris, Nash, and the others watched from a hill as the storehouse creaked and detonated, aircraft, dynamite, and all, issuing two massive jets of flame that, for a brief moment, almost resembled two abstract bird wings. Then the wind blew the red and gold tongues around furiously, with the other burning debris of Torino fanning flurries of embers everywhere into the night.

"Damn," Nash coughed.

Mina grunted, breathing heavily.

All of them rushed to the passenger's side as steam rolled from under the truck's smashed hood. Blood stained the seats as they pulled her out, laying her on the ground. Behind them, sirens whirred closer.

"Are the rest of you hurt?" Nash griped at them.

"No," Chris said, then looked at Melanie. "Baby, you good?"

"I'm scared," Melanie cried.

"I know, baby, I know," Chris consoled, cradling his daughter.

Melanie glared at Nash. "Don't take my daddy away from me!"

"Trust me," Nash wheezed. "I'm not."

"C'mon, Mina, don't die on us!" Naomi pleaded.

"The laptop," Mina gasped deliriously.

"The laptop's gone," Naomi told her. "They blew it up, remember?"

"Sam's…laptop," Mina murmured. "He hacked you…he has our video. I saw it…."

"What?" Nash questioned.

"Get the…laptop," Mina moaned, then she passed out.

"Mina? Mina!" Naomi screamed, slapping her face.

Blue and red strobe lights shone from over the hill as FBI cruisers and an ambulance skidded to a halt by them, billowing dust everywhere. Redman lurched out of one of the Humvees, his vest having suffered a few gunshots. He glanced a Mina. "Get her to a medic, quick!" He ushered Chris, Naomi, and Melanie to the ambulance. "C'mon!"

A U. S. soldier radioed his commanding officer. "Captain, we've secured the friendlies."

An unclear voice garbled back as they rushed Mina and the other civilians to the EMTs.

Nash hobbled to the silver truck and removed a laptop, opening it.

Redman approached him. "Would've been here sooner, but half of our crew turned out to be moles. They turned on us back there—it was a damned mess. What the hell happened?" He pointed at the computer. "What are you doing? You bleeding?"

"I'll be…fine," Nash grunted. "What the hell is this?"

Both agents' eyes widened as they accessed the footage.

Then they both glanced at each other with raised eyebrows.

Inside the ambulance, Mina came to on a gurney, slowly stabilizing, with an oxygen mask on her face. A couple of paramedics surrounded her, injecting morphine into her arm and staunching her wounds. Naomi and Melanie sat on the rear fender on one side while Chris stood with them.

"She needs a blood transfusion," of the EMTs said.

"We got more choppers on their way," the other replied.

"You owe me," Mina complained, squirming up in a lightheaded stupor. "All of you."

"I know, I know, I know." Chris said.

"I want a new car," Mina whimpered woozily. "I want a trip to Hawaii. I want a new house...and a swimming pool...and some ice cream...and some pancakes...and some—"

"Sounds like someone's making their Christmas list early," Chris joked dryly. "Want a flying saucer to go with it too?"

"Fuck you," Mina slurred, plopping back down on the gurney.

Naomi snorted, trying not to laugh as Nash shambled back to them. Melanie clung to her father for dear life, recognizing Nash from the trial.

"Please don't take my daddy away from me!" Melanie sobbed.

"Nobody's taking your daddy away, sweetheart," Nash panted, holding a gauze to his bullet wound. He looked at Chris. "You look like hell."

"Likewise," Chris smarted.

"Where's Sam?" Nash asked.

Chris shook his head. "Dead, I guess."

Redman trudged to them, with the folded laptop in one hand, then he put the other on Chris's shoulder. "Looks like the Vulture actually came through for you, Sullivan."

"We *had* evidence!" Naomi griped. "I had some nanny cams up in Evelyn's house, and—!"

"I know," Redman assured, looking at the computer. "It's all right here. Sam evidently hacked you and stole your video of Evelyn and Newton. Don't ask me how. Guy was a wizard."

Chris and Naomi exchanged bewildered looks.

Redman glanced at Chris. "Ready to get your life back, kid?"

Chris gazed at the towering inferno, crackling from the storehouse's ruins, a funeral pyre for their enemies, lapping up at the evening star in the sky. Naomi and Melanie watched as the spotlight of two medical helicopters from a military air base swooped towards them, spraying dust everywhere. Far off, the moon was rising, peeking over the mountains as a waning yellow sliver, a dying eye closing in the serenity of the clear heavens, without fog or clouds to pollute the pure tranquility.

The storm was gone at last, the darkness purged.

They were free. The hunt was finally over.

The mayhem was done.

Chris looked back at Redman. "Yeah. I'm ready."

XVII: The Phoenix

Theo Nash glumly studied his FBI badge in his cubicle at the bureau's headquarters at night, with his piece lying before him. He had already cleaned what few personal items off his desk, having placed them in a cardboard box, and had loaded them in his vehicle outside. The sector was vacant; agents had either gone home for the day or were currently on duty. May had finally graced the Rocky Mountains with greenery and flowers, the lifeless snow having melted away.

Producing rebirth.

And for Nash, it was time for a change.

Laura had already divorced him, all thanks to his unforgiving job, and it was only a matter of time before a cat like him spent all nine of his lives; he didn't fancy dodging bullets forever, especially from Nazi cultists. Though Sam Conroy, the Vulture, was presumed dead, only more scum kept piling up. More cases. More lives lost. More mayhem.

They weren't even making a dent.

A photo lay on his desk on top of a manila folder, showing the smoldering wreckage of Torino, taken as the sun was rising, displaying the crispy corpses of the crooked cops, the moles. The sleepers. How many more were there? What the hell was festering in the government, this disease they could not cure? He eyed a few bloodied footprints in the dirt, leading up to the hill, with something gleaming in the gravel from a camera's flash.

A ring.

The one they had found.

"He's *their* problem now," he grumbled.

"Guess I can't get you to reconsider," Redman said, walking to him with a newspaper in hand.

Nash gave a pained smirk, leaning back in his office chair. "You gonna tell me to sleep on it again, Red?"

Redman sighed. "That's up to you, kid. You're a good agent. Wish there were more like you." He slapped the newspaper on the desk. "Because we're gonna need all the help we can get."

Nash read the headline in big, bold capital letters:

CROOKED COPS MURDER KINGSTON. INCITES RIOTS NATION-
WIDE

"Whole country's about to go up in flames," Redman said, pointing at a picture of Kingston, the black man killed in front of a convenient store. "Guy just pinned his neck down with his knee, suffocated him out of cold blood. Now, we're hearing about this virus overseas. As if we didn't have enough shit to deal with in this ongoing upheaval and controversy in law enforcement already with what happened with that batshit Nazi cult in Utah last year. Dan Addison's in hot water, and I don't think he's gonna bounce back from it." He shook his head. "Can't trust anybody anymore."

"Damn," Nash said.

"I'm thinking about quitting myself," Redman snapped, looking around the empty cubicles.

"I guess I'm a coward for leaving, huh?" Nash admitted.

"Coward?" Redman said, raising an eyebrow. He shook his head again. "No. I'd call it smart, especially after that Nazi fiasco in Torino a few months back. *I'm* not gonna think ill of you for it. I can't speak for others, though. Individuals gotta speak for themselves, not stereotypes." He sighed again. "One thing I've learned is that…you don't have to be a cop in order to do good things in this world."

"Why don't *you* quit, Red?"

Redman looked at him. "I don't know. I really don't know." He peered at a woman standing at the double glass doors at the entrance. "I guess I'll get out of it sooner or later, one way or another, if they don't kill me first."

"Don't say *that*."

"No, it's the truth—that's the…that's the grim reality of it," Redman confessed. He glanced at Nash's badge. "So, what are you gonna do now?"

Nash shook his head. "That's something I'm still trying to figure out. Firefighter, maybe?"

"Well," Redman said, "you'll do all right, whatever you get into." He extended his hand. "It's been a pleasure having you, Theo."

Nash shook his hand and smirked. "Same to you, Vince."

"Bianca's waiting on you," Redman joked.

Nash snickered, rising to his feet. "Take care, man."

Redman nodded, then strode away to another office. With that, Nash absentmindedly pocketed his badge and wandered through the glass doors, meeting the prosecutor outside.

Bianca smiled. "Hey."

"Hey," Nash greeted. "How're the trials going."

"Exhausting," Bianca breathed. "But…you know, it's weird. I'm actually…happy for how Chris's case turned out. It's like he's…reborn from the ashes, like…."

"A phoenix," Nash said, his eyes widening.

Bianca squinted at him. "Yeah…kinda like that."

"Never thought I'd hear you cheer Chris Sullivan on." Nash grinned. "Sounds like Leah's been rubbing off on you."

"I'm not *that* old, Theo," Bianca said. "But…yeah, maybe, I don't know. I never noticed how cute his little girl is. He was telling me she had her birthday about a week ago. She's six now." She smiled. "They were telling me that he, her, Naomi, and Mina were all gonna take a trip to Hawaii with Mina's sister, Lucy, and her family when all this was over."

"That doesn't sound half bad," Nash replied, nodding. "You and I could take a trip."

"Is that an offer?" Bianca flirted.

"Hell, why don't *we* move out there?" Nash jested.

Bianca giggled. She puckered her lips to one corner of her mouth. "Melanie's starting to call Naomi 'Mommy.' It's killing Evelyn."

"Oh, is it, now?" Nash scoffed, feigning pity.

"But after the crap Evelyn pulled, she deserves every curse she gets," Bianca went on. "Rodriguez is helping Naomi regain custody of her daughter, Aeriel. Mina's been campaigning for rape victims, helping them cope and heal. She and her sister, Lucy, finally made amends. Chris got his zombie novels reinstated, so now they're selling like crazy—I already got the others, and I've preordered the last one he's working on." She sighed. "He's suing the news media outlets for…I don't how many millions. He and the others are gonna be swimming in dough."

"Must be nice," Nash groaned, crossing his arms.

"Well, he told me not to tell anyone, but…." Bianca bit her lip. "He, Hugh Altaha, and their church are planning on donating a large sum of that money to start a charity for Native American tribes throughout the nation. He wants to keep quiet about it, because he doesn't want to do it for publicity and come off as a showy douchebag about it…unlike Evelyn and…every single politician and celebrity who has slithered across this earth. And I respect that, I really do."

"Well…good for them."

"And he, Naomi, and Mina have all been doing interviews in Hollywood about the *Abendstern* shootout, so it's been super-busy and chaotic, but…in a good way. Naomi and Mina are getting book deals, too."

Nash scoffed. "Everybody gets book deals, huh?"

She smirked. "Guess what Naomi is gonna call hers?"

Nash smiled. "What?"

She tittered again. "*Some Bones May Remain.*"

"What's so funny about that?"

"It's how she came up with the name," Bianca laughed. "One day, she was cooking Melanie some frozen fish filets out of a package, and the label on the box said something like, 'While every effort has been made to remove the bones from this product, some bones—'"

"May remain," Nash chuckled. "How ironic."

Bianca raised an eyebrow. "What's so ironic about it?"

"We do the same thing in the criminal justice system, if you think about it," Nash explained, looking up at the stars. "We always think we got all the 'bones' out…then we realize just how many bones we missed…and how bad we messed up. *Some Bones May Remain*—I could just see that on a crime-drama novel's cover, all in big, bold capital letters."

Bianca grew silent.

Nash looked into her eyes.

"What's wrong?" Nash asked.

"Do you buy into what Sam said? About a 'blur between realities?'"

"I don't believe in parallel universes, Bianca." He squinted at her. "You don't…do you?"

"I'm not sure what to believe anymore." Bianca ran her fingers through her hair and looked away. "If I hadn't known any better, I would've thought Sam to be a…ghost, demon or something. I had him in my house, right in my sights. I fired, right at his head. No human being could ever move that fast."

"Traumatic situations…can make us…imagine things, Bianca."

"I don't know…." Bianca looked up.

Nash cleared his throat. "But…I'm happy for Chris and them. I'm jealous as hell, but…I'm happy for them."

"Yeah, me too!" Bianca replied, perking back up and stargazing with him. "They…they certainly have a lot more class about it than what Evelyn did, I know that."

"Well, maybe." Nash peered up at the expanse, with a new crescent moon setting in the West. "Stars are beautiful tonight."

"They sure are," Bianca marveled. "I wish I had more time to enjoy nature, just go into the mountains and just watch the heavens, maybe go get a telescope, take pictures of the Milky Way. I always take all this for granted every day."

"That's sounds like a date, Ms. Sterling."

Bianca giggled again. "I'd love to just quit my job and just get away, get out of the city…maybe move to Alaska or something, just you and me." She looked at him. "Start a family of our own."

Another grin slowly slinked across Nash's face. "Who are you, and what have you done with Bianca Sterling?"

They both laughed.

"I don't know, it's weird," Bianca told him. "I just feel so…good tonight, and it's not even the weekend yet. Maybe Leah *is* rubbing off of me, finally." She ruffled her long black hair with her fingers. "I guess you heard about that virus and…what happened to Kingston and all."

"Yeah. That's some bad shit."

"And with all these protests and riots starting…I don't know what the future is."

"Well," Nash said, caressing her hips with his hands, pulling her to him. "I know what *my* near future holds."

She locked her wrists behind his neck as they leaned into each other and kissed, their tongues stroking each other. He could feel Bianca's sleek body growing hotter in his embrace as her high-heeled foot popped daintily behind her, with her knee nudging his toned thigh and pushing her breasts against his tight, athletic core. Passion coursed through their veins as their hearts drummed faster. It was spring, after all. Why not get intimate tonight? Life was too short not to make love. And Bianca was so much better at sex than Laura ever was. So sensual. So elegant. He was already picturing her in her black lingerie she was planning on wearing that night. But the feminine prosecutor was far more than some cheap sex machine. She was alive, just like Theo Nash was, and he intended to treat her well. As they continued to romance each other, Nash pulled out the badge and tossed it in a trash can next to the door. He had far better things to do than be a pig in uniform for the rest of his life.

If he didn't get shot first.

It was definitely time for a change.

Inside, Redman passed Nash's old desk, taking the newspaper…then he froze, eyeing the photograph, at the bloody footprints on Utah's rugged turf. He examined the suspicious gleam in the dirt: a piece of jewelry. They had found that ring; it was in evidence, the ring that had made the Vulture brands on the murder victims' foreheads, with Sam Conroy's DNA on the band. A cold chill wracked his flesh as he studied the lone tracks; only one set of footsteps ventured up the hill and vanished.

No…there were two.

The second set was charred, seeming completely isolated from the rest of the carnage, leaving black smudges in the dirt. They branched off from the first set of bloodied tracks and meandered to the left, toward another hill…and stopped abruptly, as if the walker had disappeared into thin air.

Two. From one.

"The hell?" Redman whispered.

He strained his eyes closer. Where the second tracks ended…something like burnt raven feathers lay there, amidst the footprints.

Feathers….

He didn't recall seeing these prints, even when they were at the crime scene. They scoured that entire area for evidence. How was that possible? How did they miss this? Why didn't he see it that morning? Why couldn't he see it?

And why was it just now showing up?

"Son of a bitch," Redman cursed, taking the photo, his crazed eyes bulging. "Son of a bitch! Surely…surely, he—he couldn't have just…."

He stormed back to another office, picking through the evidence once again. Surely, it was over. Surely, they were all dead. Their charred bones lay there. Gone. It was over. The *Abendstern* cult was no more. That case was closed. But he failed to shake the morbid feeling.

That he had missed something.

Yet again.

Five o'clock rolled around in San Francisco as a gorgeous, slender auburn brunette with a light-tan complexion strutted into a nearby bar, garbed in a dark-red dress showing her cleavage with polished matching heels clacking on the hardwood flooring. Only a fraction of the evening crowd had showed up, not that she cared either way. She sauntered into a stool next to a man reading a newspaper as the male bartender helped a few customers several seats down. Slowly, her head swiveled as her unblinking, glassy dark-brown eyes scanned the establishment's modern architecture and décor. The brilliant sunset caught her gaze through one of the large windows, casting its dazzling ultraviolet splendor of blue, orange, gold, pink, and red along the clouds and through the smoggy gossamer haze beyond the prominent Golden Gate Bridge's crimson pinnacles in the distance. She then turned and crossed her legs, then casually propped herself up with her right arm on the counter, showing her manicured nails glimmering under the bar's urbane lighting. Had it not been for her fluid, lithe motions, one would be tempted to think her an eerie animatronic doll, with camera apertures for pupils, all the while wearing a charming yet unnerving smirk on her flesh-colored lips.

The bartender took notice of his new patron, walking towards her. "Hey, how ya doing?"

"I'm fine, dear, thank you," her soft, sultry voice sang with a silvery European accent. "I'll have an old-fashioned, please."

"What brand?"

She flicked the bangs of her short bob haircut. "One can't go wrong with Jack Daniel's."

"No ma'am, you sure can't," the bartender flirted, fishing for a rocks glass. "Coming right up."

"Thank you," she said, placing her purse on the counter. "I'm told it's a…girly drink."

"Well, perhaps I should 'woman up' and try it," the neighboring man said, putting his newspaper away. "I'll pay for the lady's drink, Mack."

"You got it," Mack, the bartender replied, pouring the whiskey over the ice cubes.

The woman looked at her guest: a smirking bald man with blue eyes in a gray pinstripe suit.

"It's so difficult to find such chivalry here on the West Coast," her voice flittered.

"Such a dreadful shame," the man concurred with contrived reverence. "A woman of your caliber and beauty deserves only the best…and with such a lovely accent to go along with it. Tell me, are you British?"

"Australian."

"Please forgive me."

"Oh, that's quite alright," she grinned, showing perfect white teeth as the bartender sat her drink down. She took it. "Thanks…Mack." She toasted at the stranger. "And thank you, sir." She flicked her hair again. "You see, my family was actually Irish. My ancestors moved 'down under' back in the 1800s. Alas, I do believe we've…lost our brogue along the way." She sipped the liquor. "Mmm. I love how it burns down inside of me. Makes me feel so alive all over again." She eyed him up and down. "So, tell me…what brings a suave, handsome bloke such as yourself to a place like this."

"On holiday," the man claimed.

"Really? Same here." She pivoted her head to the left, watching the vivid sunset gradually dwindle beneath the western horizon. "Have you ever been to the opera house in Sydney?"

The man's smirk vanished. "No. I'm ashamed to say I haven't. But I'd love to go," he smiled again, "and take you with me, I hope. Perhaps we could see a production of…*Carmen*?"

"*Carmen* is my favorite opera. It is *sooo* romantic." She turned to him again. "I'd very much adore that. By the way, what do you do for work?"

"Freelance, mainly," the man told her. "An entrepreneur of sorts, dealing in a variety of wares wherever I go." He squinted. "I don't believe I got your name."

"Vanya," she lilted.

"What a majestic—"

"And I smash puppies with a sledgehammer."

The man paused.

She averted her eyes up at the wall like a robotic mannequin, waiting for his reaction.

He remained silent…then grinned.

She grinned back.

"You know," the man jested. "I used to do the same thing…on Alcatraz."

Vanya busted out laughing. The man tittered like a weaselly hyena deep in his throat.

"In all seriousness, though," Vanya confessed, fluttering her eyelids, "I do, in fact, enjoy some good ol' sadomasochism in the bedroom…that is…if you've got the stomach for it. You'd be surprised how many men are absolutely squeamish."

"My dear Vanya," the man said, picking up his whiskey, "You are speaking to a man who's been through hell and back and raises hell wherever he goes."

"What a coincidence," Vanya mused. "So do I." She playfully smacked her tongue on the roof of her mouth. "Well, I think I've decided what *I* want to do tonight." She raised her glass towards his. "I propose a toast to your good will…and your good looks. I trust you'll be a good sport."

"Aye," the man said. "To good will."

Their crystalline glasses clinked together, then each took a sip.

"Mmm." Vanya hummed. "I love that punishing icy burn." She fluttered her eyelids again. "And you name is…?"

"My *real* name is Bernard Hamilton," the man lied. "But you may call me Sam."

Vanya gently tilted her head to one side. "Pleased to meet you…Sam."

197

Acknowledgments

I give thanks to God for providing me with family and friends who have supported me throughout the years. I also give thanks for my fans and their thoughtful contributions. There are so many names that I cannot list them all here. But I am grateful nevertheless for their kindness and encouragement, especially during tough times. I cannot thank you all enough for your generosity.

About the Author

Shawn Christopher Whittington specializes in crafting surreal epics about otherworldly beings, bizarre worlds, and deep subject matters. Shawn became intrigued with literature at an early age and decided to pursue a career in writing at the age of thirteen.

Inspired by the supernatural and his turbulent internal struggles, it was Shawn's prolific writing that helped him during the years where he developed a keen interest in dark fantasy and the macabre focused on the outsider. He is best known for his psychedelic vampire series, *Ravage & Requiem*, consisting of five novels.

Thank you for purchasing
Some Bones May Remain!

Be sure and check out more titles
by S. Whittington!

For more information, please visit the portfolio
website at www.swhittington.com.